Hellish Book Four: Vizibir

By Scott Dokey

DISCLAIMER

This is a work of fiction. Names, characters, businesses, places, events and incidents are either the products of the author's imagination or used in a fictitious manner. Any resemblance to actual persons, living or dead, or actual events is purely coincidental.

DEDICATION

This book is dedicated to artists everywhere with a dream and a passion. Follow your dream with all of your soul.

PART ONE:
JEREMY

You crawl under my skin and settle there
as the clock in my heart ticks.
Easing your way into my soul,
your teeth sink into me,

As you hold my heart in your teeth
and my hand in your hand.
My secret, you are killing me.
Please don't tell me how I make you better
Or how if things were different,
we'd be together.

My secret, you rest in my pocket,
held tightly in a locket
that wraps around my neck and chokes me.
I keep you hidden for a purpose,
so I can breathe at night and not feel ashamed.

For all the world is changing,
and you are standing there looking at me
With your eyes in a glare and your hands so rough

rubbing me like sandpaper across my heart

And making the trees dance
and the sun spit its rays upon my face.
Secret…keep quiet…please don't come out now.
—Victoria Marie Barracca

CHAPTER 1

Sometimes the forces of evil work in ways that are open for the entire world to see, their atrocities laid bare before God and man; individuals like Hitler and Stalin, who personified evil in its purist form. Usually, though, the evil works just under the surface of our reality, spreading its icy tentacles into all that is good. At first, it feels like nothing more than a slight tickle, only mildly irritating, but before long, it becomes a maddening itch that can never be scratched. That's how it started with Jeremy.

On a warm Saturday morning in June, little Jeremy Daniels bounded out of bed and rushed to his bedroom window, smiling wide when he saw a cloudless, blue sky overhead. As fast as a six-year-old kid can dress himself, he pulled on a pair of jeans, two mis-matched socks, and a t-shirt—that may, or may not have been dirty—then raced downstairs.

He held the carton of milk tightly with both hands and gingerly poured it into his bowl of Cheerio's, proud of the fact that he'd only spilled a few drops onto the table, all while glancing back and forth at the picture of the hungry lion splayed out next to him. A dribble of milk ran down his chin after shoveling a couple of huge bites into his mouth, almost more than his mouth could hold, then he flipped the page to a giraffe with its long tongue snaking out and eating hungrily from the hand of a small boy about his age. He smiled.

Jeremy had just plunked another huge spoonful of cereal into his mouth, turning the page to show a troop of monkeys whispering classified secrets to each other, when his dad entered the room.

A tall and thin man, who wore a serious face most of the time, Nathan Daniels was unusually happy and upbeat as he passed behind his son on the way to the counter, where the coffee maker sat with a freshly brewed pot in its belly. After pouring himself a cup, he sat down across from Jeremy, taking a long sip before putting the cup down. "Are you excited for today?" he asked.

Jeremy nodded. "First, I wanna see the lions, then the elephants, then the snakes, then the—"

Nathan chuckled, "Wow, slow down, kiddo. We'll have plenty of time to see everything."

Jeremy pouted for a second. "I know. It's just that, we don't get to do stuff like this very much. And I want today to be special."

Nathan looked at his son. "I know, but you have to understand how important my work is."

"More important than me?"

Nathan was silent for a moment. Then his phone rang.

Jeremy listened with the familiar uneasiness coiling up in his stomach as his dad answered the call while rising from the table, and walked to the corner of the kitchen, talking in his distinct business tone to the person on the other end.

Nathan looked at Jeremy for a second before he turned and walked out of the room, where he continued the conversation.

"Sorry, kiddo," Nathan said when he returned a few

minutes later after the call was done. "I'm afraid I have to go in to the office for a while today. Something's come up in this case I'm working on. I'll have to take a rain check on the zoo."

For a few minutes, Jeremy tried to be brave; tried to hold back the tears. If he had been older, he might've understood what the name Nathan Daniels meant among prosecuting attorney notoriety. But he was just a child, with childish hopes and childish dreams. He didn't know the world of grownups; didn't want to know; didn't deserve to know. Not at his age.

Finally, the dam burst and he ran to his room, crying like he had done so many times before.

That's when it all began.

***

A soft sound, like the flutter of tiny wings, drifted to Jeremy's ears, breaking through the sadness and jolting his curiosity. He looked up from his tear-soaked pillow and was surprised to see a soft, green point of light hovering a few inches from his face.

His first thought was that a firefly had somehow found its way into his room. Then he realized two things: first, it was morning; and second, the thing floating in front of him had no visible body. It was just a glowing orb that hung there in the air for a minute before it suddenly disappeared. But right before it did, it whispered his name.

Instantly, Jeremy forgot about his dad's broken promise and ran to his mom to tell her about the glowing light. Unfortunately, the condition he found her in was one of a drunken stupor, with an empty bottle of whisky on the end table next to the couch where she laid, the television blaring away and her cloudy eyes trying to focus on whatever show was playing. A cigarette dangled in her fingers, threatening to drop a pile of ashes onto the floor. Barely able to lift her head from the arm of the couch, she looked at him in a confused way while he recreated his close encounter for her.

Her words were slurred as she spoke. "What in the hell are you talking about, boy? Are you going crazy? If it's attention you're after, I'll give you attention! How 'bout I beat your ass and really give you something to think about?"

In the span of a minute, Jeremy's heart was ripped out and thrown back into the void where his father had tossed it only a short time before. Jeremy ran back to his room, which had become his harbor of refuge from this hurtful world he had been forced to live in.

As soon as he buried his head back into his pillow again, the soft buzzing drifted to his ears once more, lifting him from his saddened state and bringing a smile back to his lips. This time, the creature seemed to shine a little brighter, buzz a little louder, feel a little warmer. It darted back and forth in front of Jeremy a few times, like a crazed, happy-go-lucky insect. It flitted around, tickling the end of his nose, brushing against his cheek, and nuzzling up to his ear.

A soft voice then whispered into his ear a single word, "Vizibir."

CHAPTER 2

A soft knock sounded on Jeremy's bedroom door and immediately his little alien friend vanished.

His door creaked open slowly, and his dad peaked his head in, trying his hardest to look apologetic. "I've got to go, kiddo. Hopefully, this will only take a few hours and I'll be home before you know it. Maybe we'd still have time to go out for ice cream, or something?"

These were hollow words that Jeremy had heard numerous times before.

"Since Janice has decided to drink her breakfast today, I've asked your Aunt Sophie to come over and watch you until I get back," Nathan continued.

Sophie stepped from the hallway. She was a young lady with short, blond hair, and bright blue eyes. She resembled a younger version of his mother, only she had a clear head and a sense of self-pride—and she was sober. A pixie-like demeanor radiated from her.

"Hey, Jeremy," she said. "How's it going?"

"Okay, I guess," he lied.

Nathan turned to Sophie, "You have my number in case you need to reach me?"

"Yep, sure do."

She looked over at Jeremy. "Don't worry, Sweetie, we're going to have lots of fun today. I promise. I figured we'd watch a couple of movies, maybe make some popcorn, order a pizza? How's that sound?"

Even in his state of hopelessness, Jeremy's eyes lit up, just a little, at the mention of popcorn. The buttery smell, the salty flavor, even the popping sound echoing through the kitchen was a weakness of his. The very thought of that melted butter flowing down his throat as he crunched on a handful of the magic corn had him thinking that maybe this day wouldn't be so bad after all.

He couldn't have been more mistaken.

After a few minutes, he heard the front door close and his dad's car backing out of the garage. As he walked out of his bedroom toward the family room, he noticed that his mom no longer occupied the couch in the living room. For a long moment he was lost in sadness, not because his mother had moved, but because in his eyes, she was never really there to begin with.

Jeremy was a little more enthusiastic, even anxious, as he sat down in front of the TV, waiting for the pizza party to start. Sophie had that way about her, making everything just a little brighter during the darkness. His stomach started to rumble a little, trying to coax the pizza delivery guy through some arcane hunger communication to get there as fast as possible.

Sophie walked over to him, carrying a couple of movies in her hands.

"Okay, kiddo, which would you prefer, 'Toy Story' or 'The Lion King'?

"Those movies are for babies!" Jeremy said. "I'm six-and-a-half now. I want something with action, like the 'Power

Rangers'."

She giggled, "Six-and-a-half now, is it? When did you get so big?"

After rifling through the large collection of movies, which filled one large bookshelf in the corner of the family room, she finally pulled one out.

"If it's 'Power Rangers' you want, then it's 'Power Rangers' you'll get."

A minute later, Jeremy was watching his favorite show and thinking that this day might turn out pretty great after all. Then he realized that it was his aunt, and not his mother, that he was enjoying this moment with. Suddenly, it wasn't so fantastic anymore.

He looked at his aunt for a second, taking in her carefree, fun-loving essence, and thought that his mom was probably like that at one time. Then, somewhere along the road, the pressures of life, marriage, motherhood, took their toll and zapped all the joy from her spirit.

The ring of the doorbell snapped him from his moment of wistful thinking, and immediately he smelled the scent of pepperoni pizza wafting through the house. Apparently his stomach communication trick had worked pretty quickly.

A minute later, he heard Sophie's voice shouting from the living room; "I said, take your hands off me, now!"

Jeremy jumped from the couch and ran toward her cry. As he rounded the hallway, he saw her struggling in the doorway, trying to escape the delivery guy's grasp. Even though he wore the uniform of one of the most important people in this world, the look in his eyes and the tone in his voice was more fitting to that of a hardened criminal.

"Listen, bitch," he said. "I want my stuff back, and I want it now!"

Sophie yelled back, "You'll get your stuff back, asshole,

when I'm fucking ready to give it back, and not before!"

The not-so-nice delivery guy responded by slapping her hard across the face, sending Sophie slamming backward against the wall with a mixture of shock and rage on her face. Jeremy ran forward and kicked him as hard as a six-and-a-half-year-old could kick.

Once again, the guy's hand swung around, this time catching Jeremy on the side of the head and sending him sprawling to the floor.

As Jeremy lay there on the floor crying, with blood seeping from a cut on the back of his ear where the man's nails had caught his flesh, he heard the familiar buzzing echoing in his ear, and saw the mysterious green light fluttering before him, bigger than before. Then it shot forward and struck the delivery guy in the middle of the chest, sending him flying backward into the stone pillar that supported the roof covering the front porch. His body slumped to the ground, leaving a streak of blood behind to mark where his head had hit.

Somehow, at this time, Janice had managed to arouse herself from her drunken stupor in response to Sophie's outcry, and peeked her head into the living room.

"Oh my god," she cried. "What in the hell happened here?"

By this time Sophie was sitting up, propped against the wall. "I'm not sure. It all happened so fast."

She turned to me. "I saw it. I saw the light, right after he hit you. It flew forward and hit him right in the chest."

His mother, in all her alcohol-induced splendor, looked at Jeremy with disgust written all over her face. "What have you done, Jeremy?"

CHAPTER 3

No matter how hard he tried, no matter how hard he pleaded, Jeremy couldn't make them understand, couldn't make them believe. In their eyes, he was just a little kid with an overactive imagination. Even though the evidence supported his story—that he had nothing directly to do with the terrible accident Mr. Not-So-Nice-Pizza-Delivery-Man had suffered earlier—his parents refused to even entertain the idea that some mysterious force had come to his rescue.

His only saving grace that day was that the guy had only suffered a mild concussion from the impact. It was of little consequence to them that there was a long cut running down Jeremy's neck, or the deep bruise that had already shown its presence on his forehead where it had hit the floor when he fell. More important to them was the notion that their son was seeing and talking to imaginary creatures, a sure sign that there was something seriously wrong with his mental wiring.

For a few minutes, Jeremy did as most kids his age when their parents didn't believe them: he threw a tantrum, complete with stomping feet, pounding fist, and yelling at the top of his lungs. Then he ran to the only place of sanctuary he had in this world: his room.

His pillow opened up to his tears once more, absorbing them as it had done so many times before. The feeling of loneliness immediately engulfed him, sending him spiraling quickly into the bowels of despair, with no hope for rescue. He realized then that he had no one to turn to, no one to comfort him, and no one to believe in him.

Again, the buzzing sounded in his ears, and he looked up at the green, glowing form hovering before him. Immediately, it flew against his cheek, sending a warm tingle through his face. He brushed it away, as if a pesky fly or mosquito were tormenting him.

"Leave me alone," he cried.

Instead of disappearing back into the ether from whence it came, it flew down and tickled him repeatedly in the stomach. He tried hard to resist, but the assault was virtually non-stop.

"You don't understand," Jeremy said. "Nobody believes me. They all think I'm crazy, or like my mom said, loony in the head."

Vizibir flew softly against his cheek again and whispered his name in his ear, only this time it was followed by one other word: "friend."

Jeremy stopped moving and looked at the green, glowing orb. It looked so warm and friendly, so gentle and innocent. He couldn't help but feel a calming peace flowing through him.

Abruptly, Vizibir flew from him and circled his bedroom like a whirlwind. Jeremy had seen the Wizard of Oz, and thought for a second that he would be sucked up into some incredible tornado and deposited roughly onto some magically land, complete with munchkins, flying monkeys, and an ugly green wicked witch. Or maybe he would be catapulted out into the farthest reaches of outer space, where he would die a silent death?

Then, just as suddenly as it had started, the whirlwind stopped, and Jeremy looked around in amazement. What used to be a young boy's room in total disarray—complete with toys and clothes and small bits of food strewn about—was now transformed into a wondrous magical kingdom. The corner of his room was a giant castle made of a crazy combination of wooden blocks, Lego's, and Lincoln Logs. One of his red socks served as the castle's flag, waving high above the main tower. Army men were strategically placed around the mighty structure in anticipation of the savage attack being planned by the dinosaur horde nearby. G.I. Joe and a couple of Power Rangers waited in the wings to give support. In the other corner, a ship full of scurvy pirates went on with their looting and pillaging of an unknown vessel with no knowledge of the other conflict nearby.

When Vizibir once again whispered "friend" into Jeremy's ear, his heavy heart was lifted and replaced with one full of joy and happiness. His wonder-filled eyes failed to notice that Vizibir was glowing even brighter than before and had grown to twice his former size.

CHAPTER 4

Jeremy learned quickly that his relationship with Vizibir needed to be kept secret. Under no circumstances did he want a repeat of his parent's ridicule again. It was bad enough that they ignored him most of the time. He certainly didn't want the few times that they actually paid him any attention to be filled with accusations and diagnoses they had contrived from watching Dr. Phil too many times. So, for the next few months, while his supernatural friend continued to amaze him any chance it could, Jeremy kept his secret hidden.

Vizibir had an uncanny knack for rescuing Jeremy from the monster of despair whenever it reared its ugly head from the shadows in his mind. His vocabulary grew as they interacted more and more, and before long he was able to communicate in full sentences.

Each night, Jeremy waited anxiously for the time when the lights in his room would turn off and his parents would retire their selfish little lives to their selfish little bedroom, barely acknowledging that he existed. Then the soft green glow would spread throughout the room, signaling Vizibir's entrance and the beginning of his nightly journey into the land of make-believe. And as Jeremy began his story each night, Vizibir would nestle himself gently beside him, spreading his warmth like a magical blanket, and listened intently.

One day, though, before Jeremy was able to start into his story, Vizibir spoke up, and Jeremy became the listener.

"Once upon a time," Vizibir said, "in a land far, far away, there lived a sad little boy name Jack. Now, Jack wasn't sad because he was poor, or ugly, or short, or fat. In fact, Jack was just the opposite; a smart and handsome boy who lived in an expensive house, with every toy a child could want. The reason Jack was so miserable was that his parents didn't love him."

Jeremy sat up in bed and told him he didn't want to hear anymore. The room grew silent for a minute before Vizibir spoke up again.

"Don't worry, Jeremy," he said in a calming whisper. "Everything will be fine in the end." He followed this with the two words Jeremy had heard far too often from his parents and no longer believed: "I promise."

But since he was a child and longed for any kind of acceptance, he laid back on his bed and let his mysterious friend continue his story:

"One day, Jack was outside playing in the woods near his house. The sun was shining bright, and the birds were singing their happy songs. A gentle wind blew the leaves around on the dirt path beneath his feet."

"He followed this path through the woods to a small cave hidden in the hills behind the lake. Almost every day he went there to play make-believe house with a make-believe family, only in this family the mother and father loved their son."

A soft tear fell down Jeremy's cheek.

"Unknown to Jack, a group of three mean boys was

walking through the woods, causing trouble. They threw rocks at animals, kicked over small trees, and squashed innocent bugs galore. Then they stumbled onto Jack and his hidden cave."

'Well, boys,' said the biggest of the bullies. 'What do we have here?'

'It looks like a little sissy boy to me,' one of the other boys shouted.

The third one chuckled, 'I think he's actually playing house here.'

"The three boys laughed while Jack stood silent. A second later, the leader of the group walked over to a large rock in the corner of the cave and picked up the teddy bear that had been posing as the child in Jack's pretend family.

'Leave that alone,' Jack cried as he lunged forward to recapture his stuffed friend.

"The other two boys grabbed Jack before he could get close.

'Awe, look at the little baby playing with his baby toys!'

"The leader bully smiled as he grabbed the bear's arms, one in each hand. Jack made one last scramble to escape, but a swift kick by one of the other boys sent him crashing to the ground."

At this point, Jeremy was laying with the blanket pulled up to his chin, anxious and nervous for the end of the story.

After a pause, Vizibir continued:

'Watch this,' the leader said, and then pulled hard, ripping the arms from the defenseless stuffed bear.

Jack cried out, 'No!'

"Just then, a bright light filled the cave, followed by a gust of wind that lifted the bullies off the ground. The three of them hung in mid-air for a moment, scared to death, crying and yelling, before they were thrown away from Jack.

"When the dust settled and the bright light subsided so Jack could look around, he saw the three bullies lying on the ground in front of him, each one grunting and groaning. But that wasn't what shocked him the most—not the mysterious wind that had picked them up like they were nothing more than dead leaves; not the blinding light that had appeared out of nowhere and would have given the sun a run for its money—none of these freaked him out more than the sight of his exact double standing behind the boys, with a soft green glow surrounding him, and a sharp smile on his face."

"The Jack-double lurched forward, landing only inches from Jack, and looked curiously at him for a minute. Then he spun around, his eyes glowing blood-red, and he raised his arm and pointed at the stuffed-animal killer. The bully leader rose into the air and flew against the cavern wall like a rag doll. A sharp crack echoed through the cave as the boy's head smacked against the stone. Then he fell to the ground dead."

A small cry issued from Jeremy's mouth as he pulled the blanket completely over his head.

"There's nothing to be scared of," Vizibir said as he paused the story.

Jeremy inched the blankets down to his chin and listened timidly as Vizibir continued his story.

"Jack's double winked toward Jack before he reached down and grabbed one of the other boys. He held the boy up with one arm so that he was inches from the double's face. Then Jack's double opened his mouth wide and sucked in the boy's soul. When he was done, he let the body fall in a pile on the cavern floor.

"There was just one more bully left. The Jack double could have let this one go, sure that he had learned his lesson that it was not okay to pick on those that were weaker. But he had a responsibility to Jack to make sure he would never be hurt again. So, he raised his hand again and the third bully flew up and sailed to the back of the cave to be impaled through the heart on a long and sharp rock in the corner of the cavern floor. Blood gurgled from his mouth for a second and then he died."

"The supernatural rescuer walked up to Jack, smiling, and said just one word, 'Friend.'

"Then he disappeared. The end."

The silence in the room was deafening for a moment while Vizibir waited for some kind of comment from Jeremy about his storytelling. Even though the story had kind of a happy ending, with Jack escaping the clutches of the evil bullies, Jeremy sensed for the first time something powerful and destructive in Vizibir. The graphic depictions of the boys and their deaths sent a chill through him, and he had a feeling that something far more dark and sinister lay under the surface of his supernatural friend than it was portraying.

Just then, something even more startling happened; something that shook Jeremy to his very core. Standing in front of him in his own room, was a full-size apparition bathed in a familiar green glow, his smiling face staring back at Jeremy.

Jeremy was suddenly looking at his own reflection, only he wasn't standing in front of a mirror.

CHAPTER 5

At first, Vizibir could only keep his Jeremy look-alike form for a short time before it lost composition and transformed back to a shimmering orb. But, with each passing day, his power grew, allowing him to maintain the guise a little longer.

Initially, the doppelganger frightened Jeremy. He sensed that his supernatural friend had developed into something dangerous and unpredictable, with dark secrets he wouldn't share. But then Vizibir would do something silly, something that a six-year-old boy could appreciate, and his fears would be temporarily put at ease. At least, for the moment.

When a moving truck showed up one day at the house across the street, which had sat empty for quite some time, Jeremy watched curiously from his bedroom window, as three guys from EZ Moving began offloading a bunch of furniture onto the street in front of the house. While two of them were bringing a large sofa down the ramp, the rear overhead door suddenly flew down, almost decapitating the third man standing at the top of the ramp with a large box cradled in his arms. For a brief second, barely perceptible, Jeremy thought he heard a whisper of laughter nearby.

For the next couple of days, Jeremy watched as the new family stacked empty boxes by the curb in such large quantities that he imagined they could've built a fortress with the cardboard. Then he saw her and his heart did a little flutter. She was chasing a toad around her front yard, her blond curls bouncing softly as she ran, and he knew immediately that he'd found something that he'd been searching for. He could tell that she was a kindred spirit, the way she laughed and giggled as the amphibian squirmed from her grasp repeatedly.

Gathering every ounce of his courage, Jeremy crossed the street and proceeded to capture the elusive creature for her. When the toad responded by peeing in his hand, Becky burst out laughing and almost sent Jeremy running back home in embarrassment. But as he watched her standing there, her bright blue eyes sparkling in the sun, the happiness exuding from her mesmerized him.

"Hi, my name's Becky," she said with a smile.

"I'm Jeremy," he responded as he offered the toad to her awkwardly.

Graciously she accepted the squirmy gift from him, and in doing so, set the foundation for a friendship that he had hoped would last a longtime.

Nearly every day after that found them together doing something fun or crazy. It was as if this spunky little girl across the street had been sent down from Heaven to rescue Jeremy from his doldrums. Some days, they would head down to the small pond a couple of blocks away and watch the fish, or ducks, or whatever wildlife happened to be wandering about. Other times, they would ride their bikes all over the block until they ended up at the park, where the jungle gym would serve as a magic fortress that enslaved the princess. And sometimes they would venture to a secret little hideout they had built in the woods in the back of Jeremy's house.

It was there that Jeremy received his first kiss. He would soon learn the importance of that moment.

When Jeremy's birthday rolled around a few months later, he actually felt like he was part of a real family—at least for one day. His dad actually stayed away from work, mostly, that is, if you don't count the multitude of calls he received on his cell phone. And his mom did her best to stay sober, limiting herself to a little Irish Cream in her coffee, and only smoking a half a pack of cigarettes.

When the doorbell rang, Jeremy jumped excitedly. His heart nearly leaped from his chest when he saw Becky standing in the doorway with a large gift in her hand, and an even larger smile on her face.

Politely, Jeremy ushered her in, trying to impress her in a gentlemanly manner. As she walked past him, her arm brushed against Jeremy and a jolt of electricity shot through them, like static coming from the carpet in the foyer.

"Ouch!" Becky cried out.

When Jeremy glanced down, he was shocked to see a bright red mark on her forearm. Then he heard a soft giggle in his ear, and felt a soft tickle across his cheek. His heart sank immediately, sweat started to cross his brow, and he glanced nervously around for a second before leading her down the hall toward the dining room.

As Becky placed her gift on the table in the corner of the room with the others, Jeremy glanced at the mirror above the buffet and saw the reflection staring back at him with a wicked smirk on his face. Vizibir turned and blew a kiss in Becky's direction before vanishing.

Jeremy yanked Becky out of the room toward the backyard.

"Where do you think you're going, young man?" his mom called out as she placed the last candle on his birthday cake.

Jeremy replied nervously, "We're just going outside to play for a few minutes."

"Just don't get dirty," she said.

No sooner had the words left her mouth, and they were out the door. Becky was more than a little shocked at the abruptness of their departure.

"What in the world is going on?" Becky asked as soon as they were outside.

Jeremy was afraid to tell her what was really going on and quickly made something up. "I just wanted to spend a couple of minutes with you alone before everyone else showed up."

She leaned forward and looked into his eyes. "That is so sweet," she said before planting her lips on his.

For a brief second, he was in Heaven. Then he heard the buzzing in his ears and felt the terror rising in his stomach.

When Jeremy opened his eyes, he saw Vizibir standing behind her as big as life. The fury in his eyes clearly portrayed the hatred burning in his heart. Immediately, Jeremy pushed away from her, causing her to stumble backward with a look of shock on her face.

"I'm sorry," she said as tears streamed down her face. "I thought you felt the same way I did."

Jeremy tried to reach for her but she pulled away.

"I do feel the same way," he pleaded. "I really do. You have to believe me."

"You have a funny way of showing it," she said as she pushed past him and ran back home.

The only thing that prevented Jeremy from doing the same thing was his other guests, forcing him to put on a false front for everyone and pretending that everything was okay. When his dad came up to him and asked where Becky was, he choked back the tears and lied, telling him she had gone home sick.

The suspicious look in his dad's eyes told Jeremy that he didn't quite believe his little white lie. The sick feeling in the pit of Jeremy's stomach told him that the worst was yet to come.

CHAPTER 6

A large lump grew in Jeremy's throat as he trudged across the street, desperately trying to think about what he would say that might make up for the disaster the day before. With each step that took him closer to Becky's front door, his feeling of dread grew. He needed to tell her how he really felt, and even considered for a brief second telling her everything, including the secret about the supernatural entity whom lately he was beginning to fear.

When he knocked on the door, however, he was met with the response he had feared. "Becky doesn't feel like coming out today," her mom said flatly.

The cold look in her eyes told him not to press the issue, sending him walking back to his house dejected. The only real friend he had ever known had been alienated from him, leaving him alone once more.

Jeremy moped around the house for the next few days in a terrible funk. Vizibir showed up frequently, trying to snap him out of it, popping up out of nowhere with some silly look on his face, apparently unable to comprehend the fact that he was the reason Jeremy was in such a state of depression.

"I'm sorry," he told Jeremy repeatedly. "Please don't be sad."

Then he said something that got Jeremy's blood really boiling: "I love you more than Becky ever could."

Jeremy spun around quickly. "Don't you dare talk about Becky like that! It's because of you that she hates me right now."

Vizibir said, "Can't you see she's not right for you? All she'll do is hurt you just like everyone else."

"That's not true! Becky would never do anything to hurt me."

"Yes, she would," he countered. "She's human, and humans always hurt other humans."

The words struck Jeremy hard. He had experienced firsthand the truth in that statement. In a dark and twisted way, he was absolutely right.

Vizibir continued, "Look at the way you've been treated your whole life; beaten down and ridiculed by everyone around you, including your own mother and father."

Jeremy's innocence and naivety got the best of him, smothering him with a wave of pain and rejection that opened up a hole in his heart just big enough for Vizibir to squeeze his way back in. A warm blanket of energy surrounded him, which he mistook for security, and for a brief second, entertained the notion that maybe Vizibir was right. *Maybe Becky isn't right for me?* He thought. *Maybe no one will ever be right for me?*

But something tugged forcefully at Jeremy's heart. He didn't want to give up on her; couldn't give up on her. Desperately, he ran out of his room, down the hall, and rushed out of the house across the street to Becky's.

Jeremy pounded on the front door. He had to talk to her; had to explain everything, even if it meant losing her forever.

She deserved to know the truth.

Expectantly, he saw her mother's mean scowl again when she opened the door, her face twisted so that she resembled a junkyard dog warning off any trespasser who got too close to its territory. "I thought I told you not to come over here?" she scolded. "Becky doesn't want to see you!"

Jeremy pleaded, "Please, I just need to talk to her for a minute, and then I promise I'll leave her alone."

The woman was unshakable. "I said, no! Don't you think you've hurt her enough?"

The front door slammed shut, and with it the door to Jeremy's heart.

With tears running down his face, he started walking back toward his house. Then he heard a window raise and turned around. A glimmer of hope sparked inside his eyes when he saw Becky looking down at him.

"Make this quick, Jeremy," she said somberly. "If my mom catches me talking to you, she won't be very happy."

For a second, Jeremy froze, unable to find the right words to say, and not wanting to sound like a blubbering idiot. But then the words just started flowing out of his mouth. "I'm so sorry, Becky. I never meant to hurt you. You have to believe me. I do like you, really, I do. More than you'll ever know. Believe it or not, I was actually trying to protect you."

"What do you mean, protect me?" she asked with a puzzled look on her face. "Protect me from what?"

Becky must have sensed Vizibir's presence, because she spun quickly around. That's when she saw him standing behind her, resembling Jeremy in every detail except for the demonic grin on his face—the dark betrayal of his true nature.

Even from Jeremy's place on the ground, he heard her horrific gasp. It was followed a second later by a terrible scream, as her body flew through the open window and landed in a mangled heap only inches from where he stood. Her broken body pointed in several unnatural directions, while her lifeless eyes pleaded with him for some kind of understanding to what had just happened.

For that, he had no answer.

CHAPTER 7

In a matter of seconds, what was once a quiet Chicago suburb was transformed into a horrendous crime scene. As Jeremy sat on the ground beside Becky's broken body, her mom came rushing out of the house screaming. She stopped short when she saw the pool of blood surrounding her daughter's head and her dead eyes staring up at her.

Jeremy barely heard her cries while she kneeled beside her dead daughter's body, because he was suddenly lifted from the ground forcefully by his dad, who bore the look in his eyes of someone who had seen something so dark and evil that it urged him toward the edge of madness.

As he was ushered from the horror and raced toward their house, Jeremy dared a quick glance backward, trying to catch one last glance of his fallen angel.

His moment of grief was short lived as they rushed across the street, his dad holding him in a death-grip that would have rivaled that of Sampson or the Hulk. They were about twenty yards from the front door when his grip fell loose and a loud gasp escaped from him.

Standing ominously on the front steps, Vizibir assumed the role of a malevolent bouncer plucked straight from the depths of Hell itself. His piercing gaze shifted from Jeremy to his father as his true demonic nature manifested. Eyes ablaze with an infernal fire, a wicked grin slithered across his lips, exuding a sinister presence that sent shivers down their spines.

It wasn't until the doppelganger stepped off the porch and advanced toward them that Nathan got over his paralyzing shock and dragged Jeremy quickly toward his car, which still hummed softly in the driveway. Wrenching the car door open, he shoved Jeremy inside, and a moment later the tires squealed loudly as they launched backward out of the driveway and into the street.

Suddenly, Vizibir materialized abruptly in the middle of the street, a malevolent specter daring them; taunting them. Nathan sat paralyzed, his entire being gripped by a suffocating shock, his world reduced to a horrifying stillness. But in a sudden rush of desperation, his instincts surged back to life, propelling him forward as he stomped hard on the gas pedal, hurtling them toward the demon blocking their path.

A surge of anticipation sent shivers down their spines, the air crackling with an eerie premonition of supernatural annihilation. Bracing themselves, they awaited the violent impact, and the certain death to follow. Yet, by some twist of fate, they seamlessly passed through Vizibir's ethereal form, as though traversing an intangible abyss. But even in their deliverance, a wicked undercurrent swelled.

A gasp escaped Jeremy's lips when he cast a desperate glance backward, his heart pounding as he anticipated the torrent of scorching flames and bolts of lightning raining down upon them from Vizibir's outstretched arms. To his relief, the street behind them was empty. Unfortunately, the area was also teeming with chaos, as frantic neighbors and passersby rushed onto the scene, their collective panic amplifying the air with a maelstrom of terror.

A right turn a few seconds later took Jeremy and his dad out of view of the carnage left behind, but the image of that horrible moment remained forever burned into Jeremy's mind. Becky was dead, and it was his fault.

Once the initial shock subsided and they had put significant distance between them and the grisly scene of Becky's death, Nathan pulled over to the side of the curb, parking in front of a small coffee shop.

As they sat there in silence, Jeremy could almost hear the gears turning in his father's head as he tried to make sense of everything. In Nathan's world of municipalities and judicial supremacy, everything happened according to a strict set of rules and laws. Action led to a consequence. Every rule, if broken, resulted in appropriate punishment. But what he'd just witnessed destroyed the fabric of logic that had been ingrained so deeply in his brain. Things like Vizibir shouldn't exist! It was the first time the notion that the Universe operated on a different set of rules than what he had known entered his mind, and he didn't know how to process it.

When he finally spoke, his voice was scared and shaky; the horrified look in his eyes a contrast to the normal calm and confidence seen in them. "What the hell just happened back there?" he almost shouted.

The desperation of his words made Jeremy cringe, and he sat there for a minute, unable to speak. What could he possibly say that would make his dad understand? How could he explain something that he didn't even understand himself? Finally, three words just stumbled from his mouth, "It was Vizibir."

Nathan's jaw dropped, and his eyes widened in shock. "Are you telling me that your little imaginary friend is responsible for what happened back there?"

Jeremy answered him in a quiet and timid voice, "Yes."

"But that's not possible!" he cried. "He's not even real!"

"Yes, he is. He's very real, and he's evil." Jeremy paused for a second as he fought back tears. "He's the one that killed Becky."

That's when Jeremy saw something in his father's eyes that he'd never seen before: fear. He knew Jeremy was telling him the truth, yet he still refused to admit it to himself.

"But you saw him standing in the middle of the street? I know you saw him," Jeremy said.

A look came over Nathan's face like a light bulb had gone off in his head. "But he let us go. Why? Why didn't he finish us when he had the chance?"

"I don't know," Jeremy answered simply.

"And why did he look exactly like you?"

"I don't know."

He had caught hold of a dangerous thread of reasoning and was pulling on it desperately. "And where did this thing come from?"

"I don't know."

His voice raised a few decibels as frustration began to mount, "Is there anything you actually do know about what's going on?"

Jeremy tried to be brave, as brave as any child could hope to be, but quickly broke down and started crying again. After a moment, Nathan put the car in drive and pulled away from the curb.

"Where are we going?" Jeremy asked softly.

"I don't know," Nathan replied. "But we have to get away from here so I can sort this out."

As they traveled down an unknown street, toward an unknown destination, Jeremy witnessed his father talking to himself rather animatedly. Although his words were mostly incoherent, Jeremy managed to pick up on a few. What he heard made his heart stop. Amidst the mumbling, two words were distinct that brought more fear to him than Vizibir ever had: 'kill', and 'accident'.

It didn't take long for Jeremy to realize what he had in mind. Suddenly, his head flew back, smacking against the back of the car seat when Nathan stomped on the gas pedal. His eyes grew wide in terror when he felt the car swerving radically beneath him from side to side down the nearly deserted street, as Nathan imitated a mechanical failure that would work to cover his real intent.

Somehow, in Nathan's analytical mind, he had rationalized to himself that killing Jeremy was the only course of action possible. Maybe he thought that Jeremy's sacrifice would be the saving grace necessary to defeat this evil? Regardless of his reasoning, Jeremy's own father had suddenly turned into a cold and ruthless killer!

A large oak tree loomed suddenly before them, its long, tangle branches reaching out like giant tentacles eager to snatch them up. As they neared the fatal impact, Jeremy screamed as he dared a glance over at the man who was driving him to his death. The person he saw no longer resembled his father.

He turned to meet Jeremy's gaze seconds before impact. "I'm so sorry," he said softly, as if this last second confession would absolve him from this horrendous crime before God.

Then Jeremy closed his eyes tight and braced for death.

CHAPTER 8

Jeremy's body was wrenched violently forward as the car hit the tree full force. For the briefest of moments, his short life flashed before his eyes, and the only thing he saw was regret —regret over Becky's death; regret over his relationship with his parents; regret over bringing Vizibir into this world.

Then, in a cruel twist of fate, it was that very evil that became Jeremy's salvation.

Just as Jeremy's head was about to meet the dashboard with skull-shattering force, a field of energy suddenly surrounded him, protecting him from certain death. The sound of the horn blasting through the air cut the astonishment of his escape short. He looked toward the driver's seat and was horrified to see his dad's body slumped over the steering wheel, his hair plastered with blood and pieces of broken glass.

Slowly, Jeremy reached over and struggled to pull him off of the steering wheel. Once he had finally succeeded and quieted the screeching horn, he let out a gasp. One lifeless eye stared back at him, while the other was impaled by a long wooden spike, as if the oak tree itself had impaled him in its own defense.

For a brief second, Jeremy wondered why the airbag hadn't deployed. Then he saw Vizibir standing next to the car, and he had his answer. In order to save Jeremy's life, he had taken his father's. That struck Jeremy like a lightning bolt. His father was dead! Sure, he had always been self-absorbed and had barely paid him any attention his whole life, but he was still his father, and he still loved him.

Jeremy's breathing became short as a tightness started to form in his chest. Anxiety began to suffocate him like a giant constrictor snake before it devoured its prey. He screamed at Vizibir, "How could you?"

"But he was going to kill you," Vizibir said.

That statement stuck a knife in Jeremy's heart deeper than any regular blade could ever reach.

Sirens blasting through the air signaled the approach of police and rescue units. A second later, Jeremy saw the flashing lights and heard the screeching brakes as the emergency vehicles came to a halt near the accident scene. He was dimly aware of unfamiliar hands prodding and groping him as his consciousness began to fade. Vizibir's words echoed again in his head, *He was going to kill you.*

Then everything went black.

***

The voices in Jeremy's head sounded distant and muffled, as if he were lying submerged in a pool of water, waiting to drown in a sea of sadness. Slowly, however, they began to get louder until he recognized one of them. She was talking sternly to a man whose voice he didn't know.

Jeremy fluttered his eyes open slowly, and after the initial disorientation wore off, he saw that he was in a hospital room. Then, panic quickly set in when he tried to raise his hand to his face but couldn't. After struggling for a second, he was able to lift his head up just a little, sending a terrible shooting pain through his brain, and saw through shocked eyes that he was strapped to the bed!

The doctor immediately turned to him. "Save your strength, young man," he urged. "You've been through a lot these last few days."

Jeremy's voice was low and scratchy, and his throat was on fire as he spoke, "What do you mean, 'these last few days'? And why am I strapped down?"

Instead of a technical answer from the doctor, Janice came over and put one hand lightly on his shoulder, while the other brushed the hair out of his eyes. "Don't you worry, Dear" she said with a sweetness that didn't sound natural coming from her lips. "Everything's going to be fine."

"What do you mean?" Jeremy asked, getting more and more scared. "What's going on here?"

"Take it easy, son," the doctor said. "You've been in a horrible accident. You're lucky to be alive right now. Do you remember anything about what happened?"

It all came flooding back to him like a tidal wave: Becky's dead stare as she lay on the ground in a pool of blood; Vizibir's evil smile as he stood in the street taunting them; the sad look in his dad's eyes as he rammed the car into the tree. The problem was that he couldn't tell them any of that. Instead, he quickly changed the subject, "You still haven't told me why I'm strapped down?"

"The impact from the crash had quite a traumatic effect on you," the doctor said. "Apparently, when the paramedics arrived at the scene, they found you lying on the ground outside the car, unconscious, without a scratch on you. They said that as they were transporting you to the hospital you started thrashing around violently. They had to restrain you to the gurney to keep you from hurting yourself."

Jeremy's eyes grew wide in shock. He didn't remember any of that! Even though the events of the actual crash were burned into his brain, creating a series of images that would haunt him forever, everything went black after that. Then he had a chilling thought. What if Vizibir had taken over his body while he was unconscious? He could only imagine what kind of horrors the demon would create.

The doctor continued, "Even after you were heavily sedated, we still had to restrain you. Our only conclusion was that the psychological effect of the accident caused you to experience a series of post-traumatic stress incidents that led you to lash out. Because of the violent nature of these outbursts, we had no choice but to restrain you."

Jeremy glanced at his mom, searching for some kind of answer, any glimmer of hope to cling to. Instead, all he saw was anger and hatred burning from her eyes. An instant later, her demeanor changed completely, so that she wore the face of an angel and looked at him through the eyes of a saint. The exact opposite of who she really was.

"Just rest your little head, Dear," she said in a sweet voice that reminded him of the wicked witch that had led Hansel and Gretel to her house of doom in the woods. "Everything will be over before you know it."

CHAPTER 9

The sting of the needle puncturing Jeremy's skin didn't hurt nearly as much as the unabashed hatred radiating from his mother's eyes. As the sedative began to wind its way through him, his eyelids became lead weights, and he found it impossible to stay awake. With darkness closing in on him, it was the first time in his life that he thought the world would be a better place if he hadn't been born.

***

Jeremy didn't know who she was or where she came from, but when he opened his eyes, he knew was looking at the face of an angel. She was a young lady in her twenties, with silky blonde hair and sapphire blue eyes. But what made her so special was the kindness and love shining from those eyes. They were completely foreign to him, and for a time he felt a blanket of hope covering him.

Her voice was soft and soothing when she spoke. "You must be strong, Jeremy. There are things in this world that can't be understood. Regardless of the difficulties you face, you must always believe that everything happens for a reason."

Then he asked the age-old question, which surfaces in everyone's mind as they face a difficult period in their life, "Why me?"

The woman responded tenderly, "A good soul is hard to find. It shines like a beacon for all the world to see, lifting troubled hearts out of the gloom, and spreading warmth everywhere it goes. But it also becomes a target for the forces of darkness who are eager to extinguish anything that is pure and good. They feed off of the fear that is generated by attacking those innocent souls. That is why Vizibir chose you; he needs your energy to make him strong."

Her statements made Jeremy's heart sink, for, if that were true, he had no hope for salvation; no way to escape the evil that had attached itself to him. He was doomed to walk this life in constant fear, completely alone.

The mystery woman sensed the despair in Jeremy's eyes. "Take heart, Jeremy," she said. "Know that you will never be alone. Always remember that just as there are evil forces in the world, there are also forces of good, battling the darkness.

Suddenly the woman was gone, vanishing like a whisper into the ether from where she had come, like something had frightened her into a hasty retreat. Jeremy knew immediately that something evil had forced her away, for in her place an instant later, stood a large black mass writhing and undulating like the shadow of a coiled serpent.

A series of loud hisses emanated from the dark entity as it slithered toward Jeremy. A scream erupted from Jeremy's lips that was cut short as the mass wrapped around him quickly, cutting off his voice. With the coils tightening around his chest, Jeremy tried desperately to break free but the demon only squeezed harder. A collection of loud snaps signaled the breaking of Jeremy's ribs, bringing a silent scream from his lips as tears rushed down his cheeks.

The head of the shadow demon reared back and studied Jeremy's anguished face for a moment, reveling in his suffering, before it morphed into Becky's dead face. Her skin was rotted and peeling, while her cold eyes stared at him with deadly hatred. Her mouth moved in a soft mumble, and when she opened her lips, a wriggling mass of maggots squirmed out.

The shadow swirled for a second and then became his father's image, holding a look of scorn in one eye, while the other was just a hollow socket that bubbled black blood down his face. "This is all your fault, Jeremy," the thing hissed.

Once more, the head twisted until Jeremy was looking back at his own reflection. Vizibir's eyes held something dangerous in them, while his lips were turned into the kind of smile only a demon could carry. "It didn't have to come to this, Jeremy," Vizibir said with a hiss before he opened his mouth wide, his jaws unhinging like that of a giant serpent.

Jeremy tried to scream but Vizibir's head shot forward and swallowed Jeremy whole. As the darkness engulfed him, Jeremy thought he heard a faint voice urging him to be strong, but it was quickly silenced.

CHAPTER 10

When Jeremy woke the next morning, his lungs were on fire and his throat felt like it was full of glass. He instantly remembered the nightmare and a cloud of dread started to form around him. How could he hope to fight something so dark and so evil? He was just a kid whose own father had tried to kill him only days ago. He could only imagine what his mother would do given the chance? Sad tears formed in the corners of his eyes when he realized he was truly alone in this world.

Then he remembered the woman from his dream, the lady with eyes that had shown like beacons of light in his dark world before the nightmare had invaded and drove her away. She had given him a glimpse of hope. And however fleeting that glimpse was, he snatched onto it like it was a life-preserver, keeping his head above water so he didn't drown in the icy blackness of his despair.

His arm strained against the strap that secured him to the bed as his fingers found the button on the edge of the rail that called the nurse to his room. He could feel the woman's disdain as she entered his room a few minutes later, her eyes holding a scorned look in them as if his call had interrupted her from a life-changing orgasmic experience.

"What seems to be the problem here?" the nurse snapped.

"My chest and throat hurt," Jeremy replied hoarsely, straining against the pain spiking through him.

He could almost hear her eyes rolling into the back of her head as she pulled a thermometer from her pocket. *Why is she being so mean?* He thought bitterly. He had his answer a second later when the nurse looked at him through eyes of the blackest ink, with a sly smile on her lips, before she disappeared. A second later, the real nurse entered the room, and Jeremy sank further into his darkness, knowing he was powerless to escape the nightmare that had become his life.

***

Over the next few days, Jeremey's world was filled with the piercing looks of suspicious strangers, the stringent smell of antiseptic, and the horrible images of death resurfacing continuously in his mind. At least the doctor at some point deemed him safe enough to remove the restraints.

His mother made a few token visits, pretending that she actually cared, but the familiar stink of alcohol on her breath betrayed the fact that it was all just an act. She didn't care about Jeremy—never had, never will. He was a burden thrust on her by some malevolent act of karma that she resented with all of her being.

Finally, a week after his father's death, Jeremy was released from the hospital. His mother seemed unusually chipper as she led him down the long corridor toward the receptionist's desk. She was even whistling while she signed his discharge papers, which was almost as scary as anything else he'd been through.

Jeremy began to worry a little as they continued across the parking lot toward the car with Janice smiling like the cat that had swallowed the canary. The lump in his throat got even bigger as she proceeded to turn on the radio and sing loudly to the music, something he had never seen her do before. She actually had quite a good voice, but then again, it's been said that Satan has the voice of an angel.

The lump that had resided in Jeremy's throat quickly dropped to his stomach as they rounded the corner of their block and he saw the piece of plywood covering Becky's bedroom window, laughing at him like a wooden specter. On top of that, her parents had planted a white rose bush in their front yard, directly on the spot where Becky had died, serving as a headstone of sorts. A patch of cedar mulch surrounded the rose bush, concealing the blood-stained grass beneath it.

Jeremy had never longed for the comfort and safety of his own bedroom more than he did then. But instead of turning into their driveway so he could rush inside and bury his face in his pillow, his mom kept on driving. She went right past their house, down the street, and out of their neighborhood.

"Where are we going?" Jeremy asked worriedly.

He saw her look back at him in the rearview mirror with a smug sort of smile. "Don't worry, Dear," she said. "We'll get you fixed up and good as new real soon."

With each passing stretch of road, Jeremy's feelings of dread grew deeper. His greatest fears were realized twenty minutes later when they pulled into the parking lot of a big, red brick building. The sign on the front of the building read 'Whitmore Psychiatric Hospital'.

"Mom?" he said worriedly. "What are we doing here?"

Her answer was simple and matter-of-fact, "We're here to get you some help."

Jeremy was stunned. "But I don't need any help! There's nothing wrong with me!"

"Come off it!" she snapped, changing her demeanor instantly. "We both know that there's something going on in that messed-up head of yours. You're suffering from some sort of mental disorder and we're going to find out what it is and fix it."

"I am not!" Jeremy countered. "Everything that's happened has been real."

She turned to him angrily, "Look, you fucking little brat! The only thing I know for sure is that my husband is dead, and it's your fault!"

After slamming her car door shut, she came around to Jeremy's side and yanked him roughly out of the car. "Now, let's get one thing straight," she hissed. "You're going to go in there and do whatever the doctor tells you to, no questions asked. Got that?"

Knowing that any hint of objection would only escalate the situation, Jeremy slowly nodded in resignation as he followed her into the building. While the interior of the building was painted with bright colors designed to exude a degree of happiness and well-being, and the associates all greeted him with smiling faces, a little voice in the back of his mind told him it was all a lie. Behind the curtain lay the darkness and evil of a place built to extract every ounce of a person's will, stripping them down until only the basic fabrics of humanity were left.

What followed was a prison sentence in a white-walled room, void of any contact with the outside world, in a constant, drug-induced, state of semi-consciousness. The only good thing that came from being in such a vegetative state was that Vizibir disappeared completely for the next year.

CHAPTER 11

The next year of Jeremy's life went by in a dreamlike fog, where the harsh realities of this world gave way to a catatonia induced by the multitude of drugs coursing through his veins. Every once in a while, he was dimly aware of a stranger's touch propping him up in his bed and prying his lips apart in order to force more pills down his throat. Then he would be laid back down onto his pillow to resume his murky bliss. He vaguely remembered his mother coming to visit him a couple of times, although he couldn't really be sure it was her.

One day the fog was thinner than usual, like he was almost alive again, and as he groggily opened his eyes, he was surprised to see her standing there beside his bed.

"Good, you're awake," she said frankly. "How are you feeling?"

Before Jeremy could reply she continued. "I hope you're up for a little excitement? Today is your birthday, after all, and I have something very special in store for you."

She bent down and pulled Jeremy forward off of his pillow. "Let's make you a little more comfortable, shall we?"

A cold shiver ran down Jeremy's spine when she touched

45

him, like the hand of Death itself was upon him. A second later, she ripped the pillow from behind his back and slammed him down hard on the bed. Everything went completely dark as she covered his face with the pillow.

As Jeremy struggled for his life under his mother's force, the adrenaline pumping through his veins shook him out of his mental funk and brought him back to reality for the first time in a year. He kicked and flailed wildly with all of his might. But a young child, even when fighting for his life, is no match for a maniacal mother hell-bent on revenge, who is willing to do anything to exact that revenge, including killing her own son.

Then suddenly, the darkness was replaced by a brilliant white light, divine and serene, as Jeremy felt his last ounce of will draining away. He was ready to surrender completely. But just as he was about to push the last breath from his lungs, the pressure on the pillow suddenly withdrew, and he instinctively gasped life back into his body.

He threw the pillow from his face just in time to see his mother's body picked up and slammed into the wall in front of him with a bone-crunching thud. A wail of pain and fear erupted from her as she slumped to the floor in a huddled mass. Her respite lasted only a second, however, for then she was yanked up a second time and sent flying across the room, this time crashing into the door, but instead of slumping to the floor after the impact she was reeled back to repeat this blow over and over again.

Even though Vizibir hadn't been seen during the attack, there was no doubt he was behind it, and he wasn't going to stop until she was dead. He raised her high in the air, her feet dangling a few feet off the ground, her eyes wide with shock and bleeding. She shook violently for a second as blood started to pour from her mouth, then she dropped to the floor like a broken rag doll. Her body twitched and shuddered for a few seconds before falling lifeless.

That was when Jeremy became an orphan.

He climbed from his bed and shuffled to where his mother's body lay in a matted heap. He started to reach out to her with a trembling hand, but a shimmer nearby startled him, and he pulled his hand back quickly. He looked over and Vizibir was there, leaning toward him.

"She can't hurt you anymore," he said in a soft voice.

Jeremy looked at him in disbelief. There were no words that swam to his lips. What could he possibly say? Even though he resented the way she had constantly beat him down, making him feel worthless and unwanted, he had never once wished her dead. But there she was, lying before him in a pool of blood, unable to torment him any further, and tears of grief found their way to his eyes.

A minute later, the door burst open and a horde of hospital personnel rushed into the room. They stopped as one, completely horrified when they saw the mutilated body of Jeremy's mother. One of the nurses looked at him and cried a familiar cry, "What have you done?"

They were the same words that had crushed Jeremy's heart once before, ushered from his mother's lips. The effect of those words was magnified a hundred-fold, given the smell of death permeating the room.

"Get him out of here!" one of the doctors yelled, and seconds later Jeremy was hurried from the room and ushered down the hall toward the maximum-security ward; the section reserved for the extremely violent and suicidal.

After a straightjacket was wrestled onto him, Jeremy was thrown into one a padded room like he was a dog thrown into a kennel. A loud thud echoed through the room as the door was slammed shut, leaving him lying on the floor, a constricted mass teetering on the verge of insanity.

The silence in the room soon became deafening as he struggled to make sense of his life. Then she was there once more, the mystery woman with the deep blue eyes that sparkled like a fountain in the morning sun. She smiled her warm smile again before she spoke, "We only have a few seconds before he shows up again. I can sense him drawing near even now as we speak."

She looked into Jeremy's eyes and he was instantly lost in a sea of tranquility. For that tiny moment, his heart was relieved of its burden.

She continued, "I know it's hard, but you must remain strong. Don't give in to your fear, for that makes him strong. If you keep your heart pure, his power over you will weaken. You must have faith and believe that everything will work out in the end."

Then Vizibir was standing there.

Luckily, the woman had disappeared a split-second before the demon arrived. Vizibir paused for a moment and looked around, as if he were scanning the room for something. He turned to Jeremy with sincere sadness residing in his eyes. With a flick of his wrist, the straightjacket split down each side and fell off. Jeremy was free to move about, even though he still wasn't free of the prison his life had become.

It was at that moment, in a room built for the mentally and emotionally anguished, that Jeremy found the courage to face the demon before him and cast him out of his life.

"No one can hurt you anymore, Jeremy," he said, trying to justify his bloodshed. "You are free to live your life now, without fear or suffering, and I will always be here to protect you."

Jeremy fought hard to subdue his emotions. In some bizarre way, Vizibir sincerely believed that everything he had done was to save him. But there had been too much blood; too much death.

Jeremy looked at him and said simply, "No, you won't."

A look of shock and disappointment crossed Vizibir's face. "What do you mean?" he asked.

"It's easy. I want you to leave me alone. Forever."

CHAPTER 12

It was hours before anyone entered Jeremy's room again, and even though he desperately needed to escape, all he could do was curl up in the corner, his mind numb from the ongoing horror his life had become, and his eyes blistered red from the fountain of tears he had shed. When sleep overtook him, he tried to steer his dreams toward images of race cars and bullfrogs, fire-breathing dragons and circus tents—all the things a boy his age would enjoy. Instead, all he found was darkness and dread.

The black cloud still clung tightly to his body, wrapped around him like a thick blanket, when he heard a voice rousing him from his sleep. It belonged to Mrs. Monroe, one of the nurses checking in on him. She was a short, stout woman in her late forties, with gray hair and horn-rimmed glasses. Her thick German accent lent an added harshness to her words. "How in the world did you get out of that jacket, young man?" she barked.

She regarded Jeremy coldly as he sat there. When she saw that he wasn't going to respond, she picked up the torn straightjacket and looked at it curiously for a minute. She turned to walk out of the room, only to stop at the door and bark at Jeremy to follow her.

After winding their way along a series of twisting corridors, they came to a large wooden door. Hesitating only long enough to turn the handle, she walked into the room beyond with determination in her steps. When Jeremy paused for even a brief second at the doorway she snapped quickly, "Get in here, now!"

The room beyond was a small waiting area, completely empty except for a few chairs lined up against a wall. The neo-Nazi nurse with the personality of a rock ordered Jeremy to 'sit'.

Jeremy did as he was told and watched nervously as the nurse disappeared through a door opposite him into another room.

"You can go in now," Mrs. Monroe said a minute later as she walked by him, her eyes cold as steel.

Jeremy's hand shook as he reached for the handle. Swallowing back the lump in his throat, he opened the door and found himself entering a large office. Sitting behind a desk, his eyes studying a computer screen intensely, was a large man in his early fifties, with gray hair and a scraggly beard. A small nameplate on the desk read Dr. David Bennett, P.H.D.

The doctor steered his eyes away from his computer screen as Jeremy entered the room. When he spoke, he was visibly agitated, "We have a situation here, Jeremy, which needs to be dealt with as quickly as possible."

"But I didn't do anything," Jeremy pleaded.

"We've reviewed the security footage concerning the incident in your room and that's the reason you're here right now."

"But I don't understand?" Jeremy asked.

"Simply put, your presence here poses a danger to

everyone. My responsibility is for the safety of my staff and the patients they attend to. In order to provide that to my utmost ability, I have decided to discharge you, effective immediately. A representative from Child Services is on the way to place you in foster care."

No sooner had he finished that last sentence and there was a knock on his office door. "Come in," he called out.

A second later, the door opened and she was there—the lady from his dream. Jeremy almost leaped from his chair. "It's you!" he cried out excitedly.

When she looked at him with a confused look on her face, Jeremy wanted nothing more than to crawl under a rock.

"Have we met before?" she asked simply.

"I'm sorry," Jeremy stuttered. "For a second, I thought you were someone else."

She chuckled, "No problem. I get that all the time."

She turned toward the Doctor, "Dr. Bennett, I'm Susan Conway from CPS. I'm here for Jeremy."

Her smile made Jeremy's spirit rise just a little. If nothing else, maybe she could lead him to a place where he might feel safe and secure for the first time in his life.

After exchanging signatures on several documents, Susan led Jeremy from the office, holding his hand tightly as they walked through the hallway and exited the building amid a sea of damning stares.

Jeremy stopped suddenly when they neared a black car that looked exactly like his father's. Instantly, the terror of that day came flooding back.

"What's the matter?" Susan asked.

"I'm sorry," Jeremy stammered. "It's just that…this is just like my dad's car…like the one he…"

She hugged Jeremy tight, "It's okay. Everything's going to be better now, I promise. I'm not going to let anything hurt you."

After a minute, Jeremy had calmed down enough to climb into the car. As he settled into the passenger seat, he dared to hope that this journey would lead him to a better place, where someone would welcome him with open arms.

The initial drive lasted only a few minutes before they pulled into the parking lot of the Child Protective Services building.

"What happens now?" Jeremy asked as they walked toward the entrance.

Susan stopped and crouched down so she was eye-level with him. She put one hand on his shoulder, while the other combed softly through his hair, "Well, now we go in and meet the nice family that has offered to take you in. Then, hopefully, you can start to live a normal life."

Jeremy suddenly realized that everything had happened so fast that he hadn't had time to grieve for his mother, whether she deserved it or not. For a brief moment an overwhelming feeling of guilt engulfed him. Then he remembered that she had tried to kill him only hours before. After enduring a childhood built on suffering and neglect, his guilt quickly turned to hatred. She didn't deserve anything else.

They walked into the large building that served as the hub for several charitable and social organizations. Continuing down a short hallway, past an office for United Way, and then another for The Red Cross, they stopped just outside the doorway to a small waiting room, where Jeremy saw a couple of small children playing with some toys in the corner. The girl, approximately five, with short black hair and a sad look in her eyes, was a couple of years older than her little brother, who sat on the floor playing with a fire truck, apparently unaware of their plight. He kept brushing his sandy hair from his eyes as he played cheerfully.

"Wait here," Susan said. "I'll be back in a couple of minutes." Then she turned and walked toward an office just across the hall.

Jeremy watched a blond-haired lady walk into the waiting room. As she neared the two children she was met with mixed reactions. The little boy rushed over to her and practically jumped into her arms. "Do we get to call you mommy now?" he asked eagerly.

She glanced at the girl for a moment, and Jeremy could see a very real connection there. "Only if you want to, Hun," she replied. The girl smiled, just a little, but it was enough to know that she was going to be alright.

As they walked past him out of the room, Jeremy felt a tug on his heart as he fantasized about the family he'd never had, and feared he may never have.

CHAPTER 13

Jeremy sat in the waiting room for what felt like hours, wrapped up in his thoughts before Susan reappeared. Her eyes told him everything he needed to know.

"I'm afraid there's been a change of plans," she said solemnly.

"What do you mean?" Jeremy asked, sure that the answer was something he didn't want to hear.

She spoke slowly and deliberately, "Something happened, and the family that was going to take you in isn't able to anymore."

Jeremy knew from the tone in her voice that something terrible had happened. The little voice inside his head said that Vizibir was behind it.

"What happened?" he asked.

She looked at me for a second, "I don't think I should—"

"Please, I have to know."

A protest started to form on her lips, but she stopped. Instead, she took a deep breath to collect herself. "There was an accident; a gas leak at the Matteson's home. It only took minutes for the whole house to be engulfed in flames. That's where you were going to live."

Jeremy knew the answer, but he asked the question anyway, "Is everyone okay?"

Tears streamed down her cheeks. Her voice was deep and heavy, "No, they're not."

She stopped for a second. Fighting through the anguish long enough to continue, "The whole family—mom, dad, the two boys—they all died in the fire." Then she collapsed against the wall and sunk to the floor.

Jeremy felt the blood draining from his face, the panic rising in his chest once again. "My God," he muttered. "Not again."

Susan looked at him, "Now, Jeremy. I know that some terrible things have happened to you, but I assure you that this was nothing more than a tragic accident."

"But, Miss Conway," he cried. "I know it was Vizibir. I just know it."

She took Jeremy's hands in hers, "First, you need to call me Susan. And second, the Fire Marshall has already declared that the fire resulted from a gas leak. Even though it's all very tragic, there's nothing to suggest anything supernatural."

Tears were streaming down Jeremy's face in a torrent. "But I know Vizibir was responsible! He killed those people. I'm sure of it!"

Susan grabbed Jeremy and held him tight; assuring him that everything was going to be all right. He buried his doubts in the back of his mind, hoping beyond all hope to keep them there.

"There is a little bit of a silver lining here, if it's appropriate to call it that," she said. "We've decided that, at least for the time being, you're going to stay with me."

Jeremy's eyes brightened instantly. His mind was such a whirlwind of mixed emotions that he barely noticed the drive to her place. He was finally going to get a chance at happiness, knowing that a lot of people had died already because of him, and deep down, he wondered how many more would follow?

The house didn't actually turn out to be a house, but a small, two-bedroom apartment that sat nestled in the middle of a complex on a large wooded section of land on the outskirts of town. As they drove into the complex, Jeremy could actually feel a physical change in the atmosphere surrounding him, from the hustle and bustle of city life, to a gentle and calm peacefulness.

"Well, here we are," Susan said as they came to stop in front of a building located in the rear corner of the complex. Even though it pretty much resembled any other apartment building Jeremy had ever seen, at that moment to him it was the greatest place on earth.

The inside of the apartment was even better than he could have dreamed, filled with an array of bright colors and whimsical designs. She led him through the living room and down a small hallway with a doorway on each side and one at the end. She gestured for Jeremy to open the one on the left.

She was a little embarrassed as he went in. "Sorry, it's not exactly a young boys paradise," she apologized.

Jeremy looked around the small room, which had been used mainly for storage. Boxes were stacked in the corner of the room; trash bags full of miscellaneous items formed a pile at the end of the bed—one of only two pieces of furniture in the room. The other was a small three-drawer dresser lining the opposite wall of the room.

"Don't worry," she said. "We'll get it cleaned up in no time."

"It's perfect," he told her as he hugged her tight.

Susan responded by kissing him softly on the forehead. As

she pulled back, Jeremy caught a glimpse of something strange on her neck: three small red dots, spaced equally apart to form a perfect triangle, bordering a reddened patch of skin.

"What's that mark on your neck?" Jeremy blurted out.

She backed up a little, pulling her shirt collar up to conceal the markings. "It's just a birthmark," she said softly.

"I'm sorry, I didn't mean to make you mad."

She smiled at him. "Not to worry. No offense taken."

"If it means anything, I think it looks pretty cool."

"Why, thank you. Now, how about we drop this stuff off and go grab something to eat? How does pizza sound"

"That sounds great!"

When they arrived at The Pizza Emporium, Jeremy thought that this might be the best place ever on earth! Bright neon lights flashed crazily atop a large marquee that hung above the entrance. Music blasted happily through speakers attached in various places to the outside of the building. And the smell of pepperoni wafting through the air as he stepped out of the car nearly brought a tear of joy to his eye. His stomach responded with a loud growl of anticipation.

"Looks like we got here just in time," Susan said with a smile.

Upon entering the building, Jeremy was bombarded with sensory overload. Large screen TV's were scattered throughout the establishment, some showing sporting events, some cartoons, and a few were showing news channels. A large arcade area stood in the corner of the room, the bells and whistles from the various games mingling with the music that blasted from speakers overhead. And permeating through it all was the smell of pizza swirling like a specter through every nook and cranny of the place in search of hungry souls.

A young, bubbly girl dressed in the red, white, and blue uniform of a Pizza Emporium employee escorted them cheerfully to a booth along the front of the building.

"Well, what'll it be, Champ?" Susan asked.

"Pepperoni," Jeremy replied, "lots and lots of pepperoni."

"Ah. Excellent choice." She then handed him a pile of quarters, "Go have some fun while I order?"

It took Jeremy a few minutes to break free of the spell that held him mesmerized. But once he got over his initial excitement, it didn't take long for the controls to become an extension of his arm, and within a short amount of time, he was a master at dodging space aliens, destroying zombies and ghouls, and rescuing damsels in distress.

At one point, he paused between games to glance and see if their food was there yet. He was surprised to see Susan talking animatedly with an older man who had white hair, a short white goatee, and was wearing a long black trench coat. If he'd been wearing a brown robe instead, Jeremy would've sworn she was talking to Obi-Wan Kenobi about the ways of the Force.

Jeremy made his way back to the table and was stunned when he saw that the person Susan was talking to had exactly the same mark on his neck as she did. Although he was just a child, he was smart enough to understand that her birthmark story was a lie. Even if it was a birthmark, and they miraculously had the same one, in the same spot on their necks, there was certainly more to her story than what she had told him. This caused the shadow of doubt to start creeping in, putting questions in his head about who his new guardian really was?

She was startled when he neared the table. "Jeremy," she said awkwardly, "I'd like you to meet Andrew, a friend and colleague of mine."

Jeremy nodded guardedly in his direction. "Hello."

Andrew responded with a nod of his own, coupled with a deep, piercing look, as if he were dissecting Jeremy with his eyes.

Luckily, the waitress arrived at that moment with their food. After she had set the pizza on the table and left, Andrew rose from his seat.

"It's good to meet you, Jeremy," he said. "You're a lucky boy to have Susan here to watch over you."

His words helped ease Jeremy's apprehension a little, but not completely.

Andrew turned to Susan, "I'll call you later to discuss things in more detail." Then he walked away.

Jeremy climbed into the vacated seat and began to munch quietly on a breadstick. Susan noticed the change in his mood. "Are you okay?" she asked.

"I'm fine," I replied, "just a little tired."

"I'm sure you are. You've had a rather busy day." She let the matter drop, content to let Jeremy eat in silence.

Before long, his eyes were bigger than his stomach. Then, when Jeremy's guard was down and he was at his weakest, his stomach full and his eyes heavy, she asked pointedly, "Okay, spill it. What's up?"

At first, Jeremy was reluctant to open up, afraid that he might jeopardize the first good thing in his life he'd had for a long time. But he knew that she was the only one he could turn to, given the secret he kept buried as deep as he could manage.

"Why did you lie to me about the birthmark?" Jeremy finally asked.

She regarded Jeremy silently for a second before speaking, "I'm sorry, Jeremy. You have every right to be upset. With everything you've been through, the last thing you need is to be lied to. The truth is that it's very complicated."

"Why don't you explain it to me?"

She sighed slightly, "I was hoping to have this conversation a little further down the road, after you had a chance to get settled into a normal life, but I guess, as the cliché goes, there's no time like the present."

She took a deep breath. "All over the world, things happen that can't be explained; supernatural events that defy logic and reason. Unfortunately, they usually involve bad things happening to good people."

The reality of that statement hit Jeremy hard.

She continued, "But there are people in this world that have made it their mission in life to fight for those in trouble. The mark we bare—a perfect triangle, one side for each; mind, body, and soul—help keep us in balance and give us the strength needed to defeat this evil."

Jeremy tried as best as he could to process this information, wishing now that he'd just taken her at her word and let it go at 'complicated'.

"What were you guys arguing about?"

"The truth? He was lecturing me about getting too attached. He's afraid that you living with me will prevent me from being objective, create an imbalance, and make me weak, thus putting our lives in danger."

Jeremy grew quiet. Her words rang true. People that he had been close to were now dead, and suddenly it hit him that Susan was now in mortal danger.

She noticed the fear surfacing in Jeremy's eyes, "Don't be afraid, Jeremy. I promise that as long as I'm here to protect you, you'll be safe from your demon."

Jeremy was shocked. "But how did you know?" he stammered.

"How we know is not important. What is important is that

you trust me."

For a brief moment, Jeremy finally felt a certain safety and security in his life. Then he heard the buzzing in his ears and the fear returned stronger than ever before.

62

CHAPTER 14

Even as the scream flew from Jeremy's lips he was jumping from the booth, knocking their drinks over and ruining the last couple slices of pizza in the process. He spun around in a frenzied panic, searching for Vizibir.

Susan grabbed his shoulders, forcing him to look at her. "Stop it, Jeremy," she said firmly. "You're safe now. There's nothing here to hurt you."

"But I heard him!" Jeremy protested. "He's here, I know it! We have to leave now, before it's too late!"

She grabbed him tighter, "There's nothing here, I promise. You have to believe me."

"But I heard the buzzing. That's the sound he makes right before he appears. Then people die."

"It wasn't what you think, Jeremy. Look, on the window by our table. There's a bee buzzing around. That's what you heard—just a silly old bee."

Jeremy just stood there for a moment, staring at the insect buzzing around the way normal insects do. He looked at her, his eyes tearing up and his lips quivering, "I heard that horrible sound...and I was afraid he'd come back. I was afraid he'd hurt you."

She hugged him tightly, "Don't you worry about me. I'll be fine."

Even though he had a thousand eyes burning holes through him as they left the restaurant, Jeremy took solace in the fact that Vizibir hadn't materialized. With Susan next to him, he began to convince himself that everything was going to be alright.

The drive home was a quiet one, as Jeremy sat there smothered in embarrassment. Susan tried various attempts at cheering him up. None of them worked. She finally pulled over to the side of the road and stopped the car.

"Look at me, Jeremy. You have to stop beating yourself over what just happened. It was no big deal."

"But look at the trouble I made. Now we can never go back there."

"Don't worry about that. Their pizza was kind of greasy, anyway."

Before he could stop it, a smile crept across his face.

Susan said, "There, that's what I like to see. Now let's go home and get some rest. Tomorrow's a new day, and I have a lot of things planned for us."

Suddenly, Jeremy felt very foolish for doubting her. This woman was every bit a saint and savior, as anyone had been throughout history. He made it his mission that night to do everything in his power to keep her safe, just as she was doing for him.

***

The sound of the television in the living room woke Jeremy from a deep sleep. Figuring Susan had stayed up to watch some late-night TV, he swung himself out of bed and shambled down the hallway.

Jeremy was shocked when he saw a little girl sitting on the floor in front of the TV. Becky turned her head to look at him and he almost fell backward in horror. The whole left side of her face was caved in, leaving her eyeball hanging from its socket by a small strand of tissue. Blood oozed from the gaping hole down to her chin and dripped to the floor. When she smiled at him, all the teeth on that side of her mouth were broken and fragmented.

"Hi, Jeremy," she said happily. "Do you want to watch TV with me?"

Jeremy began to back down the hall toward his room. The dead girl who hadn't stayed dead leaped from the floor and rushed at him, "What's the matter, Jeremy? Don't you like me anymore?"

Jeremy didn't answer.

"That's okay," she said. "I have a new friend now, one who appreciates me for who I am."

Then Vizibir was there beside her, holding her hand. She looked up at him admiringly.

Jeremy was shocked. "How can you say that when he's the one who did this to you? He's the one who killed you."

"No," she shot back, "it's all your fault. You and your lies! If you'd been straight with me from the beginning none of this would have happened."

She was right. He knew he should've told her everything, but didn't. And that had cost her. Jeremy slunk to his knees and started crying.

"Enough of this!" shouted a voice from behind them. Jeremy turned to see Susan rushing down the hall from her bedroom. First, she went over to Becky and grabbed her roughly by the arm, as if scolding a young child.

"You, young lady, have no business being here. You no longer have a place in this world, so you can go right back into the ground and stay dead!"

A light flashed and Becky was gone. Susan then turned to face Vizibir. "As for you, you ought to be ashamed of yourself, picking on a little boy the way you have."

Vizibir simply smiled at her and replied, "You're not going to get rid of me that easy."

"Oh, yeah? We'll see about that." She lifted her arms and began chanting. An intense light filled the room and Jeremy had to shield his eyes or risk being blinded.

With a sharpness in her voice that could cut flesh, she shouted to Vizibir, "Now, demon, you can return to the bowels of Hell. You will not torment this child anymore!"

A bolt of energy shot from her hand and struck Vizibir in the chest. For a few seconds, he stood there, seemingly unscathed. Then slowly his form started to shift, blinking in and out of existence, becoming more and more opaque with each passing second.

Jeremy took a tremendous amount of satisfaction from seeing the look of terror on his face as he disappeared into nothingness.

But his revelry was cut short as he saw Susan slump to her knees in exhaustion. He rushed to her to make sure she was okay, and was reassured with a weak smile.

"He won't be bothering you any longer," she said weakly.

***

Jeremy woke up the next day feeling alive for the first time in his life. He half expected to see Susan curled up in the chair when he woke up, but then the scent of bacon found its way to his nose and he jumped out of bed and raced toward the kitchen.

He stopped short when he rounded the corner and saw

Susan slumped across the kitchen table. An image popped into his brain—a pool of blood under Susan's head and her dead eyes staring up at him from oblivion.

She stirred when he approached her. A plate of bacon, and another with a stack of pancakes, sat on the table a few inches from her. "Hey kiddo," she said groggily. "I guess I fell asleep."

She looked around the kitchen, "Good thing the stove was off or this could have gotten ugly, really fast."

She tried to stand up and immediately plopped back down, her body swaying like she'd just gotten off a Tilt-a-Whirl. She had deep, black circles around her eyes, and her skin was pale and blotchy.

"You don't look so good," Jeremy said.

"I'm fine," she replied with little conviction. "Just a little tired; didn't sleep well last night."

"I know. Thank you."

"No need to thank me. I was just doing what I could to protect you."

"What did you do to him?"

She smiled. "It hit him with the most powerful force in the universe. It might sound corny, but love is stronger than anything evil."

Jeremy's eyes filled with tears, and his words caught in his throat, "I love you too."

After a long embrace, Susan pushed away from him, "How about we start eating before everything gets cold?"

CHAPTER 15

Jeremy's life became somewhat normal after that, if you can call living with an occult priestess who possessed powers to banish demons normal.

It was difficult at first to adjust to a life where he wasn't in a constant state of paranoia. Because of that, Susan home-schooled him for the next few years. It took a while, but through the course of time, Vizibir's image started to slowly fade from his mind.

He grew to become a young man, free to look toward the future, hopeful once again that he might find love in this world. Since Susan had come into the picture his life had been full of bliss.

Eight years passed since their last encounter with Vizibir, and although Susan was great company, they both knew it was time for him to start having some interaction with other kids his age. So, he started his freshman year at Lincoln High School, a small private school located just a few blocks from their home.

Jeremy was fortunate that Susan had been a great teacher, making his transition to structured academia easy. While most students struggled at the beginning of the school year, trying to remember what they had forgotten over the summer, or failed to grasp the new material presented, he was like a sponge absorbing everything easily.

Reality hit Jeremy quickly. Not having much social exposure at an earlier age was a major shortcoming, and led to ridicule and scorn from other kids, who thought he was nothing more than a show-off.

A loud clang echoed through the hall when Brighton slammed him into one of the lockers one day after biology class, the handle on the locker biting sharply into Jeremy's back. The captain of the wrestling team, a short and stocky boy with large arms and a thick skull, poked his finger in Jeremy's chest as he brought his face up close to Jeremy's, twisted in a fit of rage.

"You like making us look bad, you fucking freak?"

"I don't know what you're t-t-talking about?" Jeremy stammered.

"I don't know what you're t-t-talking about?" one of the boys standing next to Brighton mimicked.

"You, answering all the questions like you're better than us," the other boy said. "That's what he's talking about."

"Are you better than us, Freak?" Brighton asked.

Jeremy pleaded, "Look, this is just some misunderstanding. I'm just trying to do my best. I'm sorry my answers upset you."

"See, that kinda sounds like you're mocking us," Brighton said. He clenched his fists tight. "Let me show you what I do to people who mock me!"

An unlikely savior sauntered up to Brighton as he pulled his arm back. She was a long, tall beauty with blond, silky hair and mesmerizing green eyes, who bent forward and whispered something into his ear. Whatever she said had a profound effect on him, because he looked at Jeremy for a second through eyes wide with shock before he turned to his group, "Come on. Let's get out of here. He's not worth our time."

They dispersed and never bothered Jeremy again.

Jeremy looked at the goddess striding toward him in amazement. "What in the world did you say to him?"

She shrugged, "I simply told him that if he didn't leave you alone, he'd be sorry."

"Thank you. But why did you help me?"

"Would you have preferred I leave you alone?"

"No, of course not," Jeremy said quickly. "It's just that...you don't even know me."

She looked at him for a second, "Haven't you ever heard the saying, 'Don't look a gift horse in the mouth'? I helped you because you needed it. Let's leave it at that. Besides, I do know you, Jeremy. I know quite a lot about you."

With that, she turned and walked away, leaving him weak-kneed and google-eyed.

CHAPTER 16

The bad thing about Jeremy's encounter with the blond bombshell was that it happened on Friday afternoon, forcing him to wait anxiously the whole weekend just for the chance to catch a glimpse of her once more. To say that he fell for her hard and fast would be an understatement.

He was practically bouncing off the walls come Sunday afternoon. When he stubbed his toe for the third time on the coffee table, barely avoiding a catastrophe that would have resulted from the glass of soda slipping from his grasp onto the beige carpeting, Susan had seen enough. "What in the world has gotten into you?"

Jeremy took a second to regain his balance. "I don't know. I guess I'm just a little clumsy today."

She studied him for a few seconds, which was the only bad part of living with Susan: her intuition. She always knew what was going on in his head, usually even before he did. Finally, she smiled, "Okay, what's her name?"

He feigned a look of surprise, "What do you mean?"

"Don't give me that. You've been off in La-La Land all day, tripping all over yourself."

He started to protest again, but knew it was pointless, "To

be honest, I don't know her name."

"Uh-huh."

"I'm telling you the truth, Mom. She just appeared out of nowhere. Friday at school, some kids were threatening to beat me up, and she stepped in and persuaded them otherwise."

The witty retort that he expected never came, instead her eyes started filling with tears, "What did you say?"

"You mean about the kids at school?"

"No, before that."

"The girl—"

"No, you knucklehead. What did you call me?"

He stood there confused for a second, unable to grasp right away what she was getting at. Then the light bulb went on.

"I called you mom. I hope that's okay? I didn't mean to upset you."

She rushed over to him; her eyes filled with tears, and gave him the biggest hug he'd ever had.

"Don't be silly," she choked. "I couldn't be happier."

They sat there, just holding each other for a long time. Jeremy's spirit soared to new heights as he felt the love pulsating through him.

Finally, she pulled away from him, "Okay, so tell me about this woman of yours..."

***

Jeremy's thoughts wandered aimlessly the whole day, making it impossible to concentrate. In between classes, he rounded each corner expectantly, hoping to catch a glimpse of his blond angel.

Every time the bell rang to signal the end of one class—and a few minutes later for the start of a new one—his heart sank just a little. Then the final bell rang and his heart dropped completely. Slowly he shuffled out of Algebra class, telling himself that he was a fool for even thinking he had a chance with someone like her. He was starting to believe that the whole thing had been a fairy tale made up in his mind to deceive his heart into feeling a false sense of youthful infatuation.

He trudged his way down the front steps of the school, resigned to a slow and heartbreaking walk home. Then suddenly she was beside him, about five feet to his left. If his head hadn't been buried so low into his chest, he would've seen her sooner.

"Hey, Jeremy," she said as she continued down the steps.

A couple of the jocks that had threatened him were coming up the stairs as they were descending, and both sidestepped the couple widely with anxious faces, and hurried into the building.

She smiled at Jeremy as she continued down the steps and down the sidewalk, while he stood there entranced. Even though the whole episode had lasted mere seconds—a spec of sand in the fabric of time—those two words and her brilliant smile instantly became one of the greatest moments of his life. If his head had flown any higher above the clouds, he would've found himself floating in the endless void of space, not caring that the oxygen had been sucked out of his lungs.

Suddenly, his tether was yanked hard back to earth when he heard the sound of screeching tires, followed by a loud scream. When he turned toward the source of the emergency, his legs almost gave out.

Pushing his way through the crowd that had gathered quickly at the intersection in front of the school, he came to the body of the girl whose name he still didn't know, but who had stolen his heart anyway, lying face down on the pavement. About ten feet from her lay one of her shoes turned at an awkward angle. For a gruesome moment, he was sure her severed and bloodied foot rested inside, but when he glanced at it a second time, he realized that it had simply flown off.

A sigh of relief escaped Jeremy's lips when he saw her slowly roll over and sit up. He rushed over to her, praying that she was okay. After shaking her head a couple of times, she tried to stand up, only to think better of it and sit back down.

"What happened?" she asked, her face twisted in confusion.

The driver of the car, a short woman in her thirties, with long brown hair, was standing over her with a frantic look on her face. "You just darted out in front of me," she said. "I didn't have time to stop!"

The girl thought for a second, as if trying to grasp at a memory. Then a look of realization swept quickly over her, "You're a liar! I remember everything. You weren't even paying attention to the road. I saw you talking on your cell phone. I had to dive out of the way or you would've killed me!"

"That's not true!" the lady said in shock. "I don't even have my phone with me."

"Then what's that?" She was pointing to a metallic pink phone that lay on the ground only a couple of inches from her foot.

A look of shock came over the lady. "That's not possible! I left my phone at home; I know I did."

Before she could protest further, the shrill of sirens cut through the air. As the ambulance came to a screeching halt, two paramedics jumped out of the front of the vehicle, while a third came around from the back. Within seconds, they surrounded Jeremy's damsel in distress and began performing their various tests and assessments to make sure she was okay.

After they had poked and prodded her, looked at her pupils, listened to her heart and lungs, checked her blood pressure, and even taken her temperature, it was determined that she was fine. Of course, they suggested she go to the hospital anyway, just for observation, to which she promptly answered 'no'.

The paramedics left her sitting on the curb while they returned to their vehicle to write up their report. This gave Jeremy a chance to get close to her.

"Are you sure you're okay?" he asked.

"I'm fine," she replied as she tossed a menacingly glance at the driver of the car, who was now talking to a couple of police officers.

One of the officers approached them, "Excuse me, Miss, but can you tell us what happened here?"

She said, "Of course. I was just crossing the street, minding my own business, when this woman comes barreling down on me, talking on her phone and not even paying attention to her driving at all!"

The officer took a small tablet from his shirt pocket. "And what is your name, Young Lady?"

Then Jeremy finally had a name he could put with the face of his blond angel. "Ciera...Ciera Vabir."

He stood there grinning from ear to ear when he heard her name.

"Would you like to press charges, Miss Vabir?" the officer asked.

Ciera looked at the driver, still visibly shaken over the whole incident. "No, I think I'll just let it go. After all, what goes around comes around, right officer?"

"That's the way it usually works."

A big, black Cadillac pulled up, and a tall, thin man stepped out. For a second, Jeremy freaked out. There, standing before him was the splitting image of his father. If it hadn't been for the bushy mustache under his nose, he would have thought it was him, resurrected from the grave to exact his revenge.

The man rushed over to Ciera and hugged her firmly, "Are you alright, Dear?"

"I'm fine, Daddy," she replied. "Just a little shaken up, that's all."

"Are you sure? Nothing broken or bleeding?"

"No, everything's fine."

She looked over at Jeremy with a smile and then turned back to her dad, "Dad, this is Jeremy. He's a friend of mine and goes to school here. He ran over to help me after the accident."

The man extended his hand, "Pleased to meet you, Jeremy. I'm Jonathan Vabir, Ciera's father. Any friend of Ciera's is a friend of mine."

Jeremy jumped slightly as his hand touched Jonathan's and a small spark of electricity passed between them, similar to a static discharge when you touch something after walking around on carpet in your socks. This alone wouldn't have been enough to cause any kind of alarm, but couple that with a slight crook at the corner of the man's mouth and a gleam in his eye, and the whole exchange seemed very odd.

He turned his attention back to Ciera, breaking the contact between them, "Let's go home, Dear. I'm sure you're exhausted from such an ordeal."

Her father reached over and opened the passenger door for her. Before getting in, she bent forward and gave Jeremy a little kiss on the cheek. "Thanks for looking out for me, Jeremy."

Mr. Vabir crossed the back of the car and opened up his door, stopping just before he climbed back in his car, "Judging by the smile on my daughter's face., it looks like we're going to be seeing a lot more of you in the future, Jeremy."

Then they drove away, leaving Jeremy's heart soaring on the wings of an eagle.

CHAPTER 17

Jeremy bounded up the stairs and through the apartment door, unable to contain his excitement! Not only did he now know her name, but her lips had touched his skin, sending a tingle through his body that he never wanted to go away.

His mood changed in an instant when he saw Susan lying on the couch wrapped in blankets and shivering uncontrollably. "Oh my god, Susan! You look terrible! What's wrong?"

She opened her eyes and tried to lift her head from the pillow with no luck. "I'm okay," she feebly. "I think I just caught a touch of the flu."

Jeremy felt her forehead and pulled his hand away in alarm. "You're burning up! We need to get you to the hospital!"

With a stubborn look in her eyes, she tried to protest, only to have that look turn to one of surrender when she tried once again to sit up.

The paramedics that arrived a few minutes later were the same ones from Ciera's accident only a short time ago and were shocked when they saw him again.

One of the paramedics looked at him and said, "Boy,

trouble sure seems to follow you around."

"You have no idea," Jeremy replied solemnly.

"Why don't you tell me what's going on here?"

"I don't know. I just got home a few minutes ago and found Susan on the couch like this."

"Has she shown any symptoms of being ill recently?"

"No. She was fine when I left for school this morning."

With each second, Jeremy grew more afraid; afraid of losing the only good thing in his life, and afraid of being alone again.

After a few minutes, they had her up on a gurney, an IV in her right arm, a blood-pressure cuff on her left, and an ice pack on her forehead.

"Is she going to be okay?" Jeremy asked as they wheeled her out the door.

"She'll be fine," the lady said with only half-hearted conviction. "Once we get her to the hospital, they can figure out exactly what's going on and get it under control."

Jeremy followed them down the stairs and into the back of the ambulance with his heart hanging by a thread. Her eyes fluttered open, and she grabbed his hand firmly as if to say, 'don't worry, everything's going to be fine'. Then her eyes closed and her hand fell away from his as she drifted into unconsciousness.

***

The waiting room felt more like a funeral parlor as Jeremy sat there in silence, hoping and praying that Susan would be alright. Maybe he was overreacting, but if something happened to her, would that mean the return of Vizibir? He had the sense that he was standing at the edge of a dark abyss which threatened to pull him down into its murky depths.

He was so absorbed in his fear that he didn't notice Andrew until he sat down next to him. "Good afternoon, Jeremy," he said, causing Jeremy to jump.

"Andrew! How did you know Susan was here?" Jeremy said.

"When she failed to show up for a meeting, I became concerned. I made a few phone calls and found out she was here."

That's when Jeremy's opinion of Andrew changed forever.

"Listen," Jeremy said, "I know we didn't exactly get off on the right foot, but I'm glad you're here."

"Thank you, Jeremy. Has the doctor been out to speak to you yet?"

"Not for a while. He came out about an hour ago, just to tell me that they're still running tests."

Andrew leaned forward in his chair, his elbows on his knees, his fingers bridged together, and sat there for a moment in deep thought. Then he asked, "Has anything like this happened before?"

"No, not really, except—"

"Except what?"

"Well...there was an incident when I found her nearly unconscious at the kitchen table one morning."

"What happened?"

Jeremy measured his words carefully, unsure how much he should tell Andrew. "I walked into the kitchen and she was passed out sitting at the table. She woke up after a minute and said she was just tired. That was a long time ago, and she's been fine since."

Andrew got up and started pacing back and forth methodically. He continued this for a couple of minutes, then stopped and turned to Jeremy, "Tell me everything you can think of—what she said, how she looked, what happened the night before."

Jeremy stiffened up at that last part. Instead of telling Andrew the truth about that night, he decided to play it off as something less dramatic. "I don't remember much of the details. It's been years since the incident, but I remember that I had a terrible dream the night before and Susan was in it."

He pressed close to Jeremy, "Please, try to remember anything and everything possible."

Jeremy went silent for a time, feeling the pit of his stomach churn as he forced his mind to un-bury the images that he had hoped would stay buried forever.

The words burned like acid as they left his mouth, "He was there—Vizibir—trying to scare me. That was horrible enough, but then he brought Becky into my nightmare. She was a girl I knew when I was younger—the first girl I had ever loved—until he killed her and took her away from me. She sat there, her skull caved in, her eyes looking at me hauntingly, and told me that everything was my fault. All the death and destruction that had happened in my life was all because of me. I felt myself start to lose it, and for a minute I simply didn't care anymore. I was so tired! I just wanted it all to go away."

When Jeremy stopped to take a deep breath, Andrew put his hand on his shoulder. As he did, Jeremy felt a warm sense of calm settle over him.

"Take your time," Andrew said.

Jeremy took another deep breath and continued, "Then Susan was there, in my dream, shining like an angel. I remember the power in her voice as she commanded Vizibir to stop. Then a blinding light filled my dream world. And then everything was silent. The next thing I knew it was morning, and I was safe and sound in my bed. Then I walked into the kitchen and found Susan the way I had said."

"Very interesting," Andrew said. "And how was she after that?"

"Okay, I guess. She was kind of out of it for a couple of days, but was fine after that."

"Did she say anything out of the ordinary to explain what had happened?"

Jeremy replied simply, "No," as the feeling of guilt began to slowly eat away at him. He knew Andrew was only trying to help, but something kept him from divulging the complete truth. Then, he realized it was fear—fear of the unknown power that Andrew wielded.

Andrew was just about to say something else, but was caught short when the doctor came in. Immediately, Jeremy jumped from his chair.

"Jeremy," he said. "Your mother is resting now. You can go in to see her in a little while."

Jeremy felt Andrew's eyes on him when he heard the word 'mother', but acted as if nothing out of the ordinary had been said. He knew Andrew was filing it away for future reference, but at that moment a lecture from Andrew was the last thing he needed.

"Is she going to be okay?" Jeremy asked.

"She's going to be fine. In fact, from what we can deduce she's perfectly healthy. We couldn't find anything wrong with her."

Jeremy was stunned. "I don't understand? You saw the condition she was in when she was brought here."

"I'm afraid we have absolutely no explanation for her previous condition. It's possible that her condition resulted from some psychological trauma she'd suffered. It's hard to say, but regardless, she's fine now. We want to keep her overnight, just for observation, of course. Barring any complications, she'll be able to go home tomorrow."

Complications have always had a way of rearing their ugly heads into Jeremy's life. He had no reason to believe the next twenty-four hours would be any different.

CHAPTER 18

Jeremy was as confused as ever. While he was relieved that Susan was going to be okay, he couldn't help but be puzzled about her previous condition, followed by her miraculous recovery. Something just didn't seem right.

When he and Andrew entered the room, he was encouraged to see her sitting up in her bed. "Thank God, you're okay," he said. "You scared me to death."

She gave Jeremy a half-hearted smile that told him she wasn't quite ready to jump out of bed and start doing back-flips soon. "Don't worry; you're not getting rid of me that easy."

He got the distinct feeling that she wasn't telling him everything, but this time he was content to let it lie. He figured that she'd tell him what he needed to know, when he needed to know it.

Andrew stepped to the bed beside him, "Can I have a few minutes with her alone, Jeremy?"

Jeremy looked at Susan, questioning her with his eyes. She nodded slightly.

"Sure, no problem," Jeremy said as he walked out of the room and found a seat on the floor next to her door.

Whatever they were talking about, he knew it wasn't anything good, and that it was probably about him.

After a few minutes Andrew came out, "Thank you, Jeremy."

He sensed Jeremy's apprehension as he scrambled to my feet. "Susan is fine...for now. While it's difficult to determine what exactly transpired, I'd be willing to bet your supernatural friend, Vizibir, had something to do with it."

"He's not my friend," Jeremy shot back defensively.

"Sorry. I didn't mean it that way. Just a little sarcasm, that's all."

He put his hands on Jeremy's shoulders, "Take care of her, Jeremy. She loves you as if you were her own son, and in every sense of the word you are. At first, I thought that would be a weakness for her, clouding her mind and judgment, and putting both of you at great risk. Now I know different. That bond has instead made both of you stronger. That strength will give us a chance to defeat the evil that surrounds you."

Jeremy shuddered to even think about Vizibir, "But I thought he was gone for good?"

"Hardly. If only it were that simple. I suspect he's just biding his time, lying low, if you will, until the time is right to spring up again. Therefore, it's imperative that you be forever vigilant. Keep your mind sharp and your eyes open to anything that seems out of place."

Then he turned and left.

Jeremy thought about what he had said for a couple of minutes before he went back in and sat down on the edge of Susan's bed. "It's not over yet, is it?" he said.

She looked at him sadly, "No, I'm afraid it's not."

Jeremy struggled to fight back the tears that had disappeared for so long. It had only taken a second for all of his past horror to come flooding back, and this time the cyclone was merciless in its attack.

Susan squeezed his hand, "Unfortunately evil doesn't just disappear with a wish and a prayer. It takes strength and fortitude, love and faith, and sometimes even a little Divine Intervention. Once we're armed with everything we can muster, then and only then will we be able to face this demon head-on and destroy it forever."

"But I thought that's what you did a long time ago in my dream?"

"I know at the time you thought I was there in your dream to protect you, but it was real, Jeremy, in every sense of the word. While you were asleep, Vizibir attacked your astral body. I had a feeling you were in danger, so I sat by your bed watching over you."

"But what could he gain by killing me in my dreams?"

"Don't you understand, Jeremy? He doesn't want to kill you; he wants to be you. He wants to take over your soul and make it his. Your death is just his back-up plan."

Jeremy sat there in stunned silence. Until then, his worst fears had always been for those around him. Now he had been told that he was actually in very real physical danger.

After a while Susan said, "Jeremy, are you okay?"

"It's just that, all this time he's never done anything to me directly. Instead, he's always attacked those who were close to me."

"By going after those you loved he was able to feed off of your fear. He was growing stronger while you were getting weaker. What he didn't count on was the courage of a little boy standing up to the darkness."

"It's you who have saved me. Without you, I wouldn't be here today."

This time, it was her eyes that misted over, and she changed the subject, "So, tell me about this woman who's threatening to steal you aware from me."

After a moment of bashfulness, he told her everything he could think of, even mentioning the near accident and the meeting with her father.

Susan's reaction wasn't quite what Jeremy had expected. Instead of showing concern for the girl who had almost gotten hit, she looked fearful.

"Why do you look so alarmed?" Jeremy asked.

"I don't know. It's just...something doesn't sound quite right."

"What do you mean?"

"I mean everything—your girlfriend, her father, the accident, my mysterious illness—it all seems strange."

Jeremy started getting defensive. "Don't be ridiculous. It's all just a big coincidence."

Susan looked at him for a second and then sighed, "I'm sure you're probably right. I'm just overreacting. But please do me a favor and be on your guard for anything that seems out of the ordinary."

The problem was that, ever since he could remember, his whole life had been completely out of the ordinary.

CHAPTER 19

Days turned into weeks, weeks into months, and each moment Jeremy fell deeper and deeper under Ciera's spell. He was head-over-heels completely in love—for the second time in his life.

His focus became solely on Ciera. Without realizing what he was doing, he began to unknowingly grow distant from Susan by spending all of his free time with her, and none with the woman who had taken him in and sheltered him from his demons.

Then one day he realized six months had passed, and he still hadn't introduced her to Susan. Maybe he was subconsciously avoiding the confrontation for fear that Susan would reject her, or find some kind of fault in her? Susan had asked on numerous times to meet her, and conveniently something had come up each time to prevent that.

Then one day Ciera showed up at their doorstep.

Jeremy opened the door after a soft knock to find her standing there with a smile on her face and flowers in her hand.

He was shocked, "Ciera, what are you doing here?"

"I know your mom wants to meet me, and I feel terrible

about always having to cancel at the last minute. So, I surprised you. I hope that's okay?"

"Of course, it's okay! I'm just a little stunned, that's all."

He ushered her in just as Susan entered the room. "Susan, this is Ciera. Ciera, Susan."

Susan shook her hand, "It's nice to finally meet you in person. I feel like I know you already, with the way Jeremy talks about you constantly."

Ciera looked at Jeremy with her eyebrows raised, "I hope he's been saying good things about me?"

Susan chuckled, "Of course. He absolutely beams when he talks about you."

"Well, your son's pretty special, too." She winked at Jeremy, causing him to blush.

"Okay ladies," Jeremy blushed. "That's enough."

"Are you embarrassed?" Susan asked.

"Of course not," he answered with mock defensiveness in his voice.

"Here, these are for you," Ciera said as she presented the bouquet to Susan. "I didn't know what your favorite flower was, so I got you a bouquet of wildflowers. I hope you like them."

"They're beautiful, "Susan said as she sniffed deeply. "Let me get a vase to put them in."

After Susan left the room Ciera turned to Jeremy, "I hope you're not mad at me for dropping by unexpectedly?"

"No, of course not!"

"I just figured it was time to quit putting it off any longer."

"You sound like you were afraid to meet her."

She hesitated for a second, "It's just that I haven't had the best luck in the family relationship department."

"Don't be ridiculous. How could anyone not find you irresistible? I know I do."

Susan returned with the flowers arranged in an obelisk shaped vase. As she set the vase down on the top of the buffet she cried out with a soft gasp, "Ouch!"

"What's the matter?" Jeremy asked.

"I must have pricked myself on a thorn or something."

"Here, let me look at it," Ciera offered. She grabbed Susan's hand and saw a little stream of blood dribbling down her thumb. "Ooh, whatever it was got you pretty good. I feel absolutely terrible."

"Don't be silly," Susan answered as she put her thumb in her mouth to suck up the blood. "It's just a little scratch. Nothing that a little ointment and a Band-Aid can't fix. How about if I go clean this up and then we can all go out for dinner?"

"I'm afraid I can't. I have a ton of homework to do, plus I promised my dad I'd help him with a few things. Is it okay if I take a rain check?"

"Sure, no problem. Just let us know when you're available."

Ciera gave Jeremy a quick kiss, "I'll see you tomorrow."

The disappointment was clear in Susan's eyes as Ciera turned and left. "I'm sorry, Mom. I think she was just a little nervous, that's all. Give her some time."

"What could she possibly be nervous about?"

"Beats me."

"Well, she seems like a nice girl."

Jeremy was just about to say something when there was a knock on the door. He opened it to find Ciera standing there.

"Is that dinner invitation sill available?" she asked.

Susan responded eagerly, "Of course! What made you change your mind?"

"Well, I figured it was time to get to know the mother of the man I love."

* * *

***

A week later, the pest control van was leaving just as Jeremy arrived home from school. When he went inside the apartment, he found Susan sitting on the couch a nervous wreck.

Jeremy rushed over to her, "What in the world's the matter?"

She hugged him tight, "Oh my god, Jeremy! It was horrible...like something right out of a horror film!"

"What are you talking about?"

"Bees! Hundreds and hundreds of bees swarming around the apartment! They were everywhere! I felt like I was trapped in the Amityville house."

"Oh my god, Susan! Are you okay?"

"I'm fine, just shaken up. Miraculously, I escaped without getting stung."

"I don't understand? Where did they come from?"

"The exterminator found a beehive just outside the balcony tucked into a corner of the awning. He said they must've crawled through a hole in the wall somewhere."

Jeremy looked around the room for a minute. All was quiet. "So, was the exterminator able to get rid of them all?"

"It looks like it. I stayed out in the hallway the whole time. I don't know what he did, but it worked. When I walked in, they were all gone. He removed the hive and said the swarm wouldn't return."

Jeremy held her tight for a long time until she calmed down. He knew something didn't seem right, but he couldn't put his finger on it. The exterminator had been right, though. The bees never returned.

What did happen as a result of the swarm was truly

bizarre. As the bees had swarmed around the apartment, they had pollinated the wildflowers. Within a few days, as they invaded every potted plant in the place, the living room was overrun. Before long, the apartment became a veritable jungle, with vines and flowers sprouting in every corner, rising through cracks in the furniture, disappearing into the baseboards, and then reappearing out of the vents in the ceiling.

When Jeremy tried to remove some of them, Susan became violent. "What are you doing?" she cried.

"It's getting too crowded in here. I just thought I'd clear some of it out. Make it less like a savage garden and more like our home again."

Susan had a desperate look in her eyes like a crack addict pleading with someone not to flush her junk down the toilet. "But you can't get rid of them! Look at how beautiful they are!"

"Don't you think it's a little too much?" Jeremy asked.

"Did you forget that your girlfriend was the one that brought them over? It would be rude to get rid of them."

After a time, Jeremy gave in. How could he argue with someone who obviously wasn't thinking straight at the time?

***

Susan grew fonder of Ciera, asking every day when she was going to come over next, like Ciera was her drug dealer and she was desperate for a score.

Weeks later, Susan's mysterious illness re-surfaced, knocking her off her feet like she'd been hit by a truck. When Ciera showed up at their doorstep unexpectedly once again, a tiny itch entered Jeremy's brain that something didn't feel right. But when Susan magically recovered, seemingly just from her being there, he let the matter drop. Whatever she had done, the end result was that Susan was better. And that's all that mattered.

CHAPTER 20

Jeremy lived with the jungle around him for nearly two months before he couldn't take it anymore. He hated to go against Susan, but he knew something wasn't right, and those wildflowers were the cause. He had to do something.

He remembered that Susan had cut her finger on one of the thorns when she'd taken the flowers from Ciera. The only explanation he could come up with was that some sort of chemical had entered her bloodstream. It had created a chemical dependency in her that could only be soothed by the fumes given off from the flowers, effectively turning her into a drug addict.

So, he took the path that many friends and family members of drug addicts had taken before him——the path of tough love. In the middle of the night, as he carried each plant out to the dumpster at the end of the parking lot, he prayed desperately that he was doing the right thing.

When Susan woke up the next morning and walked into the now-barren living room she immediately went into a terrified frenzy. "What in the world have you done?" she cried. "Where are my plants?"

"I threw them out," Jeremy said simply.

"You did what? You had no right!"

"I was only trying to protect you. There was something strange about those plants and the way they affected you."

"Who are you to talk about strange behavior? You had no right to do that!"

She was right. He had no right to do what he had done, but something bizarre was going on and he had to do something to protect her. After everything she had done for him, it was his turn to save her. Hopefully.

Somehow, he had to make her see what was going on. "Look at yourself, Susan. You're not behaving rationally. Can't you see that this isn't normal?"

She laughed a cold-hearted laugh, "Are you questioning me about what's normal? You wouldn't understand normal if it landed in your lap!"

Her words stung Jeremy deep, and it was all he could do to keep from running from the room. Even though he knew it wasn't really her talking, but some unseen force acting through her, the words hit him hard.

Before he could say another word, she was on the phone, pleading hysterically for Ciera to come over. She looked so pathetic that Jeremy had to turn his head to avoid looking at her.

After a minute, the conversation was over and Susan slammed the phone down. She looked both crazed and worried.

"What's the matter?" Jeremy asked.

"She said that she didn't have any more of the flowers, and didn't know where to get them." She looked at Jeremy desperately, "Now what am I going to do?"

"Will you just listen to yourself? It's not you talking! Something's gotten into your system and affected your mind."

A knock on the door stopped the conversation from devolving further. Susan ran to the door and threw it open.

"Ciera! Thank God you're here. I need your help!"

Ciera took Susan's hand and led her to the couch. "Don't worry," she said. "Everything's gonna be over soon. Just lie down and I'll help you get through this."

Susan looked at her with a glimmer of hope. "Do you have something for me? I feel all strange and funny inside."

Ciera put her finger on Susan's lips, "Shhh...just lie there and be still. It's almost over now."

Jeremy stood there shocked. For a second, all he could do was watch in confusion. "What's going on here?" he finally asked.

"It's simple," Ciera replied. "She's dying."

The color immediately drained from Jeremy's face, "How do you know that?"

"She has poison flowing through her nervous system right now. In a short time, paralysis will set in, then her breathing will stop, and that will be the end of that."

Jeremy watched in horror as Susan's eyes grew wide. Her breathing became shallow, and she started grasping for the edge of her couch as though she were trying to save herself from falling off a cliff into the darkness below.

Ciera leaned forward and kissed her gently on the forehead. "Thank you," she whispered.

A second later, Susan stopped moving, stopped struggling, and stopped breathing.

Panic immediately set in and Jeremy rushed to Susan's side, desperately shaking her by the shoulders in an effort to rattle the life back into her.

"No, God, no!" he cried out. "You can't die! I need you. Don't leave me."

Jeremy turned toward Ciera, his face engulfed in terror.

"What in the world just happened?" he pleaded.

Tears stung his eyes as he looked at her desperately for answers. But the sinister look she returned brought his worst fear to life. Her eyes were dark and foreboding, while a devilish smile curled across her lips.

"Funny thing about Belladonna," Ciera said as she lifted Susan's hand to reveal an ugly sore on her thumb where the thorn had cut her, "its poison works through a person's bloodstream, attacking the central nervous system. One drop is all it takes. Then the brain shuts down. What most people don't know is that the perfume given off by the Witch Hazel plant neutralizes the poison and keeps it at bay. The drawback to this is that it causes a person to lose their sanity. But if the Witch Hazel is removed from the victim's vicinity for any length of time the poison is freed to resume its deadly course."

Jeremy looked at her in shock.

"How does it feel to know that you were the one who killed her, Jeremy?" Ciera said with a hiss.

Jeremy struggled to speak coherently, his words gurgling in his throat, "But why?"

Ciera bent down and patted him on the cheek, "Jeremy, Jeremy, Jeremy...you really are such a peach. You have absolutely no idea what's going on here, do you?"

All Jeremy could do was sit there bewildered, his mind a jumbled mess. "But I thought you loved me? Why did you do this?"

Ciera replied, "Love is overrated."

He watched in horror as her face twisted and morphed into something wicked and evil. Her blue eyes turned fire red and pulsated with hatred. Sharp fangs protruded from the corner of her black lips, while a pair of small horns jutted from her forehead. Her skin was a glistening body of milky white. A forked tongue slithered from her mouth as she spoke, "What's the matter, Jeremy? Don't you love me anymore?"

Before he could respond, her serpentine tail shot forward and grabbed him around the throat. Black, leathery wings spread wide from her back, engulfing him in a shroud of death.

"I bet you're just full of all kinds of questions right now," she said. "I think there's someone else who might be able to answer those questions better than me."

Suddenly, Vizibir stepped from behind Ciera.

"Ah, Jeremy," Vizibir said. "It's so good to see you again after all this time. I've missed you terribly."

He crouched down to where Jeremy still kneeled next to Susan's dead body—the only real mother he'd ever known and loved. A cold shiver coursed through Jeremy's body as Vizibir reached out and touched his face.

"This could've all been so different, you know. Imagine the possibilities. The world would've been ours to command. We could have been together forever."

"How could I ever want to be a part of you?" Jeremy cried. "You've killed everyone I've ever been close to; everyone I've ever loved."

Vizibir looked at Jeremy for a moment then shook his head slowly in disappointment. "I was afraid you were going to see things that way."

The demon lifted his hands toward the ceiling and uttered something incoherent. A second later, his hands started to glow bright red and then burst into flames.

Just when Jeremy thought all hope was lost, the front door to the apartment burst open and Andrew rushed in. Vizibir turned around quickly and roared loudly before he disappeared just as a dagger hurling through the air struck him. It did find a secondary target, however, striking Ciera between the eyes. Instantly, her body slumped to the floor, where it disintegrated into a pile of ash.

Andrew grabbed Jeremy's hand and pulled him up quickly. "We need to get you out of here!"

"But Susan—"

"There's no time for her now. We can mourn her later. Right now, we have to get out of here before he comes back."

Andrew scooped up the dagger before leading Jeremy out the door. No sooner had they stepped out of the entrance of the building when Vizibir materialized a few yards in front of them. Andrew turned to Jeremy and handed him the knife. "Take this and run as fast as you can. It's the only thing that can destroy him. Pierce his heart and he will die."

"But—"

"No buts! Find sacred ground. That'll weaken him. He won't be powerless, but it might give you the chance you need."

Jeremy stood still for a second as Vizibir walked toward them.

Andrew pushed him forward, "Run, dammit!"

Jeremy turned and ran as fast as he could, not knowing where he was running to, or what he would do once he got there. He made it to the edge of the complex and glanced backward to see a blinding flash of light that was followed by a loud, wailing cry.

Inspiration hit Jeremy suddenly as an image of St. Augustine's Cathedral flashed in his mind. He pushed himself even faster, hoping his legs would hold up and carry him the six blocks down the street before the demon caught up with him.

CHAPTER 21

Jeremy rounded the corner and saw the large building looming before him. His breath wheezed through his lips, and his lungs were on fire. as he pushed forward even harder. When he burst through the door, he thought he could feel Vizibir's hot breath on the back of his neck and hear a dark whisper in his ear.

The church was empty except for a solitary priest occupying the front pew. The middle-aged man jumped from his meditation when he heard Jeremy's footsteps pounding through the sanctuary.

"You have to get out of here now!" Jeremy shouted. "It's not safe."

"Calm down, Son," the priest said. "Everything's going to be alright. Just relax and tell me what's going on."

"There's no time for that, Father! He's going to be here any second."

"What in God's name are you rambling about?"

"God has nothing to do with this, Father."

The doors to the cathedral burst open with enough force that they nearly flew off the hinges. The priest stood stunned as he watched an exact duplicate of Jeremy walking rapidly down the aisle toward him. Before he had a chance to utter any last second prayer, Vizibir grabbed him by the throat and raised him high off the ground.

Jeremy rushed over to him, "Vizibir, no! There's been enough killing already. Please, no more. I'll do anything you want," he pleaded. "Just please, no more death."

Vizibir contemplated for a second, as if measuring Jeremy's sincerity, then dropped the priest to the floor. The man lay on his back, gasping for air and clutching his chest.

Vizibir said, "I've done as you wish. Now it's your turn."

"What is it you want?" Jeremy asked.

"It's simple. I want you. I want to be you, completely. I want your body. I want your life. I want your soul. And I want you to give yourself to me freely, that we may go forward as one."

Every instinct in Jeremy's body told him to run. But he knew that this might be his only chance to take down the monster. Instead, he slumped to his knees in submission. He bent his head down low, carefully trying to conceal the dagger in his hands.

Jeremy said solemnly, "You win. I can't do this anymore. Do what you want, it doesn't matter now."

"So, you finally realize how hopeless it is to fight me? You can't escape your destiny, Jeremy. And your destiny is me."

Vizibir walked over to him with his arms open wide, "Come, Jeremy, it's time."

Jeremy stood up slowly and allowed Vizibir to wrap his icy tentacles around him. A deep chill passed through him, and he felt his soul being ripped from his body. He only had seconds before he would be completely helpless.

With his final act of desperation, Jeremy thrust the knife into Vizibir's chest. An ear-splitting cry erupted from the demon, and he looked at Jeremy in surprise. Vizibir staggered back as a stream of black blood oozed from the wound.

"Jeremy...why?" he said weakly. Then he slumped to the ground and fell over. His body twitched for a second and then stopped.

Vizibir was dead.

For a long time, Jeremy just sat there, his body exhausted and his brain numb. He couldn't grasp the concept that it was finally over.

The priest put his hand on Jeremy's shoulder, "The grace of God has touched you, my child. Whatever evil has plagued you is now gone. Your soul is free."

Free. The word resounded in Jeremy's brain. He had never been free. But at what cost? *What do I do now? He's taken everyone from me.* He was utterly and completely alone.

As if to emphasize that his torment was indeed over, Vizibir's body began to glow, softly at first, and then intensified until it was blinding. The ground trembled, and then suddenly the demon's body vanished, leaving only the knife lying on the wooden floor.

Jeremy reached down to pick the blade up, almost expecting Vizibir's hand to shoot up from the floor and drag him down into Hell with him. When he did finally grasp the handle, he felt the familiar tingle of energy that had once identified his demon, but after a second that too vanished, and with it the final traces of the evil that had tormented his life.

"Go home now, child," the priest said. "Find peace in your soul, knowing that you have fought a tremendous battle against an overwhelming foe and have come out victorious."

Jeremy shot back at the priest, "Victorious? That monster took everything from me! Everyone I've ever loved; everyone who's ever loved me; is dead because of him. I don't call that a victory!"

The priest was silent for a moment, studying Jeremy's eyes as if he could read his past in them. "Unfortunately, my friend, in the never-ending war between good and evil there will always be casualties. It is our duty to honor those fallen soldiers for their bravery and dedication to protecting the world from this evil. Keep their memories alive in your heart."

His words did little to ease the ache in Jeremy's soul, making the long walk home seem to take an eternity, as each step brought a different horrific memory to the surface in his mind. By the time he reached the steps to his apartment building, every terrible event in his life had replayed itself in full vivid color.

The darkness within the apartment nearly suffocated him as he made his way to the couch and threw himself down so that sleep could overtake him, and hopefully, never let him go. He was only vaguely aware that Susan's dead body should have been on the couch, and that he had walked right through a ribbon of crime-scene tape on their front door, but he couldn't think clearly enough to analyze the situation.

Sometime later, with the night sky atg its darkest, he felt a warm touch on his cheek. When he opened his eyes, he saw Susan kneeling beside him, a smile on her face, looking like an angel.

She brushed the hair from his forehead, "Oh, Jeremy, I'm so proud of you. Through all the horror, every terrible thing you endured, you remained brave and strong."

"Then why do I feel like I've failed?" he replied.

"You haven't failed at all, Jeremy. You fought hard your whole life, and in the end, prevailed against an unspeakable evil. That is hardly a failure."

"But you're still dead."

She smiled her warm and comforting smile, the same one that for so long had been his only ray of hope in his cursed life. "You know I'll always be here with you, watching over you."

"But that's not enough! Call me selfish, but I want you here beside me, in flesh and blood, loving me and taking care of me like a mother should."

"Be strong, Jeremy, and know that I love you, My Son."

Then she vanished, leaving him alone again. Tears filled his eyes as he stared at the space where her apparition had appeared.

CHAPTER 22

"You know, Jeremy," Vizibir said, "I was actually a little worried there for a moment. If the knife had struck a couple of inches higher this whole story would have played out differently. Not that it didn't hurt. It did. In fact, it hurt like a bitch. You came close, you little shit. I'll give you that. Closer than I thought possible."

He looked at Jeremy, who lay on the couch, blood gurgling from his mouth as he struggled to breathe, the result of the knife wound in his stomach.

Vizibir spread his arms wide. "But as you can see, I'm fine now. Nothing hurt, except maybe my pride a little."

Kneeling down, Vizibir spoke softly into Jeremy's ear, almost sadly, "You know, things could have been much different. All you had to do was give yourself to me. Instead, you betrayed me, and tried to destroy me. I had no choice now but to return the favor."

He bent down and kissed Jeremy softly on the cheek, "Goodbye, Jeremy."

Vizibir grabbed the hilt of the dagger and wrenched it brutally upward, nearly splitting Jeremy's body in half. A fountain of blood sprayed from Jeremy's mouth as death overtook him.

A white stream of mist issued from Jeremy's mouth, spiraling toward the ceiling. Vizibir closed his eyes, uttered a short phrase in an incomprehensible language, and inhaled deeply. Instantly Jeremy's soul halted its ascent and was tugged fiercely down toward Vizibir.

For a moment, his body shimmered and sparked, jumping out of itself as if the frequency of the two different energies were shifting to become the same. Finally, his form settled into place and he was whole. He held his right arm up and flexed his grip, testing its strength and solidity.

"Thank you, Jeremy," he said. "If it's any consolation, your soul will be put to good use. I promise."

Vizibir closed the door softly behind him, walked down the stairs and out of the building. He was a little disappointed at the fact that Jeremy was dead, knowing that his power would have been greater had he chosen to join Vizibir voluntarily. In the end, though, it was the result that was important, and he was now one step closer to his goal.

***

The glass in the mirror swirled and shimmered, and a moment later, Vizibir no longer stared at his own reflection, but a twisted, demonic face looking back at him. Large black eyes regarded him for a moment, then her black lips parted to reveal a row of silvery daggers as she spoke, "Is it finished?"

"It is, Mother," he replied.

"Good. Now it is time to move on to the next."

"Which is?"

"There's a little girl, just four years old now, who is showing much greater potential than Jeremy. Try a different approach with her. Go to her. Earn her trust, then break her down so she gives herself to you freely."

Vizibir replied, "I will do as you ask, and if needed, whatever is necessary."

The glass shimmered once more and then cleared. Vizibir smiled a cruel smile at his reflection before he vanished into the darkness, eager to begin the next chapter in his ascension.

PART TWO:
ELIZABETH

In the darkness shines no light;
Owls shrieking in the night.
All alone, no one near,
My only comfort is my fear.

In the dark, creatures walk;
With my ears, I hear them talk.
Because of the dark, I cannot see
How close, how near the creatures be.

Always hoping that me they won't find,
Seeking safety inside my mind.
Wind blows, branches break,
Hoping me they will not take.

My only sanction is the light;
Day will come and end my fright.
I lie with the blankets over my head,
Remaining still inside my bed.

When light comes and I can see,

The creatures vanish and let me be.
I am safe until the night
When once again returns my fright.
—Thomas Scott Hurst

CHAPTER 1

To say that Elizabeth differed from other kids was an understatement. Although she looked and acted like children her age, she saw things others didn't see; heard things others didn't hear; felt things others didn't feel.

The day before her fourth birthday, skipping around the backyard enjoying the new bubble blower she'd gotten as an early birthday present, chasing the shimmering orbs as they cast magic rainbows all around her, she rounded the big maple tree and squealed in delight when she saw her Nanna standing there.

"Hi, Nanna," she said as she latched onto Nanna's leg.

"Well, hello, Lizzy," Nanna replied sweetly. "And how are you today?"

"Great! I'm chasing bubbles!"

Nanna giggled, "I can see that."

"Are you coming to my birthday party tomorrow? I'm gonna be four."

"Actually, that's why I'm here, Sweetie. I'm afraid I'm not going to make it to your party. I'm just not feeling very well."

Lizzy's face grew long. "That's too bad, Nanna. I love it when you're here. You always know how to make me laugh."

Nanna bent down to give Lizzy a hug, "I know, sweety. I'm so sorry. You have yourself a wonderful birthday, okay?"

"I will, Nanna. I promise."

"Why don't you show me how awesome you are at making bubbles?" Nanna said.

She watched with a smile while Lizzy reared back and then waved the wand around in large arcs, sending thousands of shimmering bubbles into the air. As Lizzy jumped up and down clapping her hands in the air, Nanna walked toward the front of the house and was gone. Lizzy continued her bubble chasing for a while, thinking nothing more of the encounter.

The next day Lizzy's mother, Andrea, was lighting the final candle on Lizzy's cake. A soft tear hung in the corner of her eye, which she brushed away before it could fall from its perch. But a sense of sadness lingered in her eyes after. The other kids didn't seem to notice, but Lizzy did.

"Are you sad because Nanna's not here?" Lizzy asked her.

Instead of answering, Andrea stood silent for a minute, gathering herself before she said, "Why don't you just make a wish and blow out your candles sweetie?"

Lizzy closed her eyes tight for a second, then took a deep breath and blew the candles out. She looked up at her mom after, "I know I'm not supposed to tell you what my wish was, but it was for Nanna to get better. I miss her."

Andrea couldn't hold back anymore, and before the dam could burst, she excused herself and left the room, leaving Lizzy confused.

Lizzy found out later that her Nanna had died the night before from a stroke. Of course, she was shielded from the details of her death, told only that she had gotten really sick, and had gone to a place where she would never suffer again. To a four-year-old child with no concept of death, that place could very well have been some magical kingdom such as Narnia or Never-Never Land just as easily as it could've been Heaven.

It didn't take long, though, for Lizzy to put two and two together and realize that Nanna's visit had been more than a little out of the ordinary. She was smart enough to figure out that if Nanna had died Friday, then there was no way she could've visit ed her on Saturday unless she was a spirit.

With an innocence found in most children her age, she went up to her mother and asked her simply, "Did you see Nanna's ghost too, Mommy?"

A stunned look came over Andrea's face. "What in the world are you talking about?"

"The day before my birthday Nanna came to see me. She told me she was sick and wouldn't be able to be there. That was her ghost, right, since she was already dead?'

Andrea didn't say anything. Instead, she just stood there with trembling lips and watery eyes.

"Are you okay, Mommy?" Lizzy asked.

Her mother choked back her tears, "I'm fine, Sweetie. I just miss her, that's all."

"I know. I do too, Mommy."

"Plus...I wish I had seen her one last time like you did."

Lizzy didn't tell her mom that Nanna was standing right next to her, smiling her big, warm smile, and listening to every word.

CHAPTER 2

Lizzy jumped into bed and slid under the covers as her mom reached down to tuck her in. "Do you want me to read you a story before you go to sleep?" Andrea asked.

"Not tonight," Lizzy said through a wide yawn. "I'm kinda tired."

Andrea frowned for a second and then bent down to kiss her forehead. "Okay, sleep good," she said as she pulled the blanket up to Lizzy's chin.

When Andrea reached to turn off the light, Lizzy pleaded, "Can you leave the light on?"

"We talked about this, Lizzy. There's nothing to be afraid of."

"Just this one last time? Please?"

Andrea gave in and left the light on. "Okay, little lady. Last time. Goodnight."

"Goodnight, Mommy."

As Andrea left the room, she didn't see the sly smile that crossed Lizzy's lips.

It took every ounce of restraint Lizzy had to keep the giggles in check until she was sure her mom was far enough away.

Finally, she couldn't hold it in anymore and started laughing. Nanna put her finger to her lips and ushered a soft shush to Lizzy. "Quiet, Lizzy, or she'll hear you."

Lizzy took a breath. "I know. It was just funny the way you were making faces but Mommy couldn't see you."

Lizzy grew serious. "How come I can see you, Nanna, but Mommy can't?"

"When kids grow up, they get caught up in the pressures of being an adult and stop believing in things that are special. And when they don't believe, they can't see what's in front of them."

"I'll never forget you, Nanna."

"I know, Sweetie. If I had a star for every time you made me smile, I would be holding the night sky in my hand. Now, how was your first day of preschool?"

Lizzy's eyes grew wide. "It was awesome! We played all kinds of games, and had snacks, and the teacher read us a story." Then she wrinkled her nose. "There were a couple of boys there I didn't like, though. They were being mean to everyone."

Before Nanna could reply, Andrea walked into the room with a concerned look on her face. "Who were you talking to, Lizzy?"

Nanna shook her head toward Lizzy.

"Nobody, Mommy. I was just telling Nanna about my day in case she was up in Heaven listening."

A tear welled up in Andrea's eye for a second that she quickly brushed away. "Okay. Just try to get some sleep. Tomorrow's a busy day, with school and all."

"I will, Mommy." This time she closed her eyes and fell asleep with the smell of Nanna's apple pie blanketing her as she drifted off into her dreams.

* * *

***

For a while Lizzy saw Nanna everywhere, like she was watching over her, protecting her. She especially liked to visit her at night so Lizzy could tell her all about her day before she went to sleep. It was almost as if she had never left. Almost.

Then, a few months after Nanna's death things started to get strange. It was just a glimpse here and there, out of the corner of her eye. Lizzy would see something, only to turn and find nothing there. But she knew they were there, and they scared her.

One night Nanna sensed that something was wrong. "What's wrong, Sweetie?" Nanna asked.

Lizzy didn't respond because she wasn't really sure about what she'd seen. It had happened so fast and she didn't really know how to describe it.

"Don't be afraid, Lizzy. You know you can tell me anything," Nanna said.

Lizzy hesitated for a second, "I've been seeing things, lately, Nanna, just out of the corner of my eye. They disappear before I can really see them, but I know they're there. It's like they're playing hide-and-seek or spying on me or something."

"It's okay, Dear. There's nothing to be afraid of. You have a very special gift, Lizzy. You're able to see things that others can't."

"But that's what scares me, Nanna. I don't want to see things. I just want to be a kid, that's all."

Nanna smiled at her, "In time you'll learn to appreciate and control your abilities. You'll grow up to be a very special lady."

That did little to ease Lizzy's fears. Finally, she couldn't hold it inside anymore—a gut-wrenching feeling that she had been suppressing since Nanna showed up this time.

"It was you, Nanna," she blurted out as tears fell from her eyes. "Yesterday you came to see me, only it wasn't you. You were mean and evil. You said lots of nasty things to me—said you didn't love me anymore."

Nanna looked at her for a second, like she was thinking about how to answer. "That's ridiculous," she finally said. "I've never said such a thing."

Nanna's face then grew dark and sinister, "What I actually said was that 'a selfish little brat like you doesn't deserve to be loved'. Get your facts straight next time, little girl."

Lizzy sat there frozen in time as a wave of deep emotion built up inside her. Then, just as it was about to come crashing down around her and break her fragile spirit into a thousand pieces, a second figure appeared before her. It was another Nanna!

She screamed at the first Nanna with a force that shook the entire house, "Leave her alone!"

A huge gust of wind swirled around the room like a tornado, stinging Lizzy's eyes and nearly throwing her off the bed. Bolts of electricity shot around the room in random, deadly arcs, scorching the walls and shattering glass.

Andrea suddenly rushed through the door, panicked from the noise, and stopped in her tracks when she saw the deadly spectacle engulfing the room. Her face was fixed in a twisted picture of terror and fear, her mouth opened wide for an earth-shattering scream. Before the scream could erupt, however, there was a blinding flash and then everything was gone.

Shaking terribly, Andrea shuffled over to Lizzy's bed and wrapped her arms around her tight. After a long time, she finally found the strength to speak, "What just happened here?"

Lizzy started to cry, "That was Nanna...or something pretending to be her. The real Nanna saved us."

Both of them just sat there holding each other for a long time. Lizzy never saw Nanna again.

CHAPTER 3

Unfortunately, Lizzy's other visitors didn't stop with Nanna's disappearance. If anything, their ghostly visits got worse, bombarding her at a furious pace. Sure, most of them were still just glimpses here and there, like passing shadows or wisps of smoke. But others manifested themselves more prominently, appearing as full-bodied apparitions. And all of them scared her to death.

The only way to defend herself was to completely ignore them, hoping they would go away. She didn't talk much, and when she did it was only to say what was absolutely necessary. Toys and games no longer held any appeal to her. In fact, the only thing Lizzy did, all day, every day, was sit with her head down low and rock back and forth, humming softly to herself, drowning out the whispers surrounding her.

Andrea was forced to withdraw Lizzy from preschool only a short time after she had started. She pleaded with Lizzy daily, begging her to show any kind of emotion, until she herself was in tears. To see her daughter withdraw into herself so completely tore a hole in her heart.

It hurt Lizzy immensely to see her mother suffering like that, but she couldn't tell her what was really going on. She

119

couldn't let them back in.

After weeks of struggle, Andrea finally decided her only recourse was to seek professional help for Lizzy and scheduled an appointment with a child psychologist. While she held little hope that the meeting would cure Lizzy of whatever had taken hold of her, she had run out of answers.

The doctor was a weasel of a man, tall and thin, with a long face dotted with a long nose and beady eyes. Of course, Lizzy had no intention of opening up to him, or anyone else. So, she just sat there while he prodded and poked into her brain.

"Hello, Lizzy. I'm Dr. Thomas, but you can call me Simon. I'm here to help you, and together I think we can deal with what's troubling you. Does that sound good, Lizzy? Wouldn't it be good to get rid of whatever you're afraid of?"

Lizzy dared a glance at the weasel-man and immediately wished she hadn't. The crowd of entities surrounding him pushed toward Lizzy, each spirit reaching out with icy fingers to snatch onto a sliver of her soul in an attempt to renew the life it once had.

Immediately, Lizzy closed her eyes tight and willed the spirits away, refusing to give in to them or the weasel-man who had brought them to her.

"It's okay, Lizzy," Dr. Jackson said. "There's nothing here to be afraid of."

Lizzy kept her eyes shut and her mouth silent.

After a series of futile questions, resulting in absolutely nothing, the doctor took Andrea outside. They both returned a few minutes later, each with a disappointed look on their face.

Next up was the neurologist a few weeks later, whose office was located in a far wing of the hospital, making the journey down the long halls, where the shadows grew darker and larger, a trip through the danger zone for Lizzy. The whispers echoed in her ears like a symphony for the damned.

The neurologist was a small, round man with a long, gray beard and wispy hair. This time, the poking and prodding became physical, as he attached sensors to various spots around her head. Her terror grew to new heights when her body began to slide up into the metal tube for the cat-scan. All of a sudden, it felt like the world was about to collapse and smother her to death. She tried to hide the anxiety, but it was too late. As if in response to her fear, a series of crackles and sparks erupted from the machine. Lizzy screamed, and the machine shut down. The doctor and an assistant rushed in and pulled her from the machine.

Once they had recovered from the episode, the Doctor asked Lizzy to sit in the small waiting room next to his office, which was luckily, a good distance from the tube of death. Lizzy watched as he talked to her mom just outside in the hall. A couple of times Andrea glanced in Lizzy's direction, leaving her guessing at what they were saying. It probably boiled down to him telling her that Lizzy was perfectly fine; just a normal kid trying to get some attention. He could tell her whatever he wanted. Lizzy wasn't about to give in to the darkness again.

Apparently, the good Doctor had suggested a little bit of reverse psychology because Andrea certainly behaved differently after that. Instead of begging and pleading with Lizzy, she took the exact opposite approach and ignored her completely. That behavior may work with an ordinary child facing an ordinary problem, but with Lizzy it only caused her to withdraw deeper. That was the first time she had truly felt rejected by her mother. The first time she felt she didn't love her.

Days later, after Andrea tucked her into bed, Lizzy lay

there forcing herself to shut out the world around her, to keep the shadows at bay so they wouldn't sneak up on her through the cracks at the edge of reality. Then she heard something, just barely audible at first, a little buzzing noise floating around her. Slowly, it began to grow a little louder until it sounded like a bumble-bee flittering around the room.

Fear was the first feeling that caught hold of her, preparing her for the ghastly visage that was coming to torment her one more time. But then she felt a warm touch on her cheek, followed by a soft tickle on her nose and a gentle whisper in her ear.

It was one word, "Vizibir."

Lizzy felt a small tingle course through her body, winding its way from the tips of her toes to the top of her head. The sensation evoked a feeling of excitement and wonder, and for the first time in a long while, happiness.

When she looked up, she saw a small green glowing orb floating just inches from her face. She knew she was looking at something completely magic; something different than the spirits that had been haunting her.

"You're incredible," she said. "What are you?"

"Friend," it replied, and then started buzzing quickly around the room. A moment later, a rainbow of colors shimmered all around her. For the first time in a long while, a smile crossed her lips.

In the middle of her room, several toys were hovering in mid-air before settling to the floor in a tea party formation. Her favorite doll, Suzie, in her pink dress, with a blue ribbon in her hair, sat across from Spike, her teddy bear with the little tuft of hair on the top of his head. Little cups and saucers sat on top of the small table nestled between them. Vizibir floated above the table, pulsating as if beckoning Lizzy to join them.

Slowly, Lizzy slid off her bed and walked toward them. She stopped suddenly when she saw Suzie turn her head and wink at her, followed by Spike waving his matted paw and nodding.

Vizibir raced over to her, "Don't be afraid. It's just me."

It took Lizzy a second to calm down. "How did you do that?"

Vizibir's reply was simple: "Magic."

Lizzy scooted over to join her stuffed friends at their make-believe party. After a few minutes, she glanced over to see her mother standing in the bedroom doorway, a look of shock on her face and tears in her eyes.

"Are you okay, Mommy?" Lizzy asked.

Andrea paused for a moment to regain her composure, "I'm fine, Sweetie. In fact, I'm better than ever now."

Lizzy went over and gave her a hug, "You don't have to worry anymore. I'm not afraid now, so everything's going to be okay."

"But I don't understand? What happened?"

Of course, Lizzy couldn't tell her about her otherworldly visitor just yet. Not until she knew how she would react. She had humored her regarding seeing Nanna, maybe even believed her a little, but her behavior lately left Lizzy in doubt. Instead, she played dumb to get the response she wanted.

"I don't know, Mommy? Something just told me not to be afraid anymore. I don't know how it happened?"

"Well, I don't care how it happened. I'm just glad to have my little girl back."

Andrea hugged Lizzy for a long time, and it felt like they were a family again. Unfortunately, it didn't last very long.

CHAPTER 4

Thanksgiving is supposed to be a day of joy and happiness, where we give thanks for all the blessings we have in our lives. For Lizzy and her mom, it was the complete opposite—a day full of sadness and grief.

Lizzy had never had the chance to meet her father. His accident had ripped him from her life before she was even born. It had also torn a hole in her mother's heart; one that would never be filled.

It had happened about a month after Lizzy was conceived. It was just one of those freak things that no one ever thinks could happen to them. Apparently, they were late for Thanksgiving dinner at Nanna's, and he was rushing to get ready. Even though it was still morning Nanna called every meal after breakfast dinner, and they had a tradition of having a big meal sometime mid-afternoon, after they had watched all the parades and played several games. Plus, her house was an hour away.

After taking a quick shower, he stepped onto the wet floor. His feet flew out from under him, sending him sprawling backward, where his head hit the edge of the porcelain tub, cracking his skull wide open. He died instantly. His name was Jim.

So, even though Thanksgiving didn't fall on the same date each year, Andrea still felt like a trip to the cemetery was the most appropriate way to spend the holiday. It was imperative that they arrived at exactly 9:43 a.m. Not a minute early, or a minute late, for that was the exact time of his death.

Everything had gone as planned the first three years of Lizzy's life, but her fourth year was anything but ordinary, and that particular day in November began with a series of events that would have a disastrous effect on her life.

Andrea burst through Lizzy's bedroom door in a blind panic. Apparently, the alarm clock hadn't gone off, and it was already 9:00 a.m. The cemetery was a twenty-minute drive from home, so that left little time for them to get ready, plus it put Andrea in a very grumpy mood.

"Come on, Liz!" she yelled. "We need to hurry or we're going to be late. Why didn't you wake me up? You know how important this day is!"

It's not my fault, Lizzy considered responding, but thought better of it. Instead, she did her best to get dressed quickly, and managed pretty well until she pulled her tights on and snagged them with her fingernail, causing a long run that covered the entire length of her left leg.

Andrea grabbed her roughly and pushed her down on the bed, "My god, Liz! Can't you do anything right?"

Quickly she pulled the tights off, twisting Lizzy's leg as she did, which caused her to cry out in pain.

"Come on, Lizzy, don't do this now. We have to leave soon or we're going to be late. Just suck it up and be a big girl so we can go."

Lizzy's face wrinkled up, her skin got hot, her breathing got shallow, and her eyes got watery as she stood on the edge of a precipice with tears about to fall. Then she saw herself standing directly behind her mother. Sadness instantly turned to fear when she saw the look in Vizibir's eyes as she regarded her mother—pure hatred. A second later, Andrea staggered to her knees in pain, as if she had been punched in the stomach. Vizibir smiled a little smile and then disappeared.

Lizzy slid off the bed and crouched down beside her, "Are you okay, Mommy?"

She looked very disjointed for a second. "I'm alright, Dear. I don't know what happened. Something suddenly hit me right out of the blue. Maybe it was something that I ate? I don't know. But I do know that we have to go."

The long drive to the cemetery seemed like an eternity. Lizzy simply sat there with her head down low, pouting, while her mom drove recklessly in a race against time.

It was only after they had sped through town, and then twisted and turned through the maze of crypts and mausoleums at the cemetery until they came to Jim's burial plot with seconds to spare, that Andrea turned to Lizzy and said, "I'm sorry."

There's a story that mothers tell their children about how one little tiny sneeze by the smallest of creatures sets off a chain of events with disastrous results. In Lizzy's case, it wasn't a sneeze, but a simple little giggle.

She couldn't help it. She tried with all of her might to ignore it, to stifle the little snicker that had crept up on her—a little buzz in her right ear, like the hum of a bumblebee, and then it drifted to her left ear. She knew it was Vizibir.

Lizzy's hand went up and swatted at her as if she were a pesky fly. Then she flew around Lizzy's waist in a series of circles, and tickled her in the side. That's when it happened. A giggle escaped her lips, and then the volcano erupted.

Andrea's head shot around like it had been fired from a

gun, a wicked scowl covering her face, "What in the world do you find so funny?"

Immediately Lizzy stilled the laughter and put on a somber face. "I'm sorry. Something tickled me and I couldn't help it."

"Well, show some respect for God's sake! I don't want to hear another sound out of you. Understand?"

Lizzy nodded her head, content to obey her wishes.

Vizibir then buzzed up to Lizzy's ear, "Why is she being so mean to you?"

Lizzy didn't answer, which only made Vizibir pester her even more, "You don't deserve to be treated like this. I don't like her."

"Quiet down or you'll get me in trouble," Lizzy whispered as quietly as possible.

Apparently, Lizzy wasn't quiet enough. Andrea must have heard her whispering to Vizibir. That sent her over the edge. Her hand shot out like a coiled snake snatching its prey, and grabbed Lizzy roughly by the left arm. She pulled her daughter close and screamed in her face, "I thought I told you to shut up and show some fucking respect?!"

Her palm hit the side of Lizzy's face with such force that it sent her sprawling to the ground. She landed a few inches from a large headstone, and then watched in amazement as the large chunk of granite shimmered and transformed into a large television screen, with Lizzy as the audience. As she watched her dad stepping out of the shower, she realized that she was about to relive the moment of his death.

It started simply enough, with Jim walking to the sink with a navy-blue towel wrapped around his waist, his hair still wet and dripping water down his chest and back. He wiped the steam from the medicine cabinet mirror with the palm of his hand and proceeded to apply a small bead of toothpaste to his toothbrush. No sooner had he finished screwing the cap back on the tube when Andrea came rushing into the room yelling and cursing. Even though the supernatural screen Lizzy was watching came with no sound, it wasn't difficult to read her lips and conclude that she was extremely upset about something.

After she had finished her initial tirade, Jim responded to her fervently. Whatever he said apparently struck a nerve, because Andrea slapped him hard on the side of his face. The blow caught him completely by surprise, causing him to lose his balance. His foot slid out from under him on the wet floor and he fell backward. On his way down, his head hit the edge of the tub, which sat directly opposite the sink. A second later, he was lying crumbled on the bathroom floor in a lifeless heap.

The screen vanished and Lizzy turned slowly toward her mother, suddenly afraid for her very life.

Andrea stood there trembling, "But...that's not how it happened. I didn't kill your father. I couldn't have killed him. I loved him!"

Lizzy started backing away from her, "It was all your fault! How could you do that?"

"Look, Lizzy, I don't know what's going on here, but your father's death was an accident. I wasn't even in the room when it happened. You've got to believe me."

Vizibir whispered in Lizzy's ear, "She's lying. You can see it in her eyes."

Lizzy screamed at her, "You're lying! You killed him! That makes you a murderer."

She tried to scramble away from her, but her foot caught on the edge of the headstone and she went crashing to the ground. The force of the fall knocked the wind out of her and she blacked out.

Sometime later, Lizzy opened her eyes to a bright light shining at her, and saw that she was lying on a stretcher with a stranger's voice urging her to wake up. Out of the corner of her eyes, she saw flashing lights and realized that the police and fire department were there.

When she turned her head to see what was happening, an intense pain shot through her and she cried out. Andrea tried to rush over to her, but she was restrained by a couple of police officers. Another man stood with them who had brown hair and was dressed in a black suit and tie. The badge on his belt told Lizzy he was a detective, while the scar on the side of his face suggested he had been one for a very long time.

Lizzy's stomach did a little flip-flop when he started walking toward her. Her brain felt like scrambled eggs, and she was trapped upside-down at the pinnacle of a towering Ferris wheel. She had no clue what had just happened.

Vizibir whispered in her ear before the detective got close, "Don't worry. He can help. Just make sure you tell him everything."

The detective had a little southern drawl in his voice when he talked, "How are you feeling, Little Lady?"

Lizzy hesitated for a second, and then replied in a hoarse voice, "Okay, I guess."

His eyes raised to look at her forehead, "That's a pretty nasty bump you got there."

"Yeah. The premedics said I passed out for a while."

He giggled for a second and smiled, "You mean the paramedics?"

She nodded.

"Did they also tell you how lucky you are? They told me that if your head had hit the rock just an inch further down you could've died."

Lizzy stayed quiet. She didn't know whether to be happy

that she was still alive, or terrified that her mother had tried to kill her.

The detective then looked at the side of her cheek, which still stung from here her mother's hand had hit her. Instinctively, Lizzy's hand went up to cover the mark.

He sensed her apprehension and softened his voice, "It's Elizabeth, right?"

Lizzy nodded again, then said, "It's actually Lizzy. Most people call me that."

"Okay, Lizzy. I'm Detective Maddon. Can you tell me what happened here, Sweetie?"

She knew she had to tell him, but couldn't. Her brain tried to make her lips move; tried to make the words come out, but she was too afraid.

Then Vizibir whispered softly in her ear, "I'll help you."

A second later, Lizzy felt an incredible heat surge through her body. A blinding light shot through her head right behind her eyes and she was sure she was going to pass out again. But then the light faded, the heat subsided, and she felt a sense of peace settle over her. Then suddenly her body was moving on its own. Her lips moved and words flowed freely, only she wasn't the one talking. She laid there a helpless marionette in the hands of her supernatural puppeteer.

"She did it!" Vizibir said through her lips. "She hurt me. She's evil!"

"Are you saying she hurt you on purpose?"

Lizzy's head nodded in agreement. "And that's not all. She killed my dad. I heard her. She said that he died from an accident, but that's not true. I heard her talking on the phone, saying that she was glad he was dead!"

Lizzy's soul froze when she heard those words escape her lips. Even though she knew her mother was mean, and she had seen her father's death at her hands, something deep down inside told her that those words were a lie.

The detective inched forward a little closer, "That's a pretty powerful statement, Little Lady. Are you sure you heard everything correctly?"

Vizibir said through her, "I'm sure. I might be little, but I hear really good."

He patted her softly on the hand, "I'm sure you do. When did you hear this?"

Vizibir acted as if she was struggling to interpret the concept of time correctly to the detective, "I think it was about twelve-and-a-half weeks ago, but I'm not really sure?"

The detective crouched down. "Some nice people are going to take you to the hospital right now and get you fixed up. You'll be good as new before you know it."

"But what about her?" Vizibir asked.

"Don't worry, Sweetheart. Everything's going to be fine."

He spoke to the paramedics before he walked back toward the squad car where Lizzy's mother stood huddled with another officer. He talked to the officer for a few minutes and then confronted Andrea.

Lizzy watched as she pleaded with the detective. Then the officer removed the handcuffs from his belt and pushed her up against the car so he could put them on her wrist. Just as they were pushing her into the squad car, she glanced back at Lizzy, her face covered with tears, her eyes pleading for help, but Lizzy had none to give.

Then suddenly Andrea's eyes got wide just as a quick jolt course through Lizzy. A second later, Vizibir was standing next to Lizzy. Andrea's reaction told Lizzy that she could see Vizibir too.

Lizzy never saw her mother again after that.

CHAPTER 5

Lizzy woke up a couple hours later in a daze. It took her a few minutes to settle her brain down and remember what had happened. When she did, her stomach tied itself into a giant knot, while her heart felt like it was going to explode. An ocean full of tears welled up in her eyes when she realized that she was all alone.

As if on cue, Vizibir was suddenly standing beside her, wearing the same pink dress, the same ribbon in her hair, and the same sadness in her eyes. Lizzy couldn't tell if she was sincerely sad because of everything that had just happened, or if she was simply mimicking her.

"Don't worry," Vizibir said. "Everything's going to be alright. I promise."

"But what about my mom?" Lizzy asked. "What happened to her?"

"She can't hurt you anymore. The police took her away. She's going to pay for all the terrible things she's done. She'll be locked up where she can't hurt anyone else ever again."

Lizzy's head swirled even more when she heard those words, "But what about me? Who's going to take care of me?"

Vizibir simply said, "I will."

Lizzy looked at her supernatural twin doubtfully, "I don't think that will work. You got to be a grown-up to take care of kids."

Vizibir giggled, "I know that, Silly. What I mean is that I know someone who can help. In fact, he's here now."

A tall man with blond hair and deep blue eyes walked in. Wearing a gray pin-striped suit, shirt and tie, and carrying a leather briefcase, he looked like something right out of Law & Order. His smile was wide and confident as he walked over to Lizzy, and she felt a spark tingle through her as he touched her hand. "You must be Elizabeth?" he said. "I've heard so much about you."

Lizzy glanced nervously at Vizibir, as if to say *'Who is this guy?'*

Vizibir simply smiled back at her.

"Forgive me my manners, Young Lady," the man said. "My name is Damien, and I'm Vizibir's Father."

Lizzy looked shocked. Until that moment, she hadn't actually thought about the fact that Vizibir came from somewhere; had actually been born from a mother and father. The whole concept twisted her brain even further.

"Don't worry," Damien continued. "Everything I've heard has been absolutely wonderful. And from what I see here, I don't think you understand how special you truly are. I can see it in the sparkle of your eyes, and in the way your body glows."

Lizzy's eyes lit up, "You mean I'm glowing?"

She lifted her hands to her face, turning them over and over. "I don't see anything," she said in a disappointing tone.

Damien chuckled, "It's not something a normal person can see. But certain people, such as myself, have a special ability which allows us to see things others can't. What we see is like a blanket of color that surrounds everyone. It's called an aura, and it changes color according to the condition of the soul it is attached to. It tells us if that person is happy or sad, healthy or sick, loving or angry."

"So, what does my aurora look like?" Lizzy asked eagerly.

He looked at Lizzy for a second smiling, "Yours, precious girl, is the brightest one I have ever seen—radiant white, pure, and delicious."

Lizzy watched him turn toward Vizibir, who responded with a sly, devilish smile of her own, one that was a little too eager and enthusiastic. Lizzy half expected her to start licking her lips, but then Vizibir shook herself ever so slightly and her expression returned to normal.

Damien pulled her aside and talked to her for a couple of minutes before returning to Lizzy's bedside, "Vizibir has explained everything to me and I believe I can help. Obviously, the most pressing issue right now is that you need a place to live and someone to watch over you."

Lizzy lowered her head sadly, "I guess so."

"Well then, I have the perfect person in mind. Her name is Lilith, and she loves children, especially beautiful little girls like you. I'm confident the two of you will hit it off great. I'll make the call and see if she can be here later this afternoon."

Just then, the doctor came to usher everyone out. Vizibir disappeared as soon as he walked in.

"I'm afraid that's enough for now," the doctor said. "This little lady needs her rest."

Damien turned to leave, "I'll be back later, Lizzy, then we can talk some more."

No sooner had the door closed, and the Doctor was sitting beside Lizzy's bed, wasting no time sticking his tongue depressor down her throat and shining his infernal bright light into her eyes. "So, how are you feeling today?"

Lizzy just shrugged. Her irritation grew as he pulled the bandage away from her forehead with no concern for the obvious pain it was causing her. When she let out a little yelp and winced from his rough handling, he continued as if it was no big deal. It was obvious that he just didn't care.

She knew that something bad was about to happen when she heard the soft buzzing in her ears. Lizzy looked up just in time to see Vizibir standing directly behind the doctor with a furious look on her face.

Lizzy shook her head, hoping it would be enough to prevent an outburst that was certain to lead to disaster. It didn't do any good. She knew that Vizibir was determined to make the uncaring doctor pay for his lack of bedside manners. She closed her eyes and braced for the chaos that was about to ensue.

A second later, the bed shook violently for a quick moment, causing the mean doctor to grab hold of the bed rail next to him. As soon as his hand touched the metal, the rail flew sharply downward, severing two of his fingers and crushing the rest of his hand into a mangled mess of flesh. His blood-curdling scream sounded more like something from a haunted house theme park instead of a hospital.

Vizibir winked at Lizzy and was gone.

CHAPTER 6

It was nearly an hour later before Lizzy was finally alone again. Within seconds of Dr. No Manners' accident, several hospital personnel came rushing in. A few moments later, the injured doctor was sitting in a wheelchair, crying in pain. One of the nurses came over to make sure Lizzy was okay, while another nurse bent down and scooped up the severed fingers with a pair of tongs and placed them in a plastic container.

As he was wheeled from the room, the doctor turned back to Lizzy with a look of fear on his face, like she was the cause of his injury.

A minute later, a couple of orderlies came in and transferred Lizzy to the unused bed in the other half of the room. They handled the bloody bed delicately as they wheeled it out of the room, afraid to touch the railing for obvious fear that they too would fall prey to the death trap.

They shut the door behind them and Lizzy was alone once more. She closed her eyes, hoping to isolate herself from the rest of the world, if even for only a little bit. All she wanted was enough time for her headache to go away and to make sense of the craziness going on around her the best that a child her age could hope to.

Vizibir's buzzing cut her quiet time short, however, and she was starting to get annoyed at her constant interruption. But then she felt a cool touch on her forehead, followed by a slight tingle that started at the bottom of her chin, rose to the top of her head, and then spiraled its way down her spine until it reached the tips of her toes. As the sensation melted away from her, she felt more peaceful than she had ever felt in her life before. And her headache was completely gone.

Vizibir spoke up after a few minutes, "Are you feeling better?"

Lizzy nodded, still keeping her eyes closed, "Thank you."

"You're welcome. I couldn't stand to see that grumpy old man mistreating you."

She opened her eyes and stared at Vizibir incredulously, "But you didn't need to hurt him like that!"

Vizibir responded simply, "Yes, I did."

"But...why?"

"Don't you know that everyone gets what they deserve? He hurt you, so I hurt him. It's as easy as that."

"He didn't do it on purpose. He's was just a grumpy old man. Plus, my Nanna used to say that two wrongs don't make a right."

A little red spark flashed in Vizibir's eyes for a brief second, and then was gone. "Your Nanna isn't here anymore, is she? And if I remember right, she wasn't very nice to you the last time you saw her."

Lizzy's heart crashed to the floor with a heavy thud! Nanna had been the most important person in her life. Even after her death she was there to comfort and uplift her, until that night when she appeared as something warped and evil. Now Lizzy missed her more than ever. She was too caught up in her grief to wonder how Vizibir had known about Nanna in the first place.

She didn't realize she'd been crying until she felt Vizibir's hand on her shoulder. "I'm sorry," Vizibir said. "I didn't mean to upset you. I'm just trying to protect you, that's all."

"I know," Lizzy sighed. "But you can't keep going around hurting people like that, you understand?"

"Yes, I understand. But you also must realize that I love you and will always do whatever's necessary to keep you safe."

Lizzy was stunned for a second. She didn't know if Vizibir meant those words, or even understood the meaning behind them? Or was she being played with like a cat plays with a mouse before it gets bored and eats it?

"We're the same, Elizabeth. Together, there is nothing we can't do. And I want you to know that I will always be right beside you whenever you need me."

"But...why me?"

"What do you mean?"

"I mean, why did you choose me? Out of all the gazillions of girls in this world, why me? Damien even said I was special, but what makes me more special than anyone else?"

For a second, she simply smiled at Lizzy. "You have a gift that very few people in this world possess, and that's the ability to see and feel things that others can't. That's why you could see your Nanna after she died, and why you can see me now."

"So, does that mean that no one else can see you?"

"That depends."

"On what?"

"On whether I want them to see me or not."

"I don't get it?"

"Let me put it this way: You see me because of your gift, so it doesn't take much effort on my part to show myself to you. But in order for others to see me I need to focus my energy a little more. That's why I don't show myself to others very often."

Lizzy tried to make sense of Vizibir's words, but she still had the feeling there was more to it, like things weren't quite what they seemed.

Her thoughts were cut short, however, when a strange woman entered the room that sent a lump into her throat.

She was the tallest woman Lizzy had ever seen, easily topping six feet tall, and probably closing in on seven. She reminded her of Cruella De Vil, with her long dark hair graying at the temples, her long spindly arms, and her thin and lanky legs. In fact, she didn't actually walk into the room as much as she strode in, stopping at the foot of Lizzy's bed to give her a steady look.

After a minute, she spoke up in a low, throaty voice, "So, this is her?" Even though she was looking at Lizzy, it was clear that she was addressing Vizibir.

"Lilith, I want you to meet Elizabeth. Elizabeth this is Lilith, a very special friend of mine."

Once the formal introductions were out of the way Lilith relaxed and smiled a wide, toothy smile, "It's a pleasure to meet you, Elizabeth."

"Same here," Lizzy managed to squeak out nervously, not sure yet what to make of the toothpick lady standing in front of her.

"Is everything set?" Vizibir asked Lilith.

Lilith simply replied, "It is."

"Great!"

Vizibir turned to Lizzy, "It looks like Damien has found a new home for you."

For a second, Lizzy had mixed feelings. Everything had happened so fast. Her entire world had been turned upside down in an instant and she didn't know how to respond.

Then she realized she wouldn't have to be alone anymore and her eyes lit up.

Vizibir continued, "Lilith has agreed to take you in and give you the home you deserve. Isn't that great?"

Lizzy's hope disappeared as quickly as the light goes out in a room when you flip the switch. Suddenly, she felt like she was being lured into the den of a monster preparing for its feast, and she was the main course!

A cold shudder ran through her body.

***

After Vizibir and Lilith left the room, Lizzy lay there pondering her future. She couldn't help but feel that something wasn't quite right. Maybe she was just being paranoid? Or maybe it was because she was still just a child and didn't understand people very well? *But Vizibir isn't exactly a person, is she?* And she suspected that neither Damien or Lilith were either.

When another doctor entered her room, a lump rose in her throat. The images of torture plastered on the previous doctor's face—the blood splattered all over the bed; the severed fingers lying on the floor still twitching before the nerve endings finally died—were all still very fresh in her mind.

This man, however, differed from Dr. No Manners. He actually seemed to have a personality. His name tag read Dr. Randolph, and he smiled at Lizzy as he sat down next to the bed. He was an older man, with a gray beard and bald head, and acted genuinely interested in her when he spoke, "Hello, Elizabeth. I hear you've had quite a bit of excitement today."

"Yeah, you could say that," Lizzy said softly.

He started flipping through the chart at the foot of the bed and Lizzy noticed some curious marks on the back of his right hand.

"What are those?" she blurted out.

The doctor held his hand up so she could see it more clearly. "They're birthmarks," he said with a hint of pride in his voice. "And what's really neat about them is that if you connect the dots, you get an exact triangle, the perfect balance of mind, body, and spirit."

"What does that mean?"

He smiled at her, "It means that I've been blessed."

"Wow, that's cool. You mean you have some kind of special powers or something?"

"I'm actually a lot like you are, Elizabeth."

Lizzy was shocked, "You know who I am?"

Their conversation was cut short when Lilith and Vizibir reentered the room. Instead of normal and solid, Vizibir was more ethereal, her body shimmering with a ghostly hue so that she was invisible to the new doctor.

The doctor rose from his chair as they approached the bed, "Well, it looks like you're well on your way to a full recovery."

He bent forward slightly and whispered softly to Lizzy, "If you need me...", and he handed her a card with his name and phone number on it. He then turned and headed toward the door, looking directly at Vizibir as he left.

The glare she gave him as he left was as sharp as a laser. Once he was gone, she approached the bed completely solid. "What were you and the doctor talking about?" she asked with a hiss.

She must have sensed Lizzy's fear because she softened her tone, "I'm sorry. I just want to make sure everything's okay before we get you settled into your new life."

It hit Lizzy hard once more that her mom was gone.

Everything had happened so fast. She knew what she'd seen, but suddenly, it just didn't feel right. She didn't know what to believe anymore, or who to trust. Unfortunately, she also didn't have any alternative but to continue down the path that she'd been thrown upon and hope she wasn't traveling to her own funeral.

"So, Lizzy," Vizibir said much more softly this time. "Exactly what did you and the Doctor talk about? Anything in particular before we go?"

"Nothing special. He just asked how I was feeling and checked my eyes and pressure and stuff. And I noticed some funny marks on his hands, that's all."

A hint of surprise shone in her eyes for the briefest of seconds and she glanced at Lilith questioningly.

"What kind of marks were they, Dear?" Lilith asked in a steely voice.

"Just some little dots on the back of his hand. He said they were birthmarks and that he was blessed, whatever that means?"

"Did he say anything else?"

"No, that's when you guys came back in. But I think I saw him look at you, Vizibir, when you were all shiny and stuff. He acted like he could see you. Does that mean he's like me?"

Vizibir shot back, "No, he's nothing like you!"

Her voice scared Lizzy again, and she knew that if she didn't change the subject fast, Vizibir would search out the Good Doctor and probably do a lot worse to him than the first one. "When are we going to get out of here? I'm starving, plus I wanna see my new home."

That seemed to do the trick because almost immediately Vizibir's mood changed. "Actually, we're leaving right now," she said happily.

As if on cue, a nurse came in, pushing a wheelchair toward

the bed. "But I don't need that," Lizzy protested.

The nurse responded tenderly, "It's just a precaution, Dear. Any time a head injury is involved we like to be extra careful."

By now Lizzy's imagination was working overtime, because for an instant, she thought she saw small fangs jutting from the side of the nurse's mouth as she talked. Lizzy blinked and her mouth was just a regular mouth—an old and wrinkled mouth, sure—but still just a regular mouth.

The sigh that escaped Lizzy's lips was a verbal surrender to all the madness she had witnessed, and her will didn't possess the strength to fight any longer. She sat up and allowed the imaginary vampire-nurse who also had sharp pointy fingernails to help her into the chair.

CHAPTER 7

Damien was sitting in the lobby talking to a man and woman emphatically. He stopped the conversation short when the group arrived and he sprang forward to meet them.

"Hello, Elizabeth. Are you feeling better?" He asked.

Lizzy shrugged, "I guess."

He kneeled down, so that he was at her level, "I know things have been pretty crazy lately, but it's going to get better, you'll see. Lilith here will take good care of you, and you'll be happier than you've ever been in your whole life. I promise."

I doubt it, Lizzy thought, but didn't say anything. What good would it have done? She was stuck on a crazy rollercoaster, and the attendant had the left the park.

Without another word, he wheeled Lizzy out of the hospital with Lilith walking alongside. They didn't have to go very far. When he stopped, Lizzy couldn't believe her eyes. In front of her was the longest and blackest car she had ever seen.

"Is this your car?" she asked excitedly.

"No," Lilith responded. "It's our car. Remember, you're part of the family now."

Maybe this wasn't going to be so bad after all, Lizzy thought.

***

The long ride took them through the broad countryside, along twisting back roads, to a very secluded stretch of land that seemed to be lost from the rest of the world. During the ride, Lizzy couldn't keep herself from staring wide-eyed at the inside of the limo. The seats were a rich, black leather, and across from where she sat was a large screen TV, which just happened to have her favorite episode of 'Spongebob' playing. Then she saw the sunroof above her and gave Lilith a questioning look.

"Why not," Lilith said as she pressed a button on the console next to her. The glass slid backward, allowing the cool air to charge into the car. "Go on," she prodded. "See what it feels like to be truly free."

Lizzy stood up on the seat and stuck her head out of the car. She giggled as she waved her arms around, pretending like she was flying.

When they came to a stop a few minutes later, Lizzy jumped out of the car and found herself standing at the foot of a large set of steps that led up to a sprawling mansion. It sat atop a large hillside which overlooked a dense forest on the west side and a sea of rolling hills to the east. The structure was shaped in rectangular sections that looked like an Italian villa, with two wings jutting from each side, large angled bay windows, and a columned porch. The air surrounding the hillside was notably cooler because of the higher elevation, stirring Lizzy to pull her coat tighter around her.

Lilith started up the steps toward the house, apparently unaffected by the cold. Lizzy ascended behind her and caught sight of an enormous black dog running toward them from the corner of the house. As big as a bear and as dark as midnight, it closed in on Lizzy, snarling and gnashing its teeth intending to rip her to shreds.

"Loki, halt!" Lilith shouted. The massive animal stopped instantly, frozen in its tracks. She walked over to the beast and spoke a few words to it in a low, guttural language that sounded like a cross between German and Russian. The animal responded by crouching down low and inching its way toward Lizzy. Instinctively, she shuffled backward a few feet.

"Don't be afraid," Lilith urged. "He won't hurt you."

Lizzy wasn't so sure. Then the beast known as Loki rolled onto his back, like normal dogs do, and waited for Lizzy to scratch his belly. Either that or he was tricking her so he could chomp her hand off as an appetizer when she reached for him.

"See, he's just a big baby," Lilith said.

Lizzy swallowed a big gulp and inched her way over to the hell hound. He immediately sat back up so he could sniff her hand. She almost screamed instinctively when his massive jaws opened, until she felt his big, black tongue slobbering all over her.

"What did you say to him?" Lizzy asked.

"I simply told him that you were part of the family. Now he'll protect you with his very life."

Tentatively, she ran her hand down to his stomach and began scratching. He responded by laying his head to one side so that his tongue dangled out of the side of his mouth. A cascade of drool pooled on the ground beside his head as he panted happily.

Lilith barked another command and Loki jumped to attention. A tall, thin woman with fiery red hair and deep green eyes came out of the house, running toward them.

"I'm so sorry, Lilith," she said. "I didn't know Loki was out. Plus, I wasn't expecting you so soon."

"No problem," Lilith replied.

Then she turned to Lizzy, "Elizabeth, this is Circe. She helps me take care of things around here. Circe, this is Elizabeth. She's going to be living with us."

Circe crouched down toward Lizzy, "Hi, Elizabeth. I'm sure we're going to be great friends."

"Please, call me Lizzy. I hate the sound of Elizabeth...it's too grown up."

Circe chuckled, "Okay, Lizzy it is."

She grabbed Lizzy's hand and led her toward the front door. "How about we go upstairs so I can show you your room?"

The whole time Loki was licking Lizzy's free hand eagerly, his tail wagging back and forth. She still didn't know if he just being overly friendly or if he was sampling her for a snack later.

The interior of the mansion was spectacular. As soon as she stepped inside the foyer, she was completely overtaken with the aroma of wildflowers mixed with rich mahogany wood. A black and white tiled marble floor stretched the width of the massive room, which featured twin staircases on each side that curved upward to greet both ends of a runway that served as a balcony along the front of the second floor. Directly below the balcony stood a massive black door, gaping against the pale white walls like a giant tunnel leading into some unknown abyss. Two other doors placed along the East and West walls led to the other wings of the house.

"Wow!" Lizzy exclaimed.

Circe smiled, "Wait until you see your room. You're gonna

love it."

She started toward the base of the stairs to the right. Lizzy followed her a few steps and stopped, "Where does that door go?" she asked, pointing to the big, black door.

"That leads to Lilith's room. That is the one room in this house that's off limits. You're free to roam about anywhere else, but her room is strictly forbidden."

Instantly, Lizzy's imagination began to work overtime. She started dreaming up all sorts of creepy and bizarre ideas of what might be behind that door. Monsters and nightmares waited at the fringes of her mind. Luckily, before Lizzy got too carried away in her paranoia, Circe continued on.

She led Lizzy up the winding staircase toward a long hallway. Instead of the tiled marble floor, the hall was covered with a deep brown plush carpet. The walls were painted a muted gray, giving it a very earthy, underground feeling.

A myriad of assorted paintings adorned both walls, but instead of cheery pictures of meadows and seascapes, these were of strange and bizarre images painted in drab and dreary colors. As Lizzy struggled to find the meaning of most of these, one, however, caught her attention. It appeared to represent the Garden of Eden, which she had learned about in Sunday school, only this one was a little different. Adam and Eve seemed to be arguing over something, except that the woman who was supposed to be Eve didn't look quite right. She actually looked a little bit like Lilith. Lizzy's skin crawled.

After a moment, Circe continued to usher her down the hallway, past a pair of doors on each side, to the solitary door at the end.

"I hope you like it," she said as she opened the door.

The room beyond was, in every way, the perfect definition

of a fairy princess bedroom. A large, pink canopy bed stood facing the door and was bordered by a white mirrored dresser on one side and a matching armoire on the other. A shelf unit along one wall was filled with at least a hundred dolls and stuffed animals. A huge chest beckoned from the opposite corner; its lid opened to reveal a mound of other toys waiting to be played with. Lizzy squealed in delight.

"I take it, you approve?" Circe said.

"It's amazing!"

"Go look out your bedroom window."

The only window in the room was located on the wall just to the right of the toy chest. When Lizzy looked out, she was excited to see a huge backyard with a swing-set and a jungle-gym big enough for a schoolyard. There was also a merry-go-round and a sandbox to complete the private little playground. A silver chain-link fence enclosed the whole play area. To the left of that was the biggest swimming pool she had ever seen. A paved patio area surrounded it, with several lounge chairs placed about for sunning and relaxing. She squealed again.

"Wow, we even have a pool!"

"I guess that means you like to swim?"

"Well, I'm not very good at it...but I like to play in the water."

Circe chuckled, "We can teach you how to swim, if you like. You can be our little mermaid princess."

"You mean like Ariel? I can be a mermaid just like her?"

"Lizzy," she said, "We can help you be anything you want to be."

***

Her head was swimming with excitement later that night as

she lay in her new bed, trying to fall asleep. Instead, all she kept thinking about was the playground, and the swimming pool, and the new toys that were now scattered all over the floor of her room, and the delicious spaghetti and chocolate cake they had for dinner. She was about to go into sensory overload.

Then one thought crept into her brain, a dark intruder infringing upon all of her joy, and once it was there everything else disappeared back into the eternal ether where thoughts are born: she had to find out what was behind that door.

CHAPTER 8

The rays of sun peeking through the window woke Lizzy up. As she sat up in bed, she was startled when her arm bumped against something. She was a little creeped out when she saw that Vizibir was lying next to her, wearing the exact same pajamas.

"Good morning, Sleepy Head," she said cheerfully. "I hope you slept well?"

"Yes. I slept great!" Lizzy replied, which actually wasn't a lie. In fact, she felt completely refreshed and better than she had in a long time. But then something scratched at the back of her mind and she knew things weren't quite right. She had absolutely no recollection of falling asleep the night before, and had not dreamed one single dream in her sleep. Normally, she would've welcomed a peaceful night's sleep, except that she was a little girl who saw things others didn't. As a result, she had always dreamed, every single night of her life as far as she could remember. Suddenly, she felt a little hollow inside.

Vizibir sensed her worry and asked, "What's wrong?"

Lizzy shrugged, "It's nothing, really. It's just kind of weird that I didn't have any dreams last night. I always have dreams."

"I did that, Silly."

"What do you mean?"

"I put a little something extra in your chocolate milk last night to help you sleep. With everything that you'd gone through recently, I didn't want you to have any nightmares your first night here."

Lizzy was shocked, "You drugged me?"

"I would like to think of it more as protecting you," Vizibir replied.

But Lizzy wasn't buying it. Who in their right mind would drug a little child? But then again, she wasn't dealing with a normal person, and she was starting to think that maybe Vizibir wasn't in her 'right mind' either.

"Protect me from who?" Lizzy asked.

"Why, from everything, of course. In case you haven't noticed, I've been keeping the other spirits away from you."

Lizzy hadn't realized that since Vizibir's mysterious arrival, all the other shadow-things that used to hang around, hoping for her to acknowledge them, were gone.

"There are all kinds of mean and nasty things out there, waiting to get their hands on someone like you. Unfortunately, if you're not aware you might not see it before it's too late."

"What does that mean?" Lizzy asked.

Vizibir thought about it for a moment, "Take your lovely Doctor, for instance."

"You mean the one who got hurt? Well, he certainly was a jerk. I didn't like him very well, that's for sure."

"No, not him. The other one. The one with the birthmark."

"But he was nice. I liked him."

"That's how they get you. They act all nice and friendly in order to get close to you. Then, when it's too late, they swoop in and rip you to pieces."

Lizzy didn't believe her, but didn't know what else to say.

Vizibir continued before she could disagree, "I know for a fact that those tattoos are a symbol for a secret group of people known to commit horrible acts of violence. They claim to be a religious group protecting the world from evil, but in reality, they're nothing more than murderers."

Lizzy's heart felt like it was being wrenched in two. The doctor that had helped her last had seemed so sincere, and acted like he was genuinely concerned for her wellbeing. But everything Vizibir had done felt like she was really looking out for her. She didn't know what to think.

As if she was reading Lizzy's mind, Vizibir continued, "I think your doctor was one of them. You need to stay away from him."

"But he didn't seem bad."

"That's the way they operate. They act all happy and helpful on the outside, but on the inside they're like a snake waiting to snatch you up and squeeze the life out of you."

Vizibir sensed the tension rising in Lizzy and changed the subject. "But, enough of that. Let's get downstairs before breakfast gets cold."

She grabbed Lizzy's hand and pulled her out the door. A couple of minutes later, they were standing in the kitchen doorway, looking at a mountain of food piled on the table. Every kind of breakfast food imaginable was there: pancakes, waffles, French toast, bacon, sausage, scrambled eggs, doughnuts, pastries, hash browns.

Instantly, Lizzy's mouth began watering.

Lilith was sitting at one end of the table, reading the newspaper, while sipping a cup of coffee. Circe was putting a pitcher of orange juice on the table when she spotted them. "Good morning, Sunshine," she said excitedly. "We didn't know what you liked, so we made a little bit of everything."

"It all looks wonderful," Lizzy said.

"Well, come here and sit down," Lilith said as she motioned to the chair next to her. "Circe and I certainly can't eat all of this by ourselves."

Lizzy's stomach made a loud growling sound, and she sheepishly made her way to the end of the table. Suddenly, a loud shriek flew from her mouth as she pulled the chair out and saw the biggest, blackest, hairiest spider she had ever seen in her life. She stumbled backward and nearly tripped over Loki, who had taken up residence nearby.

Circe dropped the plate of cinnamon rolls she was adding to the collection of food, much to Loki's delight. Then, in his enthusiasm to snatch up the goodies, he bounded right into Lilith's chair, nearly knocking her to the floor. Her eyes burned a fiery red as she shot up, suddenly appearing much taller than she really was.

"What in the world is going on here?" she boomed in a low, rumbling voice. But then her demeanor changed when she saw the source of all the commotion.

"You silly girl," she said as she reached over and scooped up the giant arachnid. "It's just Diego. He's pretty much as harmless as they come. Wouldn't hurt a fly...well, maybe a fly? He does have to eat, after all."

Then she looked down to her hand and started talking to the creature the way a normal person would talk to a child, "Now, you know better than to go wandering around here unsupervised, Mister. You need to be more careful or next time you're liable to get sat on."

Suddenly, Lizzy had no appetite.

Lilith glanced over and saw the obvious disgust that was written on Lizzy's face. "Circe," she said. "Can you please put Diego back in his home for me?"

Circe answered, "Sure, no problem."

She gathered Diego in her hands without the slightest hesitation. Then she started speaking the same kind of baby-talk as Lilith, and Lizzy knew for sure that she was now living in a freak show. When Circe headed out of the kitchen toward the study at the end of the hall, Lizzy made a mental note to avoid that area at all cost.

Since she was already pretty jumpy, when Vizibir suddenly appeared and touched her hand, sending a little jolt of electricity scurrying through her again, Lizzy let out a little shriek.

"Lizzy, you need to calm down," Vizibir said. "I told you that nothing is going to harm you as long as I'm around. Okay?"

Lizzy took a deep breath to calm herself, "Sorry. I'm fine now. It's just that bugs have always kind of freaked me out."

"Spiders are not bugs," Lilith snapped. "They are very special creatures essential to the growth and evolution of the entire planet."

For a second, Lizzy imagined a world filled with spiders of all shapes and sizes scurrying around everywhere and almost passed out.

"That's enough, Lilith," Vizibir interrupted. "Lizzy has been through a lot lately. She's just a little unaccustomed to our way of life around here."

Lilith turned her icy stare toward Vizibir for a brief second before softening. She was just about to say something else when the doorbell cut her off.

A minute later, Circe rushed back in and whispered something in Lilith's ear. Lilith's eyes got wide for a second and then turned a deep shade of red. She scurried from the room quickly, with Circe and Loki right behind her. Lizzy should have known better than to follow them, but couldn't help herself.

When Circe opened the door, Lizzy was surprised to see Dr. Randolph standing there dressed in a gray trench coat that made him look more like a secret service agent than a physician.

"What are you doing here?" Lilith hissed.

For a second the doctor shrank back from her, but then he quickly regained his exposure, "Why, I simply came by to see how Elizabeth was doing."

"I know who you are, and why you're here," Lilith shot back.

"Then you know that my only concern is the girl's safety."

Lilith wrapped her arms around Lizzy and pulled her close in an attempt to mimic a concerned mother, "As you can see, Lizzy is perfectly fine here."

"Then you won't mind if I have a little chat with her, will you?"

Lizzy heard Vizibir's buzz in her ear and felt the electricity in the surrounding air. She caught a quick glimpse of her shimmering outline standing a few feet away from the doctor. What surprised Lizzy the most, though, is that Dr. Randolph looked straight at her and immediately started muttering some strange words and pulled some kind of weird amulet from his pocket. Hanging from a thick golden chain was a large circular disc with the same series of dots inscribed on it that was on his hand. As he chanted, the amulet began to glow and white lines appeared between the dots, forming two overlapping triangles, anchored at each point by one of the six dots.

The air crackled and hissed as Vizibir's form rippled and shimmered sporadically. Then, she was pulled toward the amulet as if she were being sucked up by a giant vacuum. Lizzy watched in stunned silence as particles of her face broke apart and floated toward the magic object. At first, she wasn't sure how to react. On one hand, she had the very real feeling that Vizibir wasn't what she professed to be and couldn't be trusted. On the other hand, it was very creepy to see someone's face disintegrate. So, she screamed like the little girl that she was.

Loki suddenly charged out of the house and leaped at the doctor, ripping his throat out before he hit the ground, effectively signaling that breakfast was pretty much over.

CHAPTER 9

As the dying man's body twitched and convulsed, Lilith strode forward and reached down to pluck the amulet from his hand. She squeezed it tight until it shattered into a thousand tiny pieces and threw the pieces into the wind.

"You should have known better than to mess with us, Magi," she said to the dead man.

Vizibir's form began to slowly regain its composure, her face melding back into its former self. She shot Lizzy a look that said, 'sorry you had to see that', just before she disappeared.

Lizzy made the mistake of looking back one last time toward the dead man and was rewarded by seeing a little twitch from the hand that had held the amulet, as if even in death he were trying to complete his Holy mission.

"Why don't we go up to your room and relax for a little while?" Circe suggested as they walked through the foyer toward the stairs.

Lizzy expected to see Vizibir sitting on the bed when they walked into the room, but she was nowhere to be seen. Lizzy plopped down on her bed and buried her head in her pillow.

"Are you okay?" Circe asked.

"I don't know," Lizzy replied as she turned over and wiped the remaining tears from her eyes. "What just happened?"

Circe looked at Lizzy for a second, searching for the right words to say, before simply saying, "We told you the Magi were evil. The doctor was trying to destroy Vizibir, and once he was done with her, he would have turned on us as well. Loki simply protected us."

"I don't understand. Why are they after Vizibir?"

"How should I say this? Vizibir is...special. Somewhere, someone got the idea that she's dangerous, and so she's hunted and persecuted."

"What exactly is she? I mean, she certainly isn't human. Even I know that. And she disappears like she's some kind of spirit or something."

"I guess you could say she's more spirit than form right now. But she's growing, getting stronger, and she needs your help."

"But what can I possibly do to help?"

"Just be there when she needs you. After all, everybody needs help sometimes, even special ones like Vizibir."

Circe gave Lizzy a big hug and went back downstairs, leaving her alone staring at the ceiling and trying to figure things out. But the reality was that she was too young, and her brain was too small to wrap itself around everything that she had gone through. None of it made any sense.

A while later, hoping that a little fresh air would help clear her thoughts, she headed downstairs to the backyard and plopped herself down on one of the swings. The sun was high in the noon sky, and the warmth on her face helped to lift her mood a little. She looked up and saw a few scattered clouds dotting the sky. She started making shapes out of them, the way Nanna and her used to do. As soon as she thought about Nanna, though, she became sad and teary-eyed again.

A little buzzing in her left ear distracted her, and for a moment she was sure that Vizibir was going to show up next to her. Then a bumblebee flew in front of her nose, causing her to jump. That's when she realized that, because of the vast amounts of wildflowers spreading throughout much of the property, there were bugs of all shapes and sizes scurrying everywhere. Suddenly, she became paranoid once more.

She turned her head to the right to look at the woods that lay just beyond the yard and was startled to see a young boy about two years older than her, with sandy brown hair and bright green eyes, standing there. "Hello," he said.

Lizzy regarded him suspiciously, "Where did you come from?"

He shrugged and then sat down on the swing next to her, "Around. I live close by. Are you okay?"

Lizzy was silent for a minute before she got the nerve to speak to him, "I don't know. I feel like I'm caught in some bad dream and can't wake up."

"Don't worry. It'll all work out okay?"

"How can you be so sure? You don't even know me, or what I've gone through."

"True, but I think that everything always works out for the best in the end. We just have to believe it will."

"That's easy for you to say. You haven't gone through the terrible things that I have."

"Maybe that's true. Maybe it's not. I bet we've both gone through some pretty tough times."

Hearing those words made her feel a little better, even if they did come from a total stranger. "You need to trust Lilith and Circe," he continued. "They'll take good care of you."

"But they kind of creep me out."

"Why?" he asked with a puzzled look on his face.

"I don't know. They just seem weird. I guess Circe's okay, but Lilith is pretty freaky, with those long spindly legs and boney arms."

He laughed at her.

"What's so funny?"

"Nothing. I've just never heard anyone described her that way before. I guess it does kind of fit, though."

"You sound like you guys are pretty close."

"You could say that. We have a kind of special bond between us."

"What kind of bond?"

"She's helped me get through some tough times dealing with my father, who is not a very nice person to be around."

Absently, Lizzy's hand went to the cut on her forehead as she remembered the terrible ordeal at the cemetery. "What happened?" she asked him.

Instead of answering, he just sat there, looking down at the ground.

"You don't have to say anything," she said.

He looked at her sadly, "Thanks. Maybe some other time? It still kinda hurts to talk about it."

Then he got up from his swing and started walking to the back of the property toward the woods. "I gotta go. I'll see you later."

Lizzy called out before he got too far, "Wait, what's your name?"

"Tyler," he called back as he disappeared into the woods.

CHAPTER 10

Lizzy didn't remember walking over to the pool, but suddenly she was there, standing behind a group of three girls who were looking intently into the water. As she stepped closer, each of them turned their heads in unison—three dirty faces, topped with scraggly hair that hung down to cover their faces. Their once white Sunday dresses were now mottled gray and tattered and torn.

Click-clack, Clickety-Clack.

They spoke as one, their icy voices cutting through Lizzy like a dagger, sending chills violently up and down her spine, "Don't go down there. You must never go down there."

She started to question what they were talking about when they continued, "We tried to warn him, but he wouldn't listen. Now he walks in darkness. Stay away from the darkness."

They stepped aside so Lizzy could see what they had been looking at. She gasped in horror when she saw the body floating face down in the pool. The gray trench coat immediately brought the image of Loki's savage attack back into her mind. When Dr. Randolph rolled over in the water and reached out to her—his head struggling to stay attached to his body—she screamed in terror.

Seconds later, she was dimly aware of someone shaking her. She opened her eyes to see Circe kneeling beside her with a look of concern on her face. Lilith stood beside her, silent.

Lizzy looked around to get her bearings and saw that she was lying on the ground near the edge of the pool. A puddle of water surrounded her. What surprised her the most, though, was that it was pitch black outside. The last thing she remembered was that it had been a bright, sunny afternoon.

"What on Earth are you doing out here in the middle of the night, Young Lady?" Circe asked, her wet clothes suggesting she had jumped in to save her.

Lizzy stammered for an answer, "I don't know. I don't even remember coming down here. It seemed like just a few minutes ago it was daytime and I was playing on the swings with a boy I met named Tyler."

Lilith said, "You must have blacked out. It happens when someone is overly stressed. Short-term memory loss is common after such a tragedy as the one you've gone through. You should be okay soon." Lilith paused for a second, "What made you cry out like that?" Lilith asked.

That's when Lizzy saw the tiny piece of white ribbon—the same kind that had dangled from the girls' dresses—lying on the wet pavement next to her hand. Something told her to be careful about what she said. "I don't remember," she lied. "Just that I was having a bad dream and something was after me."

Lilith and Circe exchanged questioning glances, and Lizzy took the opportunity to shift her hand over the ribbon.

When Lilith reached down to help her up, her skin felt cold and leathery. "Come on. Let's get you out of here before you catch your death. And we wouldn't want that."

The look in Lilith's eyes seemed to add a 'not yet, anyway' to the end of that statement.

As they stepped through the backdoor into the kitchen, Lilith turned to Circe, "Why don't you make Lizzy some of your special hot cocoa to help warm her up?"

Lizzy hadn't even realized how cold she was until Lilith mentioned it. Her mind was still troubled by the ghostly images of the three girls and the mangled face of the doctor lunging at her from the pool.

Lilith led Lizzy to the table, and a minute later Circe came over with the largest cup of hot chocolate Lizzy had ever seen. Large puffs of white marshmallows swam atop the dark, creamy liquid. "You'll be drifting off to dream land in no time, sleeping better than you ever have before."

Lizzy took a tentative sip, and as soon as the liquid met her lips she was in heaven. She drank the rest of the cup eagerly, pausing just enough so that she didn't burn her throat. Within seconds of her downing the last drop, her eyelids were getting heavy. Then everything went dark, and it was a darkness that consumed her completely.

***

Lizzy woke up the next morning in a daze. She had no recollection of being moved upstairs into her bed. When she moved her head, it felt weird and detached, like it was a giant balloon floating above her body, held on by a tiny little string.

As she rolled out of bed and her feet touched the floor, she felt a tingle shoot through her legs. With each step, she seemed to be sinking deeper and deeper into a dream. The world around her was soft and fuzzy, like her eyes were having trouble focusing, and as she walked toward the stairs, she had the distinct sensation that she was tilted slightly to one side, like she was walking through a funhouse.

The stairs even felt funny, soft and spongy. She remembered the hot chocolate from the night before and wondered what kind of special ingredient Circe had mixed in. That thought flew quickly from her head when she heard the sound— a soft *click-clack, click-clack*.

Lizzy stopped at the bottom of the stairs and listened for a minute. It seemed to be a rustling, scratching sort of sound, the kind an insect might make as it skittered across a wooden floor, and it sounded like it was coming from Lilith's room. As she got closer, the noise grew louder, making every inch of her skin crawl. She was just about to commit the cardinal sin and open the door when Circe appeared almost out of nowhere.

"It's good to see you're finally up, Lizzy," she said enthusiastically.

Lizzy gave a big stretch and yawn to cover up her close call. "How long was I asleep?" she asked.

"For quite a while. We were getting a little concerned. You seemed to be running a slight fever and were mumbling in your sleep."

"That's funny. I don't really remember anything. What happened?"

Circe took Lizzy's hand and led her toward the kitchen. "That's not important. What matters is that you're up and around and feeling better. Plus, I have a surprise for you."

Lizzy tried to sound excited, aware that surprises lately hadn't turned out very well. This one was different, though, because when she entered the kitchen, she was happy to see Tyler sitting at the table munching on a blueberry muffin.

When he saw Lizzy, he put his muffin down and smiled, causing her heart to do a little flutter. He pushed a plate of muffins toward her, "Hi Lizzy! You've got to try one of these blueberry muffins Circe made. They're incredible!"

Although she wasn't a big fan of blueberries, because Tyler had suggested it, she chomped down on one of the muffins right away. She was instantly thrown into a state of pure bliss. There was a light sugary glaze with a hint of vanilla on top, and the whole thing just melted in her mouth. It sent her straight into muffin euphoria. Before she knew it, the whole thing was gone, and she found herself absently reaching for another one.

"Be careful," Circe warned. "Too much of a good thing can be bad for you."

As she was just about to pop a second muffin into her mouth, she was dimly aware of the scurrying sound again—*click-clack, click-clack, clickety-clack*—somewhere off in the distance. She briefly wondered what kind of scary monstrosity waited for her in the shadows. Neither Tyler nor Circe acted like they heard the sound. Either that, or they were so used to it that it melded together with all of the other normal everyday sounds so that it didn't even register in their brains anymore.

She tried to concentrate on the sound, hoping to distinguish where it was coming from, but as soon as she took another bite of her muffin, she totally forgot about everything else, like she was under its sugary spell.

Tyler grabbed Lizzy's hand and pulled her off her chair, dragging her toward the back door. "Come on," he said eagerly. "I've got something I want to show you."

Lizzy glanced back at Circe, who responded with a smile, "You kids have fun. And Tyler...don't do anything I wouldn't do."

He winked at her and they were out the door.

"Where are we going?" Lizzy asked as they headed out the door.

"You'll see soon enough. It's going to be awesome."

As they neared the edge of the woods Lizzy slowed down. The darkness beyond was suffocating. "We're not going in there, are we?" she asked in a squeaky voice.

"Of course, we are. You're not afraid, are you?"

Lizzy tried to sound strong, "Not really. I just don't like bugs is all. And I really hate spiders."

"Look, Lizzy, there's nothing to be afraid of. I know these woods inside and out. I'll protect you."

Tyler started to take a couple of steps down a small path into the woods, but stopped when he noticed that she wouldn't budge. He pulled one of Circe's muffins from his jacket and Lizzy's mouth watered instantly. "Here, I think this will help."

"How did you get that?"

He smiled a little devilish smile, "I snuck it when Circe wasn't looking. I'll split it with you."

Immediately after the first bite, her trepidation disappeared and her inhibitions withdrew. With her senses dulled once again, she followed Tyler into the dark woods.

The path through the woods was narrow, and wound its way through thick bushes and over fallen trees. After several agonizing bruises on her legs from stumbling into rocks and trees, and an equal number of scrapes and cuts on her arms from branches that seemed to be reaching out for her, they finally emerged into a small clearing.

Lizzy watched in awe as a young doe stood drinking delicately from a little stream that ran from one end of the clearing and disappeared into the woods on the other. Butterflies and dragonflies filled the air with rainbows of colors, and a slight breeze spread the smell of roses and lilacs all around. She felt like she was in a magical place found only in fairy tales.

"Wow, this place is awesome!" she said.

"Yeah, it's pretty cool, but it's not what I really wanted to show you. Come on, it's this way."

She followed him across the clearing toward the spot where the stream disappeared into the woods and down a small footpath until they came to the mouth of a small cave. Tyler walked toward the entrance.

"You want me to go in there?" Lizzy asked nervously.

"Come on, it's fine."

"But it's so dark in there!" she said, trying desperately to keep herself from entering the mouth of darkness.

"Don't worry. I got the whole lighting situation under control."

Against her better judgement, she slowly made her way down the little slope that led to the entrance. She caught a brief glimpse of something white out of the corner of her eye, and turned to see a small piece of white ribbon caught in a branch nearby. Something familiar clicked in her mind and she reached for the fabric. Just as her fingers were about to grab hold, a swift breeze blew by and sent it flying away.

Then she heard it again—*click-clack, click-clack, clickety-clack.*

CHAPTER 11

Lizzy proceeded with caution to the mouth of the cave, while Tyler waited for her a few feet inside, holding a flashlight to guide the way. He grabbed her hand, "Come on. We've got to hurry or we'll miss the show!"

The stream twisted to the right, while they wound their way around a series of narrow tunnels until they finally came to a large cavern with a small pool in the center. The little stream that had traveled in the opposite direction of the cave now broke through the wall of stone at the far end of the cavern in a small waterfall to feed into the pool.

Tyler turned off the flashlight, which startled Lizzy for a second until she realized that a small opening in the ceiling of the chamber about fifty feet up let enough light in that she could see around her.

"It won't be long now...just another minute or so," Tyler said.

"What are we waiting for?" she asked, but was cut off.

"Shhh—"

Then the sun hit its zenith right above the opening, and a large shaft of pure, white light shot down as if from Heaven and pierced the black pool. Instantly, the chamber was transformed from a dark and dank earthen place to an underground light show. Prisms of light shot all around, creating a myriad of dancing colors and shapes.

Lizzy's eyes were so focused on the surrounding spectacle that her ears didn't hear the sound in time. *Click-clack, click-clack, clickety-clack*—the sound echoed throughout the chamber—and when she finally noticed it, she couldn't discern where it was coming from.

"Ow!" she cried out when she felt a sharp, stabbing pain in her thigh. She turned around to find four pairs of big, black eyes staring at her from their perch atop the head of the biggest spider she'd ever seen. As more of them scuttled closer, she heard the clattering sound again and knew it came from their countless legs scurrying against the hard rocks of the cavern, coupled with the incessant chomping of large fangs.

I really hate spiders, she thought before she passed out.

***

Lizzy woke up to find herself in a hospital room once more, only this time she wasn't lying in a bed. She was floating in mid-air above it!

A young woman was lying on the mattress, hooked up to all kinds of machines. As Lizzy looked at her, something about her seemed familiar, and then she realized in horror she was looking at an older version of herself.

Her first thought was that she was in a coma about to die, which explained why her spirit was floating above her body. She studied herself for a moment, trying to figure out what had happened to her to put her in such a state.

Her attention was snapped back to the present when a nurse came in. The fear inside her turned to terror when she realized the nurse was Lilith, and that she was injecting some kind of black fluid into the IV.

Like a life preserver thrown to a drowning person, a ribbon of white silk drifted before Lizzy. She reached out for it but it darted away toward the door to the room. When Lizzy turned to look, she saw the three girls from her dream standing there. They motioned simultaneously for her to follow them, then turned and walked away down the hall.

An instant later, she was standing outside the room in the hall, watching Lilith. Suddenly, Lilith went stiff and stopped what she was doing. Something rippled beneath the back of her blouse, like a creature was crawling around inside her skin. Her hair had drifted over to one side, exposing the back of her neck, where a large insectoid eye opened up and looked directly at Lizzy. Quickly, Lilith spun around, the snarl on her face revealing a row of sharp, dripping fangs.

Lizzy expected Lilith to come charging at her like a savage animal, fangs gnashing, claws ripping and tearing, but instead she stood there, a low growl emanating from her as she looked straight at Lizzy, or rather, straight through her, like she knew she was there but couldn't actually see her, at least not with her 'regular' eyes.

Then the three girls were right in front of Lizzy once more with their heads hung low, as if in sorrow or shame. They spoke in unison once again, "The darkness is drawing near. Open your eyes and flee the darkness."

The girls turned and walked down the hallway, the long white ties on their dresses dragging on the floor, leaving a black oily trail behind them.

Lizzy followed them down the twisting hallway and then found herself standing before a solid oak door with a placard on the wall that read 'Chapel'. Slowly, she opened the door and peered inside.

It was a small room with a half dozen pews stretched across the middle. In front of the pews lay an altar with a simple crucifix hanging above it. Sconces holding small, electric candles were evenly spaced along the walls, while two larger ones adorned each side of the crucifix, giving the room a soft, warm glow. It was a room that was made to give hope to those that entered when hope seemed lost.

The three girls were all kneeling in front of the cross, their heads bowed in reverence, praying as one. At first, Lizzy couldn't understand what they were saying, but then the words got louder:

"Our Mother, who art in Hell, cursed be thy name.
Thy darkness consumes; the whole World to doom.
Suffer this day a Death to see.
The Serpent's blood a bane to all,
Master and Lover to Him you call.
A scourge upon your head we pray;
The Demon Mother to slay."

Lizzy stood there speechless as they got up and turned to her. "It's time to push through the darkness," they said as one.

"Who are you girls?" Lizzy stammered.

"We are her firstborn children, the Daughters of Lilith, Demon Queen, and Cohort of Satan. As a pledge to The Father of Lies, she devoured us, and is now waiting eagerly for you."

Click-clack, click-clack, click-clack, click-clack, clickety-clack, clickety-clack.

The girls looked up at Lizzy, and for the first time she saw their faces. Parts of their flesh had been ripped off, their necks torn apart, and their eyes just empty sockets, "Go now; break free!"

Click-clack, click-clack, click-clack, click-clack, clickety-clack, clickety-clack.

Then the three girls opened their mouths and a hoard of black spiders surged out of each one. The flesh in their arms and chest broke open and more spiders scurried from within. The chattering increased in volume until it was the only sound in the universe—*Click-clack, click-clack, click-clack, click-clack, clickety-clack, clickety-clack.*

A flurry of hairy legs surged over Lizzy. She tried to turn, only she wasn't in the chapel anymore, but was trapped in a small compact space with wooden walls all around her. She was lying in a coffin, buried alive! Not only that, she was no longer a child, but had aged and was now the woman in the hospital bed. A panicked scream flew from her mouth as the army of arachnids covered her from head to toe.

Feverishly, she kicked and clawed to get out. With each passing second, the death-box seemed to grow smaller, constricting the life from her. With her strength fading fast, Lizzy gave one final burst with all of her might. Then, when all hope seemed lost, her hand burst through the barrier and she was rewarded with a gush of fresh air.

Fiercely, she clawed her way through and found that she was actually standing upright and not laying horizontal like she had thought. Thick, gooey mucus oozed out of the opening as she pushed her way out. When she hit the floor, she cried out as a thousand muscle spasms wracked through her body at once.

After a few minutes, the pain subsided and Lizzy looked up to see that she had just clawed herself out of a giant cocoon. Sticky strands of thick, thread-like material clung to her body as she crawled her way to safety. The floor to the room was covered in dirt and rocks, and immediately she thought she was back inside the horror cave. Then she saw a door on the far side of the room and scrambled for it.

She was only a few feet from what she hoped was salvation, when the sound stopped her dead in her tracks: *Click-clack, click-clack, click-clack, click-clack, clickety-clack, clickety-clack*—a throng of chittering and chattering descending on her. She was afraid to look back, knowing now the source of the sound, remembering the long, hairy legs scurrying across the cave floor, the beady eyes regarding her hungrily, and the venomous fangs that had brought her to the brink of death.

When she did look, she saw scores of spider-beasts the size of large dogs bearing down on her. Desperately, Lizzy reached for the doorknob in a last-ditch effort to escape, only to be stopped by the icy voice she had feared from the first moment she heard it.

"And where do you think you're going, Young Lady?" Lilith said.

Lizzy turned toward the sound of Lilith's voice, half expecting to see her standing there with a bloody axe in her hand and a demented look in her eyes. What she saw was a million times worse. Already freakishly tall before, she now towered over Lizzy. Her eyes burned with rage, while her lips snarled around sharp fangs that jutted from the corners of her mouth. Her human body ended abruptly at her torso and then was transformed into a monstrous spider-like abdomen. A large mouth in the middle chomped at Lizzy hungrily, while her eight hairy legs scurried toward her. *Click-clack, click-clack, click-clack.*

"Well, well. It looks like Sleeping Beauty has finally risen from her slumber. A little early, mind you. But we'll make do."

Lilith inched closer to Lizzy, blocking her path to the door. "Now, you probably have about a million questions? I'm going to save you the trouble and spell it out for you in condensed form. Yes, this is really happening. And yes, you are going to die. Now, the way you do so is entirely up to you. It can either be slow and painful, or quick and easy."

"What do you want from me?" Lizzy cried.

"What else do you think the Queen of Hell would want? Yes, I know it sounds cliché, but I want your soul, well I don't but my son does. You should feel honored to be part of such a grand plan as the end of the World."

A scream erupted from Lizzy as Lilith reared up, bringing the spider mouth close. "Time to go back to sleep now, Lizzy. Just know that you will be serving a higher purpose."

Suddenly, the door blasted open and a blinding light engulfed the room. A fierce howl came from Lilith's direction, and then strong hands lifted Lizzy up and dragged her away.

"Hurry," a rough voice said. "We don't have much time before she recovers."

They exited the room, and even though her sight was blurry, Lizzy was startled to see that they were standing in the same foyer she had been amazed at the first time she had entered Lilith's massive estate.

Lizzy's rescuer draped a coat around her as they ran for the entrance. The huge door gaped at her from behind as they rushed toward safety. It had been as she had feared the first time she laid eyes on it—a doorway to Hell.

CHAPTER 12

Rain pelted them as they rushed outside. They had only gone a few yards when an ear-splitting cry erupted behind them.

Lizzy spun around as she cupped her hands over her ears. She barely had the strength to look up as she dropped to her knees under the pain. Circe was standing in the doorway, her mouth opened wide in a siren's scream, with Loki next to her barking and gnashing his teeth viscously.

Her death scream continued longer than humanly possible and grew in intensity with each second until the ground beneath them started to shake. A stream of blood oozed between Lizzy's fingers as it poured from her ears. For the second time in a matter of minutes, she was sure she was going to die.

When the scream stopped, Lizzy figured Circe was merely catching her breath and gearing up for round two. Her ears were ringing so badly that she hadn't heard the gun fire next to her. After a few seconds had passed, she looked up just in time to see Circe's body crumble to the ground from a bullet to the chest.

With an otherworldly roar, Loki charged at them. The man fired at the beast, but Loki jumped to the right and dodged the bullet. The Hell-hound leaped for the man's throat, and Lizzy had a flashback of Dr. Randolph's grizzly death. But this man wasted no time firing another shot, and a resounding yelp flew from Loki as the bullet found its mark and he went tumbling to the ground.

Before she had a chance to process what was happening, Lizzy was dragged to her feet once more. The man ushered her down the walkway toward a black car. After shoving her inside the passenger's seat, he raced over and jumped in. Seconds later, they were speeding away from the place she could only describe as Hell on Earth.

They drove in silence for a couple of miles until the ringing in her ears subsided and Lizzy found the strength to speak. "Thank you," she said softly.

The man looked at her for a second before returning his gaze to the wet road ahead, "The name's Ben, and unfortunately it's not over yet."

"What is going on here?" Lizzy cried. "I don't understand anything. The last thing I remember I was just a little girl. Then I was having crazy dreams. And today..."

Ben was silent for a moment. "I know this is all difficult for you to grasp, but please know that nothing you have done is responsible for anything that has happened."

"Why me, though? I was just an innocent little girl."

"It's not just who you are, but where you come from."

"I don't get it?"

"In order to know who you are, you must first know what you're up against. There is a lost scripture that tells of Adam's first wife. When Adam betrayed her for Eve, she vowed her revenge and gave herself over to Lucifer. As payment, He ordered her to devour each child she bore him until she gave birth to a son. Three daughters were destroyed before the son was born. That son would grow to become the one that he would send into this world to lead humanity toward the end of days—the Antichrist born flesh. The demon's name is Vizibir, firstborn son of Lucifer and Lilith."

"You're telling me that Vizibir is the Antichrist? That can't be right. Vizibir is a girl."

"Vizibir can be anything he wants to be. Lucifer is the Father of Lies. It stands to reason his offspring would carry the same trait."

The rain continued to splash against the windshield in buckets, bringing visibility down to almost zero. A cold chill had settled in Lizzy's bones, both from the rain outside and the horror she had been through. "That still doesn't explain what I have to do with any of this?"

Ben replied, "What we have learned is that Vizibir needs the power of three souls born from the House of David, in order to grow to his full strength."

Lizzy's eyes suddenly grew wide as she heard the buzz in her right ear and then felt her body being taken over by Vizibir once more. She was helpless as the demon's voice issued from her mouth, "I think that's enough of the history lesson for now, Magi."

Ben turned toward her. "I was wondering when you'd show up?"

Vizibir hissed, "I see you're just as eager as your brother to die."

"You'll pay for my brother's death, Demon!"

"He was an arrogant fool to think he could come into my own domain and defeat me? He deserved to die. And now you'll follow his same fate."

Lizzy was helpless as she felt herself surge forward and grab hold of the man who had almost saved her. Her hand thrust through his chest and grabbed hold of his still beating heart. With a quick pull, she ripped it from his body, and

Lizzy watched in horror as Vizibir brought the pulsating organ to her mouth. Under the demon's control, her mouth opened wide and chomped down eagerly on the bloody organ.

Without the guidance of a navigator, the car lurched forward, spinning out of control on the rain-soaked pavement. Then, suddenly, Vizibir left Lizzy's body, giving her back the ability to scream.

Desperately, she grabbed the steering wheel and tried to get the car under control, but the dead man's body slumped sideways against her, pushing her back into the passenger's seat and up against the door. The car became airborne as it spun off the shoulder of the road, before crashing down onto the hill and tumbling toward a small ravine below.

***

The bright light shining in Lizzy's eyes gave her hope that she had finally died and gone to Heaven. The smell of gasoline and burning oil suggested that she had instead gone to Hell. When she heard a voice calling out, she realized that she was still very much alive, and still imprisoned inside her nightmare.

She opened her eyes and saw that she was pinned inside the burning wreckage of the car, which somehow had landed right-side up. Ben's lifeless body had been thrown halfway out of the car with his upper torso extended onto the hood at a right angle so that his dead eyes looked back at her. It instantly brought the taste of his blood back into her mouth, and it was all she could do to keep from throwing up.

As the voice got closer, she realized that it was more than just one voice, it was multiple voices of a rescue crew, and the bright light that she'd hoped was the afterlife turned out to be a helicopter searchlight.

A minute later Lizzy heard a voice calling out, telling her that 'everything was going to be alright' as a flashlight shone through the broken glass. While the rescuer tried to pry the door open, she heard the hiss of fire extinguishers outside. When the door wouldn't budge the man reached in and grabbed hold of her arms so he could pull her out through the window. She caught a brief glimpse of his eyes through his mask and thought they looked familiar somehow.

The strong hands pulled Lizzy to safety just seconds before the car exploded into a huge bonfire that lit up the night sky. Quickly she was ushered up the slope to a group of paramedics who eased her onto a stretcher, which was then pulled up the steep hill by a rope. As she was moving up the slope, she looked over and saw a second stretcher sitting below with a black bag on it that contained Ben's body. She said a silent prayer for him even though she was convinced that prayer no longer helped.

After being bounced around for a few minutes, she was loaded inside the back of an ambulance with the same paramedic who had helped her out of the burning vehicle. As he attended to her—checking her blood pressure, cleaning the cuts on her face and arms—she caught the familiar sparkle in his eyes, and couldn't stop thinking that she knew him.

"Everything's going to fine, Liz," he said suddenly.

Lizzy looked at him in shock.

"No need to be alarmed," he said. "It's me, Tyler."

"But how—"

"A friend told me you were in trouble, so I rushed here to help."

Lizzy thought about Ben. Somehow, he'd been able to find her. Maybe they were working together? But that didn't make sense either?

"Who could have known what was going on?" She asked.

"That doesn't matter. The main thing is that you're safe now."

Her mind was a blur. There were really only two people who knew the kind of horrors she had faced. One of them was now lying in a body bag, and the other was the cause of her nightmares.

The back door of the ambulance burst open when they arrived at the hospital, and a pair of orderlies pulled the stretcher from the vehicle. They rushed Lizzy inside as Tyler fed them instructions. Just as the sliding doors closed behind them, she caught a warm smile from him, and then he disappeared from view.

From there she was wheeled into the emergency room where a couple of nurses took her vital signs and performed the same tests that Tyler had, before informing her that the doctor would be right in. She waited nervously, not having the best experiences with doctors in the past.

He was a thin, middle-aged man, with salt-and-pepper hair and wire-rimmed glasses. The first thing he did was grab the clipboard at the foot of the bed and scan the chart hanging there. After a few seconds, he came over and gently turned Lizzy's head from side to side so he could examine her injuries.

"From what I've been told, Young Lady," he said, "You're very lucky to be alive."

I've heard that before, Lizzy thought bitterly as she recalled the incident at the cemetery that had started her on her rollercoaster of madness.

"Now, do you know your name?" the doctor continued.

"Elizabeth," she said hoarsely.

"Good. Do you know where you are?"

"At the hospital."

"And do you remember what happened?"

She knew that the Doctor was just asking routine questions to gage the extent of her injuries, but she didn't know what to say at that point. Then she heard a buzzing sound and nearly jumped off the bed. To her relief the Doctor simply looked down at the pager fastened to his belt.

After the buzzing stopped, he looked back at Lizzy, "We're going to do a quick ultrasound right now to make sure there's no internal damage. After that, we'll move you to a private room and you can get some rest."

After plopping the cold gel onto her stomach, then sliding the scanner around her abdomen and chest for a few minutes the doctor was finished. "The good news is that there doesn't appear to be any internal injuries. You do, however, have a couple of cracked ribs, and judging by the bruising on your left wrist, I suspect it to be fractured as well. Don't worry though. We'll get you bandaged up and you'll be as good as new in no time."

As he left the room, Lizzy muttered to herself, "I doubt it."

An hour later, a young intern came in. "Hi, Lizzy," he said with a smile. "How about we get you fixed up?"

Her paranoia kicked in immediately, "How did you know that?"

"Know what?"

"My nickname. That's what people call me—Lizzy."

"Sorry, it was just an impulse. I have a little sister named Elizabeth, and that's what I call her. I didn't mean to offend you."

She felt stupid. "No, you didn't. I guess I'm just a little on edge right now."

"Well, that's to be expected, considering what you've gone through. Try to get some rest and you'll feel better in the morning."

The pain killers knocked her out cold. The next thing she knew it was morning and there was a man sitting on a chair next to her bed; a man she recognized from a long time ago.

CHAPTER 13

The man leaned forward in his chair, resting his elbows on his knees. He turned his head to face Lizzy, and she saw the scar on his left cheek. Instantly, she recognized him.

"I know you!" Lizzy said.

"Yes, you do," the man replied. I was there when you were a little girl."

"You took my mom from me!"

The detective was silent for a moment before continuing, "I'm sorry, but I had no choice. She put you in danger."

"But now I know that everything was a lie. She didn't do what I thought. The person who told me made everything up."

"And who is that?"

"Before I tell you everything, do you know if my mother is okay?"

The detective looked at Lizzy for a minute before answering, "After we took her away, she was put into custody for child endangerment. After that, she suffered a mental breakdown and was transferred to a psychiatric facility. I lost track of her a couple of years later."

"So, she might still be alive?"

"Probably."

Lizzy was silent for a minute. There had been so much death; so much chaos surrounding her life and it had taken everything from her. Finally, she said, "When this is all over, Detective, can you do me a favor and find her for me? Tell her I'm sorry for everything."

The detective looked at her and said, "When this is over, hopefully you can do that yourself."

Lizzy replied, "I doubt it."

The detective sighed, "Okay, then let's get to it."

He removed a small tape recorder from his jacket and turned it on. "Why don't you start from the beginning and tell me everything?"

Tears welled up in Lizzy's eyes as she took a deep breath and prepared herself to relive all the horrors that she had experienced. After finding the courage to utter the first few words of her story, the avalanche started, and the words rambled out. She had to stop at times to grab hold of herself and stop the trembling from overtaking her body and throwing her into an uncontrollable seizure of remorse.

Finally, a long time later, her story was complete, arriving to a conclusion at their present point in time. The detective turned off the recorder and sat back in his chair, quietly contemplating the story he had just heard. It was nonsense, all of it, and he knew it. Somehow, he had to get her to tell the truth.

Lizzy watched the detective earnestly, trying to judge whether he believed her or not. "Now you know it was all a lie told by that demon."

"All I know is what you've told me. There's no evidence to support your claims. What I do have is a dead man lying in the morgue with a hole in his chest."

Lizzy started crying again, "I told you what happened. She

possessed me. I had no control over what happened."

The Detective was getting impatient, which made his voice grow louder, "Dammit! I'm tired of this demon possession shit! Stop this nonsense and tell me what really happened!"

"But I'm telling you the truth!" Lizzy cried. "Why won't you believe me?"

The Detective stood up, slamming the chair backward a few feet and overturning it. He pointed at Elizabeth as he headed for the door, "I'll be back in a few minutes. While I'm gone, I suggest you rethink your story and come up with something a little more believable."

He then stormed out of the room.

***

Lizzy was startled when she looked up a minute later and saw Tyler standing at the foot of the bed. "Tyler! What are you doing here?"

Instead of answering her he shook his head in disappointment, "Lizzy, Lizzy, Lizzy. Look what you've done now."

Lizzy was confused, "I don't understand? What do you mean?"

"Look around you Liz. You've betrayed everyone that was ever close to you."

"How can you say that? You said you were close to Lilith, so you must know what she really is, and what she tried to do to me?"

"You know, Liz, I thought you were a lot smarter than this. I thought you would have figured everything out by now."

"Figured what out?"

"Who Lilith is."

The buzz preceded the transformation by a split-second.

Lizzy watched in horror as Tyler suddenly changed into her mirror image. She screamed as Vizibir climbed on top of the bed, straddling her. "You really disappoint me Liz, I thought we really had something special between us."

All Lizzy could do was cry over and over, "No, no, no. I give up. I can't do this anymore."

Vizibir smiled, "Mother will be so proud."

Elizabeth's eyes grew wide, "Lilith is your mother?"

"Ding, ding, ding. We have a winner!"

"But...that means—"

"Yes, Lucifer is my father. And now the time has come for you to play your part in the final plan to bring about the end of the World."

Vizibir suddenly leaned forward until she was inches from Elizabeth's face. She opened her mouth and drew a deep breath in. As she did so, a white stream of energy was expunged from Lizzy's mouth. A second later, it was all over and her lifeless body lay on the hospital bed staring up into the ether.

Just as the transfer was complete Vizibir stiffened, sensing that someone was watching her. She whipped her head around and scanned the room, but found it empty.

Apparently, another player had just entered this game.

PART THREE:
MATTHEW

Wading through my personal hell
  Always wondering how far I fell

Depth and despair waiting for me
  A lifeless death is all I see

Empty faces with longing minds
  Always wondering what's inside

Eyes of anger from an empty soul
  Life goes on, while you're on hold

Feeling cold, your blood runs hot
  The sun won't rise upon that spot

A crying soul, an endless night
While here you are in a hellish fight

As death approaches, there you stand
Digging your grave with soiled hands

* * *

If this life, than death is better
Than being here writing this letter…
—Michael Scott Baker

CHAPTER 1

Matthew never knew his father. He'd been told he was a great man, though, and apparently died saving the world from some sort of evil. His name was Michael. He was a hero.

The problem is, how do you live up to those kinds of standards? How do you walk in the shadow of greatness you've never even seen and not let it swallow your spirit? In the eyes of Matthew's mother, Mary, he was perfect. Matthew, though, not so much.

Instead, he was considered a slacker; unmotivated, uncaring, and selfish. Of course, Mary would never come out and say as much, but he could see it in her eyes. It didn't help that he behaved just like most eighteen-year-old boys and rebelled against any kind of authority.

He couldn't explain why he behaved the way he did. It wasn't that he hated everyone, or was angry at God for taking his dad away, or even that Mary was forced to work two jobs to make ends meet. Most of the time he just felt restless, unsatisfied, like there was some bigger force out there, a greater purpose for his life, and that all the daily little mundane things were meaningless. So, he had been labeled a loser because he didn't try.

Then, when the nightmares started, it was all he could do to keep from lashing out at everyone, including his mother, who was trying to keep him in line but failing miserably. As a result, a giant rift had been torn between them.

Matthew knew, even before he did the stupid things he was doing, what kind of effect they would have on her. But it didn't matter. He had tried everything else, and nothing had worked. The drugs and alcohol had become a necessity. They were his last hope; his final desperate attempt to keep the darkness away.

***

Suddenly, someone was shaking him violently and shouting. It took a moment for the fog in his brain to lift, and then he recognized his mother's voice, "Matthew! Please wake up!"

For a second, he panicked. He tried to open his eyes, but couldn't. His eyeballs felt like they had rolled into the back of his head and his eyelids were sealed shut. Desperately he pawed at his eyes, trying to rub the sleep from them. Finally, he fluttered them open and saw his mom hovering over him with tears in her eyes.

"Thank God," she sighed. "Are you okay?"

Slowly, Matthew sat up in bed, "I think so. What happened?"

"I was scared to death. You just kept on shaking and crying out in your sleep. I couldn't wake you!"

"I don't remember a thing. What was I saying?"

She hesitated for a minute, still trying to gauge whether he was really okay, "At first, I couldn't quite understand. Then you started repeating one word over and over. I thought you were saying visitor, but then I listened closer and it sounded like you were saying Vizibir. What in the world does that mean?"

Matthew tried to remember any small wisp of his dream that might help him understand what was going on. One thing he was pretty sure of, though, was that Vizibir was a name, and it was one he should fear.

"I have no idea?" he replied. "Could be anything?"

"Are you sure you're okay?" Mary asked, her eyes still full of worry.

"Yeah, I'm good," Matthew answered. "Let me just lay here for a minute, then I'll be down."

Mary nodded and left him alone to his thoughts.

He had told her that he needed to be alone for a minute to calm down, but in reality, he didn't want her to see how terrified he really was. The look she had given him—a combination of sadness and fear—didn't help him feel any better.

After a few minutes of trying to figure things out, the only thing he succeeded in was giving himself a headache. With a sigh, he swung his legs out of bed and sat there for a minute, running his hands through his sweat-soaked hair. He started to reach for the bottom drawer of his nightstand where he kept a stash of pills hidden— mainly Norco's and Lude's to help dull his brain in such a time as this—when something on the table caught his eye. He looked closely and saw a large gold ring lying there that he hadn't seen before. The front of it was adorned with a black onyx triangle, sporting a gold cross in the center. Two diamonds lay side by side at each point of the triangle. When he placed the ring on the middle finger of his right hand, it fit perfectly.

After studying the ring for a minute, he threw on a t-shirt and some sweats and went downstairs. He found his mom sitting at the kitchen table drinking a cup of coffee and reading the newspaper. She looked up at him when he walked into the room, "How are you feeling?"

"I'm fine," he lied as he poured himself a cup of coffee and joined her at the table.

"You want the sports section?" she offered as he sat down.

"Sure," he replied, even though he wasn't really in the mood to read. But, then again, he wasn't really in the mood for talking either. *Maybe if I keep my nose buried in the paper, she won't ask me any more questions?*

"That's a nice ring," she said. "Where'd you get it?"

"It was just sitting on my nightstand. I thought you put it there?"

A look of concern clouded Mary's eyes. "I've never seen it before."

The doorbell rang suddenly, giving him a chance to escape the conversation. Matthew quickly got up from the table and almost raced into the living room. He was startled to see a priest standing in the doorway. With long, blond hair, and deep blue eyes, he looked like he belonged in a rock band instead of the Church.

"Matthew Carpenter?" the Priest asked.

"Yes, can I help you?"

"Actually, I need to speak to your mother. Is Mary home?"

Matthew was just about to answer when his mom rounded the corner, "Who is it, Matthew?"

She stopped when she saw the Priest, "Can I help you?"

"My name is Father Andrew, and I have something very important to discuss with you. Is there someplace we can talk?"

She hesitated for a second, clearly starting to worry, "What's going on?"

"I'd really rather not talk about it in the open," Father Andrew replied. "You never know who might be listening."

A look of desperation in the Priest's eyes suggested to her

that whatever the situation was, he obviously felt it was serious. She led him back into the kitchen, but when Matthew tried to follow, the Priest interjected, "I'd like to talk to your mother alone, Matthew, if that's okay?"

Mary was hesitant at first, but then nodded.

"Okay," Matthew said begrudgingly. "But I'll be in the next room if you need me."

"Thank you, Matthew," the Priest answered.

The living room was right next to the kitchen, so Matthew flopped down on the couch. He grabbed a magazine and started absently flipping through the pages, hoping to catch a little of what was being said. They talked in hushed tones, making it hard to decipher, so he did what most people would do in his place and inched as close as he could to the kitchen without being spotted.

Mary's voice suddenly cracked, like she was on the verge of tears, "I can't go through this again."

The Priest said, "But he has the ring. Don't you see, he's been chosen?"

"I didn't give that to him."

"That's the point. It validates the fact even more that there is a Higher Power at work here."

"Look, I'm tired of all this Higher Power shit. I've already lost my husband. I don't want to lose my son as well."

Matthew had heard enough and stepped into the room, "Would someone please explain to me what the fuck is going on?"

Father Andrew stopped and looked at him for a moment, trying to decide what to say. Finally, he turned to Mary, "I'll leave this to you. Please contact me as soon as possible so we can figure out our next move."

He set a business card down on the table in front of her and then got up to leave.

"Matthew," he said as he extended his hand. "It's been a pleasure to meet you, and I look forward to talking more in the future."

He addressed Mary, "I'll see myself out."

Matthew watched the man leave before he turned to his mom questioningly. She looked back at him with tears threatening to burst from her eyes, "I think it's time we had a long talk about your father."

CHAPTER 2

Matthew's first reaction was total disbelief. Her whole story about angels, demons and the apocalypse sounded like something from a fantasy novel. To say that his father had been part of some epic hero's journey to save the world from destruction, and had then been exalted to a higher plane of existence as an angel, was a little much to swallow.

"You're joking, right?" he blurted out. Immediately, he regretted it. The hurt on his mom's face made him feel like someone who'd just kicked a puppy.

"I'm sorry," he said. "It's just a little hard to understand."

"I know. Trust me; I've been in your shoes. I didn't believe it at first, either. Even when I was there with him as he struggled, unable to help at all, I still had doubts."

Mary stopped for a moment, keeping the tears at by, before she continued, "Then he died, Matthew. Your father died. But something incredible happened...he came back to life. And he was so magnificent, more beautiful than anything I've ever seen before. He had been chosen for a higher purpose, just as you have."

Matthew just sat there, not sure what to say. Every ounce of his intuition told him she was telling the truth, or at least she believed she was. "What in the world does that mean, a higher purpose? Does that mean that I'm going to die too?"

Tears started streaming down her face like rivers born of sorrow. "I don't know what that means," she sobbed. "I only know that I love you, and I'm afraid of losing you."

She collapsed onto the couch and buried her face in her hands.

Matthew's heart felt crushed. He was so caught up in his own problems and fears that he failed to see how all of this was affecting his mother. He hugged her as hard as he could, and she responded by holding him tight, almost afraid to let go. Then, after a few minutes, she did just that.

He looked at her for a moment, suddenly amazed by the strength and depth of love that poured from her. Something he had taken for granted. He was sure that there had never been another person in this world that had loved as strongly as her.

"It'll be okay," he said.

She smiled half-heartedly, "I know. It always is, right?"

Matthew smiled back at her, "That's what you always tell me."

"Apparently, it's time for me to practice what I preach."

"What do you mean?"

"It means that I need to have faith and let things happen as they will. And you need to talk to Father Andrew so we can figure out what's going on."

As if on cue, the doorbell rang again.

"That may be the father now," Mary said. "I told him to come back after I'd had a chance to talk to you."

Matthew got up and went to the door. Instead of the rock-n-roll priest standing there, the man facing him was a short, thick man with pitch black hair and beady eyes. "I'm sorry to bother you," the man said. "I'm not from around here and I think I've gotten lost."

Suddenly, Matthew felt a tingle on his hand and looked down to find the mysterious ring on his finger glowing bright red.

"Never mind," the beady-eyed man said. "It looks like I've found the right place."

The man closed his eyes and started shaking violently. At first, Matthew thought he was having a seizure, but then his skin started melting from his face, and he knew it was time to run.

He slammed the door and raced back into the living room. "Run!" he yelled.

Mary jumped from the couch and stood there in shock for a moment, frozen in confusion. "What's going on?" she asked.

Matthew barely had time to grab her hand and run to the stairs when the front door crashed open. Quickly, they scurried up the stairs without waiting to see what was after them, running into Matthew's room and closing the door tightly before pushing the dresser over to block the door, hoping it would slow down the monster chasing them.

They both held their breaths as they listened anxiously for movement outside. A minute later, heavy scraping out in the hallway, like massive claws striking the wood flooring, echoed through the house. The sound stopped at the bedroom door and was replaced with a low snort. Mary inadvertently let out a gasp, alerting the creature on the other side of the door to their presence.

Immediately, the dresser started shaking as the creature pounded on the door feverishly. They both knew that with a few more blows, the door would come crashing in.

Mary turned to Matthew, "Listen to me, you have to hide...quickly. I'll draw the creature away while you run for safety."

Matthew looked at her in shock, "You can't be serious? There's no way I'm leaving you here to die."

"Matthew, it's the only way. Whatever your role in this is, you must be strong, and you must survive."

"But there has to be another way," he pleaded.

"We don't have time to argue, Matthew. I've gone through this before, and I know what's at stake. This is the only way. Now, please listen to me and hide."

Tears were streaming down Matthew's face as he looked at his mom, unable to move. How could he let her sacrifice herself for him? But he also didn't want his last act toward her to be one of defiance.

Before he could stop her, she shoved him to the ground just as the creature burst through the door. Quickly, Matthew scurried under the bed while Mary jumped to the other side of the room.

"Where is the Boy?" the creature growled in a low, gravelly voice. Its skin was a mottled brown covered with patches of black. Green saliva dripped from the enormous mouth that covered its skinny face. When it spoke, it revealed two rows of jagged teeth.

Mary didn't answer. Instead, she backed up further into the room. Matthew could see the creature's feet as it closed in on her—large, yellow talons ending in razor-sharp claws that shredded the carpeted floor as it walked.

"Tell me where the boy is and I'll make sure your death is swift and painless."

Mary grabbed a baseball perched against the desk in the corner. "Go fuck yourself, you ugly bastard!"

She took a desperate swing at the demon, but the thing swatted the bat away effortlessly. It grabbed her by the throat and lifted her off the ground, bringing her close to its face.

"You'll never win," she gasped in a final act of resistance before her windpipe was crushed.

Her body landed on the floor a short distance from the bed. A stream of blood poured from her mouth toward him. He tried to stifle the cry that came out, but everything had happened so fast that he couldn't.

The creature whirled around and tossed the bed aside. It almost laughed when it spoke, "So, you're the mighty hero who would destroy my master's plans?"

Desperately, Matthew scooted away from the demon, "Look, there's been some terrible mistake," he said. "I have no idea what you're talking about."

The demon seemed to enjoy this little piece of information, "How ironic that the supposed savior of the world will die, completely ignorant, before the battle even begins."

Matthew brought his hands up to block the demon as it lunged for him. As he did so, his right hand struck against the splintered bed post, knocking the face of the ring to one side. A bright beam of energy shot out, hitting the demon in the face. It cried out in pain as it stumbled backward. Then it went silent and crumbled to the floor. As it fell, Matthew saw Father Andrew standing there holding a long, silver dagger dripping with black ooze.

The Priest looked down at Mary's dead body, closed his eyes, crossed his chest, and sent a silent prayer for her soul.

"Matthew, I'm truly sorry for your loss," he said. "Unfortunately, we have to leave, now!"

"But we can't just leave her here like this."

"We have no other choice. Where there's one demon, there's certain to be more."

Matthew tried to protest, but the priest grabbed his arm and ushered him toward the door. As he was being pulled along, he saw a picture lying on the floor that had been taken a few years ago of him and his mom at the Grand Canyon. She had never looked so beautiful. Matthew snatched the picture from the broken glass and stuffed it in his pocket.

As Matthew walked out of the house with the long-haired priest his heart hurt like it had never hurt before.

Images bombarded Matthew in rapid succession, pummeling him with horror upon horror: a little girl lying dead in the grass, her head bashed in from a two-story fall from her bedroom window; a young man lying on a couch, blood flowing from a knife wound in his stomach; a young lady ripping a man's heart out with her hands before her car crashes into a ditch; giant spiders and spider demons. And through the entire dream assault, one name kept repeating over and over again—Vizibir. He knew this was the source behind his mother's death.

When Matthew woke from his terror-filled sleep, he realized they had been driving non-stop for hours, heading toward up-state New York, where Father Andrew assured him, they would be safe. After he had driven as far as he could without falling asleep at the wheel, he pulled into a small motel.

The starless sky overhead made it feel like the whole universe had passed away with Mary's last breath. A feeling of despair overcame Matthew as he considered for a brief second that life wasn't worth living anymore. Then he realized that if he gave up, her death would've been for nothing.

While the outside of the motel was dirty and grimy, the inside was worse. Puke green wallpaper covered the walls of the room, except for the places that had peeled away, revealing the drywall underneath. The tan carpet was stained with every color imaginable, while smoky clouds had become embossed on the ceiling. Two full size beds and a small dresser were the only pieces of furniture.

If he hadn't been so tired, he would've thought twice about laying on the bed. Instead, he threw himself down on the closest one and buried his head in the pillow.

Father Andrew sat down on the edge of the bed. Silence filled the air for a minute before he spoke, "I understand what you're going through, Matthew."

Matthew snapped, "I'd rather not talk about it right now."

"Okay, I'll leave you alone. I truly am sorry for your loss."

Matthew knew he probably should've said something, apologized for being short with the man, thanked him for saving his life, anything; instead, he just kept quiet and let sleep overtake him again.

Another nightmare hit him hard and fast. The last thing he remembered as he woke up in a blind panic was a young lady lying in a hospital bed, screaming for her life as a ghostly version of herself crawled on top of the bed toward her. The ghost pressed its face forward, opened its mouth wide, and sucked the life right out of the girl. In a few short seconds, the girl lay lifeless on the bed. Then the specter looked right at Matthew and smiled.

As he sat up in bed, trying to calm his nerves, Father Andrew woke up. After a yawn and a stretch, he sat up as well. "Are you feeling any better?" he asked.

Matthew still didn't feel like talking, but knew he couldn't avoid this man forever. "I'm okay," he responded. "But have you heard the name Vizibir before? Or Lilith?"

The Priest's eyes grew wide and his face whitened as if he'd seen a ghost, "Where did you hear those names?"

"I've seen them in my dreams. I think they're the ones behind this whole thing. They're the reason my mom is dead."

The Priest went silent for a second as he contemplated this information. "I'm afraid this situation has just gotten a lot worse," he finally said.

Like it could get any worse? Matthew thought grimly. *My Mom is dead and I'm on the run from demons. What else could happen?*

The Priest continued, "Until now all we knew was that you were in danger, or at least we suspected it was you. We didn't know for sure until yesterday."

"You keep saying 'we' like you have a mouse in your pocket."

The Priest smiled for the first time since he had barged into Matthew's life, "I guess I should explain myself a little. Since time immemorial, there has been a struggle between good and evil. But it was after David slew Goliath, whom Lucifer had hoped would carve a path of destruction through the Israelites, that he grew furious and unleashed countless abominations upon the world. In order to battle this new form of evil, Solomon formed a secret sect of individuals upon whom he entrusted the greatest secrets given to him. They are called the Magi, and their mission is simple: To protect the earth from evil."

"Are you telling me you're a part of a secret organization of religious sorcerers?"

"Something like that."

"And your job is to protect the world from evil?

"Correct."

"Well, I'd say you're doing a pretty shitty job so far!"

Matthew got up and stormed into the bathroom, slamming the door behind him.

The inside of the bathroom was even more disgusting than the main room. Urine stains dotted the floor surrounding a toilet that looked like it hadn't been cleaned in months. The mirror above the sink hadn't fared much better. A white, dull film covered the surface of the glass, making it seem like you were looking through a fog bank to see your own reflection.

Matthew gripped the edges of the sink and stood there for a minute, trying to get himself together. He felt around in his pockets, hoping for a bag of something that he might've stashed away, but found nothing. He sighed as he felt another headache coming on.

He ran his hand on the glass to try to clear a spot where he could see his reflection. About the only thing visible through the grime were his eyes, dark and sad, filled with pain and regret.

As he stared into them, a whirlwind of emotions coursed through him. He felt guilty for lashing out at the Priest the way he did. After all, it wasn't his fault that some demon thing had attacked them; or that his mom had chosen to sacrifice herself to save him. And that's what was really at the heart of his anger—that even after all the shit he had put her through, she still loved him enough to die for him. Deep down, he was furious with himself for the way he had treated her. She had deserved better.

Matthew was snatched from his brooding when he suddenly felt a tingle on his right hand and looked down to see his ring glowing again. He charged out of the bathroom and showed Father Andrew.

"It looks like it's time to go," the priest said as he rushed toward the door. A quick check through the small windows beside the door was all they had time for before they ran outside and sprinted for the car.

Outside, night was about to give way to a new dawn as a handful of purple fingers stretched above the horizon. As the two men looked around nervously for signs of trouble, they didn't see anything out of the ordinary until the threat was right on top of them. A swirling mass of blackness, as dark as ink, zoomed downward, at first appearing like a crazed funnel cloud hell-bent on destruction. As they looked closer, they realized they were actually looking at a giant swarm of insects. They had just enough time to dive into the car and close the door before the swarm slammed into the vehicle.

The impact felt like being hit by a missile and being riddled by bullets from an automatic weapon at the same time. The roof of the car buckled and bent under the onslaught. When one of the insects tried to crawl through a small hole in the windshield, Matthew gasped when he saw that it wasn't an ordinary insect at all. It was shaped like a giant locust, with long prehensile stingers at the end of its abdomen. Its body shimmered between gold and metallic purple, even in the predawn light. Venom dripped from the gnashing teeth that filled its bulbous head.

Father Andrew shouted, "The ring! Use the ring!"

It took a second for Matthew to grasp his meaning until he remembered the 'accident' in the bedroom. Quickly, he turned the ring, hoping for similar results. He must have turned the ring in the opposite direction as before, because instead of a white energy blast, this time blue flames shot out. As soon as the flames struck the demon it disintegrated. The flames continued outward, shattering the windshield and sending shards of glass flying toward the swarm. While the glass spray took out several demons, the holy flames behaved like heat-seeking missiles, tracking their prey and extinguishing them.

After a few minutes, they were all gone, leaving both men sitting in the car afraid to move. Finally, Matthew turned to Father Andrew, "Now what?"

CHAPTER 4

Matthew thought it was weird watching the priest next to him talking on a cell phone to some unseen party about their situation. The guy seemed so out of place, with his long hair and rock-star persona, but when the conversation switched to Latin and he held the rosary around his neck tightly, Matthew knew he was the real deal.

After a few minutes, he hung up and turned to Matthew, "Apparently, they are now tuned in to the frequency of the ring. It's acting like a GPS, giving away our location."

"That's easy enough to fix. I'll just get rid of the ring."

"I'm afraid it's not that simple. For one, we need the power of the ring to defend ourselves. And two, I think you'll find that the ring is now a part of you. You'd probably have to sever your finger to get rid of it. Even then its power might prevent that from working."

"Then how do we stop them from finding us?"

"My associates say that the emblem on the face of the ring, when pressed in, acts as a cloaking device, putting a barrier around you that can't be seen. In effect, it makes you invisible to their radar."

"How do you know that?"

"I told you we've been entrusted with powerful secrets that may aid us in our fight against evil. Solomon left us information about the ring and its power."

Matthew was shocked, "There's a user's manual for this thing?"

He nodded, "Kind of. You'd be surprised at the information that's available if you know where to look. Now, I suggest you press the button so we can get out of here."

Matthew was just about to press the emblem when it began to glow again, "Too late," he said, stating the obvious.

"Hurry, press it now. Maybe we can throw whatever it is off before it sees us?

Matthew pressed the button quickly, and it immediately extinguished the light. They heard a loud buzzing coming from somewhere nearby and knew they'd be sitting ducks if they stayed in the car

"We need to get out of the car," Father Andrew said. "We're too exposed out here."

The priest started to reach for the ignition but Matthew stopped him. "No," he whispered. "That'll just give us away."

The first rays of the sun started peeking out above the horizon, filling the morning sky with deep rays of red and orange. It was still fairly dark where they were, so they quickly slipped out of the car and ran for the corner of the building just as their vehicle exploded behind them.

When they dared to peek at their new attacker, they saw a giant fly-like demon hovering in the air on large insect wings. Tufts of thick black hair sprouted from various parts of its body. Two of its six appendages resembled long, thin human arms, while the other four were the limbs of a fly. Its head was only vaguely humanlike, with four sets of large round eyes on each side, and a hooked horn where its nose would be.

"What is the deal with all these demonic insects?" Matthew whispered.

"What else would you expect to be crawling out of Hell?"

"Since you put it that way..."

The manager of the mostly deserted motel made the mistake of running outside to check out the explosion and was immediately set upon by the creature. The demon sped toward the skinny old man, who was wearing a ratty blue bathrobe, and impaled him in the chest with its curved horn. Then it reached in with its long wiry tongue and ripped the man's heart from his chest and gobbled it down.

They waited anxiously in the shadows for nearly an hour, hoping the creature wouldn't find them. A couple of times, they had to change locations as the demon drew perilously close. Luckily, they were able to avoid its many, bulbous eyes, and after a while it gave up its search and returned to whatever hole it had crawled out of.

When it finally seemed safe, they stepped from their hiding place and walked toward the metal heap that used to be their car.

"It looks like we're stuck here for a while," Matthew said. "Any ideas?"

The Priest responded by pulling his cell phone out and punched a few buttons.

"Of course, you do," Matthew said.

Matthew watched the priest as he spoke in his phone and was amazed at how he had managed to stay so calm, given what they had just gone through. Then he realized that he, himself, hadn't gone off the deep end completely, and that surprised him even more. Maybe the fact that everything had happened so fast had been a saving grace? He hadn't had time to lose his mind.

Father Andrew ended his phone call and turned to him, "Our transportation should be here soon."

They walked around the outside of the motel for a few minutes until they came across a couple of chairs leaning against the wall near the office.

After a couple of minutes to clear his head, Matthew finally asked the priest the question he'd been holding in, "What do you know about my father?"

Father Andrew thought long and hard before finally speaking, "I didn't know your father personally, but from I've been told, both Heaven and Earth can rejoice because of his sacrifice."

"Yeah, yeah, I get it. He was a great man, fought evil and saved the world...blah, blah, blah. That still doesn't tell me who he really was."

"I think he was probably a lot like you—a little lost in this world, not sure of himself, rebellious, looking for answers."

His assessment was right on point and brought a pang of regret to Matthew for his past actions. "Do you know what happened to him?"

"From what I've been told, he was a tortured soul, bombarded by nightmares that nearly drove him mad. It apparently led him to drug and alcohol addictions as he tried to quiet the turmoil coursing through him."

"Well, that sounds familiar."

"Eventually, he came to understand that these visions were actually messages sent to him so that he could help lead the war against evil. After a time, he understood his role in the scheme of things and came to accept it. He surrendered his life on this plane so that he could lead the charge against the Four Horsemen. Then, during the battle, he sacrificed himself once more to defeat Armageddon. It was this sacrifice that exalted him to become the new Archangel."

Matthew's mouth dropped, "Are you telling me that my dad is actually the Archangel Michael?"

Father Andrew smiled a soft, warm smile, "Yes, that's exactly what I'm saying. He is the perfect example of how strong the power of love is, and how that love can transform a man, and in turn, transform the world. His undying love for your mother, and his need to protect her at all costs, are what propelled him to carry on his mission. He gave up everything for the one he loved and was justly rewarded."

"Wow, talk about a hard act to follow. How am I supposed to live up to that?"

"The answer is easy, Matthew—you don't. Each individual must follow his own path, make his own choices, and create his own legacy."

"That's easy for you to say, but I don't really recall having any kind of a choice in this.'

"There's always a choice."

Matthew was just about ready to go off on the priest when a black sedan came speeding toward them.

"I'm assuming this is our ride?"

"You assume correctly," Father Andrew answered.

The vehicle skidded to a halt in front of them, kicking up dirt and pebbles in a rocky spray at their feet. The drivers' side window slid down and a girl about Matthew's age, with short black hair and piercing green eyes, stared at him for a second. "So, this is the one, huh?" she asked.

Father Andrew nodded, "Grace, this is Matthew. Matthew, say hello to Grace."

Grace asked Matthew, "You ready to save the World?"

"It's not like I have a choice."

She smiled at him, "We always have a choice."

Matthew looked at the Priest, "Now, where have I heard that before?"

Matthew was about to slide into the backseat, when Father Andrew climbed in first, and he was awkwardly forced to make his way to the front passenger's seat.

He was more than a little curious as he sat there quietly, stealing little glances here and there while she was driving. Then he caught her doing the same thing, and they both started blushing like they were in high school again. To ease the tension, Grace cranked up the volume on the radio and refocused on her driving.

If the Priest objected to the music blasting through the car, he didn't show it. Matthew got the sense that he had been around Grace enough to know how to handle her. Or maybe he had grown tolerant and had simply resigned himself to letting her do whatever she wanted? Whatever the case, it was certainly a strange relationship the two enjoyed.

After a few minutes of loud and mind-clearing music, Grace turned the volume down and looked in her rear-view mirror, "Where to, Pops?"

Father Andrew growled at her, "You know I hate it when you call me that. It sounds disrespectful."

She persisted, "Okay, whatever you say, Pops."

"You are so much like your mother."

Matthew sat there in stunned silence at their exchange, while Grace just giggled. Then Father Andrew grew irritated, "That's enough, Grace Luanne Henson."

"Hey!" Grace exclaimed. "No need to play the middle-name card here."

It was Father Andrew's turn to smile, "You gave me no other choice."

He paused for a second and then said, "Take us home."

Grace nodded, "I figured."

"In case you haven't figured it out," the priest said to Matthew, "Grace is my daughter."

Matthew was a little confused.

Father Andrew clarified, "I wasn't always a priest, Matthew."

It made sense. *I guess everyone finds their calling in life at different times,* Matthew thought.

"So, where is home?" he asked.

Grace said, "Home is where it all comes together. We should be there soon."

Matthew glanced up through the windshield toward the sky and saw a gigantic dark cloud blocking the sun. Instantly, he recalled the swarm of demon locusts that had attacked them a few hours earlier. Maybe he was just being jumpy, but the thought crossed his mind that the storm brewing up ahead was anything but natural.

"I think you might want to step on it a little," he said.

CHAPTER 5

They crossed into New York, flying along the Sheridan Expressway until they exited onto the Cross Bronx Expressway. Matthew had no idea where they were going, but Grace navigated the busy freeways better than any Nascar driver could have. Finally, after a long stretch, they came to a stop in front of a large office building with the letters H.O.M.E. engraved on the front.

"This isn't quite what I expected when you said we were going home," Matthew said.

Grace replied, "You didn't actually think we were going back to our house, did you?"

"I didn't know what to expect, but it certainly wasn't an office building. What does H.O.M.E. stand for, anyway?"

Father Andrew answered, "To the public this is a non-profit organization. The letters stand for Help Our Mother Earth. Some of the offices are leased to various charity organizations with environmental interests."

None of this makes any sense! What does any of this have to do with the Anti-Christ? "That's great and all, but I don't get what this has to do with anything?" Matthew asked.

"That's just a cover, silly," Grace said. "The real meaning is

216

a little more esoteric than that. Besides, it's more about what's under the property, than what the building's about."

"Now you've really lost me."

Grace chuckled as she got out of the car and walked toward the front door.

Matthew felt Father Andrew's hand on his shoulder, "Don't let her abruptness throw you off," he said. "She's really a kitten once you get to know her."

A minute later, they were standing in front of the receptionist desk, with a vision of beauty sitting behind it. Long, blond hair cascaded around her thin face and down her shoulders like waves of satin. Her blue eyes sparkled like the bluest ocean, and radiated pure love. Matthew couldn't help but stare.

Father Andrew cleared his throat to bring him back to the present. "Gloria," he said, "Can you tell Sam that we're on our way."

"Already done, Father," she said.

A few feet in on the left, was a wall with two sets of elevators and a solid steel door with a security panel on it. After Father Andrew punched in a security code, the steel door swung open. Grace went first, and as Matthew followed, he couldn't help but steal one last glance at the beauty behind the desk. As he did, he heard Gloria say to Father Andrew, "You're going to have your hands full with this one."

The priest replied, "Don't I know it."

Once the door had closed Father Andrew stopped Matthew, "In the future I would suggest you avoid staring at Gloria like a love-struck monkey."

"I did no such thing," Matthew exclaimed.

Grace snickered, "Please. If your tongue were hanging any lower, you'd be licking the floor. Plus, you still have a little drool dripping from the corner of my mouth."

Out of embarrassment, Matthew ran the back of his hand across his mouth and pulled away a line of saliva.

"Don't be too hard on yourself, though," Father Andrew said. "After all, she is an angel, a Cherubim to be exact."

Matthew choked and started coughing. After a minute, he was breathing normally again, thanks to a hard slap on the back by Grace.

"You okay there, Sport?" she asked.

Matthew glared at her, which only made her chuckle. This girl certainly was a handful! Even though the scowl on his face said one thing, his brain screamed another. But the last thing he needed right then was to get involved with someone.

"Aren't cherubs little, fat angels that shoot arrows at people to make them fall in love?" he asked.

Father Andrew sighed, "That's just society commercializing the idea of love in order to make a buck. The real Cherubim are the keepers of celestial records, and the protectors of God's sacred knowledge. In fact, Lucifer was a Cherubim before his fall."

Grace added, "And if you stare at her too long your brain will turn to mush, your insides will melt, and you'll turn into a pile of goo."

Matthew turned to Father Andrew in shock.

The priest laughed, "Calm down. She's just messing with you. Although you do have to be careful not to get lost in her gaze or you could conceivably go mad."

When Matthew turned back, Grace had stormed off down the hall. "What's the matter with her," he asked.

"I'd say that she might be a little bit jealous."

Father Andrew walked past him, "Come on. Sam's waiting for us."

Matthew followed him about twenty yards until the hall

took a sharp turn right, and then abruptly ended at an elevator. Grace was waiting there with her arms crossed.

Father Andrew stepped forward and pressed his thumb into a fingerprint scanner on the wall next to the elevator. The doors opened, and they entered the small chamber. A lighted panel inside the elevator showed three unmarked buttons. The priest pressed the bottom one and immediately they descended.

After a few minutes, they came to an abrupt stop. The doors opened up to a narrow passage cut out of the earth. It stretched forward about forty yards until it disappeared into a blank wall. A row of soft bulbs hanging from an electrical line overhead created a soft glow on the cut rock walls.

As they stood in front of the wall, waiting for something to happen, the earth below them rumbled steadily. It sounded like a snoring giant lay just beneath their feet. Matthew looked back and was startled to see the elevator disappearing into the ceiling. The whole passage was descending!

He almost lost his balance when the descent stopped and the passage started to swing around. When it came to a stop, they were staring at another stone wall. This time, however, the wall shimmered and then disappeared.

Matthew followed Father Andrew as he walked forward, with Grace right behind him, as they stepped out of the passage into a large circular room. Measuring at least fifty feet in diameter, the room was like a combination library and studio apartment. A plush couch and loveseat sat in the center of the room, while the back-left quarter was filled with rows of shelves overflowing with books. In front of them were a couple of large wooden desks, each one with a desk lamp and a computer sitting on top.

To the left was a small recreation area with a large flat-screen TV hanging on the wall, and a large black leather recliner facing it. The right side of the room was basically the living area, with a small kitchen area in the front half and a bedroom area in the back. The only other door in the room was on the opposite wall.

It seemed like it would be a pretty cool place if not for the fact that it was about a hundred feet below ground, hidden within a secret society, and that the person occupying the room was an old man with long gray hair, wearing a tie-dye t-shirt and floating about a foot off the ground while meditating.

Matthew stood there watching the meditating hippie for a moment, wondering what the proper etiquette was for approaching a floating man, when he noticed the ring on the man's right hand. It was exactly like his!

"That's the same ring as mine," Matthew blurted out.

The hippie opened one eye for a second, closed it again, and then slowly settled to the floor. "Actually, your ring is a copy of this one, more or less," he said as he jumped to his feet.

"Matthew," Father Andrew said, "I'd like you to meet Solomon."

The old man extended his hand enthusiastically, "Please, call me Sam. It's much more...current."

Solomon excitedly put his arm around Matthew's shoulder and ushered him over to the couch, "I'm so happy to finally meet you, Matthew. We have so much to talk about, and very little time to do so."

Matthew was shocked at the abruptness, "Please, don't tell me that you're the actual King Solomon?"

He smiled, "That would be me."

"But that would make you three thousand years old!"

"Actually, three thousand twenty-one years, three hundred forty-eight days, to be exact. I have a birthday coming up in a couple of weeks."

Matthew sat there stunned, "How is that possible?"

"Suffice it to say that I'm here today because of a little bit of spiritual enlightenment, coupled with some divine intervention. If we have a chance sometime, I'll tell you the whole story, but for now the most pressing matter is to teach you the intricacies of your ring, and to discuss your next plan of action."

He stopped for a second, "Forgive me my manners. You guys must be starving. Why don't you relax for a minute while I make us something to eat?"

Grace and Father Andrew sat down on the couch next to Matthew. "Are you okay, Matthew?" the priest asked.

"I don't know. This is all just so much to handle right now. I mean, how can someone be three thousand years old?"

Father Andrew thought about it for a minute, "Once you achieve ultimate enlightenment, you're able to accomplish things that were once thought impossible."

"I get that. I just can't comprehend it."

Grace interjected, "He's not always here on Earth. He comes down now and then to help when times get scary. It's kind of his penance for amending his past behavior.'

Matthew still didn't understand what was going on.

"Didn't you pay attention in Sunday School?" She asked.

Feeling foolish, Matthew shrunk back on the couch, "All I remember is how wise he was, and a story about two women and a baby. Beyond that, I don't really know?"

Father Andrew said, "It's true that Solomon is considered the wisest man to ever walk this earth. The kingdom of Israel flourished under his reign for many years. But like so many men before him, and so many after, he gave himself over to temptation and turned his back on God. In the blink of an eye, he lost everything."

Solomon returned carrying a plate of sandwiches and a bowl of potato chips. After setting them down on the coffee table, he grabbed a sandwich and sat down on the love seat next to them. "I hope ham and Swiss is okay?"

"It's fine," Matthew replied, not realizing how hungry he was until he saw the food in front of him.

Solomon said, "Everything they said is true. Fortunately for me, I was given a second chance. Now I serve as a protector of His wisdom."

Matthew grew silent for a minute as he considered Solomon's statement, wondering how God could be so compassionate and yet let someone as wonderful as his mother die? He squelched the urge to open his mouth and let those very words spew forth. Harsh words wouldn't help anyone at the moment, and would only bring his spirit down again.

Solomon sensed his struggle and quickly changed the subject, "Now, about that ring of yours?"

He leaned forward on the loveseat and Matthew extended his hand so he could get a better view. "The ring has seven different abilities," He continued. "A couple of them you've already experienced."

"Yeah, sort of."

"Pressing the center cloaks you from the demons. There are also three power settings clockwise, and three counter-clockwise. A couple words of caution, though: first, each power can only be used once a day, and second, the use of any of the powers will cause the cloaking field to vanish."

"Well, that totally sucks!"

"I know it's unfortunate, but the energies of this world have their limitations. It was either that or the bearer of the ring suffer horrible injuries as the different energies course through his body at the same time. Besides, it only takes about thirty seconds for the ring to reload after you use it, so you just need to make sure you're not vulnerable during that time."

"Makes sense, I guess. This is all still pretty new to me. What other things can the ring do?"

"Good question. First off, after every use, the ring resets to its original position. There is a slight delay at each point, giving you a chance to advance it further, or to aim the ring at your target. Now, the settings clockwise are holy fire, levitation, and then mind control. Counter-clockwise, they are lightning, earthquake, and then invisibility."

Matthew was speechless. All that power literally in the palm of his hand.

"Use the ring carefully. For when you do, you unleash the full force of nature with the fury of God behind it. If we had more time, I would suggest a little practice before you venture out. But I'm afraid we simply don't have that luxury."

Solomon turned and addressed Grace and the Priest, "Father, Grace, it's been a pleasure, as always." He turned back to Matthew, "Well, I've shown you all I can for now. The rest is up to you."

"You're leaving? But I still have so many questions. Where do I go next?"

Solomon patted Matthew on the shoulder, "Everything will be fine, Matthew. Your ring is linked to mine, so if you ever find yourself in trouble just say my name into the ring and I may be able to help. Besides, I'm leaving you in very capable hands."

Then he snapped his fingers and disappeared, leaving Matthew standing there in shock. For a brief second, he thought he was finally going to get some answers. Instead, he was left with more questions.

He looked at the Father Andrew and Grace, "Now what?"

Grace answered, "I think maybe a trip to the circus is in order."

CHAPTER 6

Father Andrew and Grace were sitting at one of the desks searching the internet vigorously, while Matthew remained on the couch and suddenly found he couldn't keep his eyes open. *Just a quick nap,* he thought as he laid down. Within seconds he was asleep.

***

When the darkness lifted, Matthew was looking over the top rail of a crib where an infant boy, barely a few weeks old, slept soundly, nestled inside a blue blanket. A banner hanging on the wall above the crib read 'Happy Birthday Caleb!' Next to the crib stood a dresser with several photographs on top, depicting a happy Mother and Father holding their bundle of joy. It was obvious that he was loved.

Then suddenly Matthew was the infant in the crib, looking up at the jungle animals hanging from the mobile over his head. A figure came into view above him, temporarily blocking out the light. He reached down and picked Matthew up, sending a shock through his body. "I think you'll do nicely," the man said.

A vapor of smoke drifted forward as the man blew gently on his face.

Matthew was violently wrenched out of the baby's body to find himself an onlooker once more. Then he felt a tiny sliver of smoke travel down his throat into his lungs.

His chest constricted, and he fell to his knees in the middle of a coughing fit. At the same moment, he heard the baby choking and wheezing. The strange man looked at Matthew, flames dancing in his eyes; his face burning with fury.

He charged at Matthew and grabbed him by the throat, lifting him off the ground. His face was inches from Matthew, spitting acid saliva as he spoke, "This will not happen to me! Your father might've succeeded in defeating Belial, but I am not him, and you are not your father!"

He let go and Matthew went crashing to the floor, struggling to breathe. His body started to shake violently, and he thought for sure that he was going to die. Voices surrounded him, calling out his name, like the voices of the dead calling him home. Then his body was being shaken back and forth by an unseen force. Cold water suddenly splashed in his face, jolting him from his nightmare and leaving him in a state of momentary shock.

When he opened his eyes, Matthew found himself lying on the floor. Slowly he crawled back up to the couch, still trembling from the dream assault.

"Are you okay?" Grace asked worriedly.

Matthew stammered, "I think so. Just give me a minute to calm down."

Father Andrew asked, "What happened?"

"I don't really know? I was dreaming, only it seemed so real. First, I was in a nursery looking down at a young child. Then suddenly I was the child, and I could sense an evil presence in the room. He lifted me from the crib and I could feel the unnatural heat coming from his hands. The scary part is that he somehow sensed that I was an intruder and wrenched me from the infant's body. His fingers clamped on my throat and he screamed at me about someone name Belial and my dad. If I didn't know any better, I would swear that the Devil himself was there in my dream."

Grace cried out when he lifted his head up, "My god, Matthew, your neck!

The Priest rushed over to the bedroom area and quickly came back with a small mirror. Matthew snatched the mirror and was horrified when his reflection showed burn marks on his neck clearly shaped like long, boney fingers.

Father Andrew looked at him fearfully, "It appears that your nightmare just now was not merely a dream, but was very real."

As Matthew sat on the couch shaking from the horror he'd just experienced, Grace ran to the sink and came back with a glass of water. "Here, drink this. It'll help."

Matthew's hands were trembling as he brought the glass of water to his lips and some of the liquid sloshed to the floor.

"Do you remember anything important that might help us figure out what's going on?" Grace asked.

Matthew shook his head, but the truth was he didn't want to remember anything. Every crisis that he faced pushed him closer and closer to giving up. All he wanted to do was crawl into a hole and hide.

He replied, "Everything's pretty fuzzy right now." Then he put his head down into his hands, "I can't do this anymore. How can I possibly hope to fight against Lucifer? He told me right to my face that I wasn't my dad. And from what I've gathered, he was right!"

The room suddenly filled with light, and everyone had to shield their eyes to avoid being blinded.

A moment later, the light dimmed and Matthew found himself looking at an older version of himself. The person looking back at him had the same eyes, the same hair, the same chin, and looked to be about ten years older. "You can do this, Matthew," the man said. "You have strength inside you that haven't realized yet."

"Who are you?" Matthew asked.

"You already know the answer to that."

Matthew sat there stunned. It was too much! How could this possibly be? But his very conflict provided the answer he was afraid to admit. "Dad?" he said as he slid off the couch, crying.

He felt a hand on his shoulder and looked up to see Grace standing there. "We'll leave you two alone," she said before she and her father walked out of the room into the hallway outside.

When Matthew first learned of his Father's exploits, he shrugged them off as fantasy. That was the easiest way for him to process everything. But now he suddenly felt very ashamed of his disbelief, and also very humble.

Michael continued, "I was just like you, Matthew, facing my own darkness with no hope to survive. But then your mother saved me from that darkness and brought me back to the light. I couldn't have done it without her."

Matthew lost it again when Michael mentioned his mom and started crying.

"Please, don't mourn her death, Matthew," he said. "She sacrificed herself so that you could live. There's no greater love than that."

"But...I treated her like shit! All she ever did was love me, and all I ever did in return was hurt her. Now she's gone and I'll never get the chance to say I'm sorry."

When Matthew looked up again, he was surprised to see

his mom standing there, shining like the sun and smiling at him. "Please, don't beat yourself up, Matthew. I'm the one who should be sorry. I should have told you everything from the beginning, but I didn't. I thought I was protecting you. Instead, I put you in even more danger."

"Don't be silly. No one could have known that any of this would happen."

"That's not true. With everything your father had gone through, I above anyone else, knew what to expect, and should have prepared you for it. But I was afraid. I thought I could go through life with blinders on and ignore what was going on around me. I just didn't want to see you hurt. In the end, my selfishness caught up to me."

Matthew looked at her, blinking back the tears, "Instead I lost you."

"Please don't look at it that way. I did what I had to in order to keep you safe, and I would make the same choice again."

"But now I'm all alone."

"You'll never be alone, Son," Michael said.

"I know that, but it's just not the same."

Father Andrew and Grace came in at that moment, pulling Matthew's gaze away momentarily. When he looked back, his mom and dad were gone. On the floor in their place was a gold chain with a medallion that showed a sand dollar on it. He remembered the story of the gift his dad had given his mom just before he went away. As he put the chain around his neck, he swore that he would keep the necklace close to his heart for the rest of his life.

"Is everything okay?" Grace asked.

For the first time, he could honestly answer her, "Yes."

CHAPTER 7

Matthew sat back on the couch, trying to make sense of his place in the world. He was so overwhelmed that his brain was a tangled mess. Once again, he found himself longing for something that might ease his turmoil. Anything would help.

Then, in the middle of the maelstrom in his mind, a memory suddenly ignited, "His name was Caleb," he blurted out.

Grace asked, "Whose?"

"The boy in my dream. His name was Caleb. I saw it on a banner over his crib. That might mean something, right?"

Father Andrew replied, "Maybe."

He thought about it for a minute, then got up and went over to one of the computers, where he started typing feverishly.

"What're you working on, Pops?" Grace asked.

She was shocked when he didn't respond to her quip with his usual deadly stare. Instead, he went on searching the web intensely. After another minute, he stopped, "I think we've found our man."

Matthew got up from the couch and waked over to the workstation. The headline on the screen read, 'Peace

Advocate to Run for U.S. Senate'.

"I don't get it," he said. "What does that have to do with anything?"

Grace grabbed a Bible from the desk behind them. She flipped it open and scanned through the pages until she came to Daniel 8:25 and read out loud:

'And through his policy also he shall cause craft to prosper in his hand; and he shall magnify himself in his heart, and by peace shall destroy many.'

"If I understand correctly," Matthew said, "this is claiming that the Antichrist is going to be someone who stands for peace. Doesn't that contradict everything we've been told about his reign of evil?"

Father Andrew answered, "Many theologians believe that this does, indeed, refer to the Antichrist. The consensus is that he will rise to power on a platform of peace, and once he has achieved this position of power, he will use his influence to gain dominion over all. Think of him as a wolf in sheep's clothing."

"Okay, let's say that what you've said is true, how do we know this is the guy?"

To answer his question, the priest navigated to another page, this one showing a younger version of the same man. The article, though, was much more gruesome than the previous one. The heading read, 'Tragedy strikes prominent family during drive-by shooting'. It went on to tell how Caleb Albright's Father had been targeted because of his battle against local gangs. Several leaders were prosecuted and imprisoned. The gang's retaliation took the lives of Caleb's Mother, Janet, and his little sister, Giselle. His Father, Samuel, wasn't even in the car. The article stated that Caleb had been shot in the back of the head, but somehow survived, ending up in a coma. A few days later, he regained consciousness.

After a couple months of treatment, he had made a full recovery.

Even though he didn't quite understand everything, he got the main idea, "So you're thinking that Vizibir switched places with the real Caleb while he was injured?"

"That's my guess," the Priest replied. "I'd even guess that Lucifer orchestrated the event in order to manipulate the prophecies. It wouldn't be the first time he's done so. By forcing the Apocalypse on us, he plans to create a godless world."

"We have to make sure that doesn't happen."

"I agree."

While they were talking, Grace grabbed the mouse and continued browsing other articles. She was scrolling through an article concerning a new technology that Caleb Albright was developing that involved injecting nanotechnology into a person's skin that would store that individual's personal information. This even fit in with the prophecy of creating a universal worldwide buying system.

A picture came on the screen that caused Matthew to gasp. "Wait. Go back up," he urged Grace. She scrolled back until the picture filled the screen once more. There she was, standing right next to Caleb Albright.

"What's wrong?" Grace asked.

"Well, now I know for sure that we have the right man."

Father Andrew asked, "Why do you say that?"

Matthew pointed to the left side of the screen, "Because that woman standing next to him is Lilith, the Demon Queen from my dreams."

As Matthew stared at the picture, he was terrified when Caleb turned his head and smiled at him. "Did you see that?" he asked nervously.

Grace replied, "See what?"

When Matthew looked again the picture was normal. *Now I know I'm losing it,* he thought.

Suddenly the power went out, throwing them into darkness. A backup generator came on a few seconds later, bringing the lights back on, but only at half power. Strange shadows danced along the walls in an eerie display. A siren started wailing through a series of speakers in the ceiling. Then the room started trembling.

Matthew turned to Grace, "I have a bad feeling about this." A second later, his ring started to glow.

"Time to go!" Father Andrew said as he grabbed Matthew's arm in one hand and Grace's in the other. He rushed them toward the door at the back of the room.

The bathroom beyond was almost too small for the three of them to fit, but after they had all squeezed in, Father Andrew grabbed the towel bar on the wall opposite the door, and pulled down. The wall opened to reveal a tunnel that stretched forward about fifty feet before curving to the left out of sight. The tunnel was illuminated by a soft, natural phosphorus glow that gave them a sliver of visibility.

As they entered the tunnel, Father Andrew pressed a small button on the right wall. "Hopefully that'll buy us a little time."

"What did that do?" Matthew asked.

"It created an illusion that concealed the doors presence from those looking at it."

Grace rolled her eyes, "Christ, Pops! You could've just said that it makes the door invisible."

They heard a loud explosion coming from the outer room that sounded like the whole place had been blown apart. Without another word, the three of them bolted down the tunnel. They had no idea what they were running from, but certainly didn't want to find out.

They ran as fast as they could around the bend, and Matthew noticed that the slope of the tunnel seemed to be rising gradually. After a few minutes, they came to a four-way intersection.

"Okay, which way?" Matthew asked.

"We go right. The other passages are decoys; dead ends that are designed to confuse pursuers in the case of infiltration."

"But won't they see our footprints or something?"

Father Andrew pressed another hidden button on the wall. "As we pass, a small stream of dust will shoot out to cover our tracks. But we have to hurry because it only lasts for thirty seconds."

As they charged down the tunnel, Matthew glanced back to see the last bit of dust settling on the floor, making it look as if no one had traveled that way for ages.

"How much further?"

Father Andrew replied, "Not too far."

The tunnel took a turn back to the left, and after a few minutes they were at a dead end with a tall ladder leading upward.

"Ladies first," Matthew said.

Grace looked at him with a sneer, "Don't get any funny ideas." Then she turned and started up.

Matthew had thought she was cute before, but when he saw her swaying back and forth as she climbed, his hormones suddenly went into overdrive.

He followed her up, and about half-way up she glanced down at him, "Keep your focus, Big-boy! We're not out of the woods yet."

His face flushed as they resumed their ascent. He then looked down to make sure Father Andrew was following them, and was shocked to find him right below, moving like a man half his age.

After ten grueling minutes, Grace finally reached the top, only to find a blank ceiling. She looked down, "Okay, Pops, now what?"

He called up, "Side of the ladder, third rung from the top on the left. Flip the lever there."

She fumbled for a few seconds, "Got it."

A soft whoosh, and the ceiling slid back to reveal the open sky. The black clouds above them told them that a storm was coming. But they knew the tempest was already there.

They scampered out of the shaft, eager to be on top of the earth instead of under it. They were in an empty field across from the H.O.M.E. building, or at least what was left of it. It looked like it had been the target of an armored attack. Half of the building lay crumpled to the ground where a massive explosion had torn through the structure. Fire leaped from numerous windows where the glass had blown out.

They heard a chorus of guttural sounds coming from the tunnel below. Father Andrew rushed a few yards to the left and pushed aside a large rock. He pressed the button that was hidden underneath. The ground grumbled and the opening immediately closed again.

The shaking continued for a long minute, and then it abruptly stopped. "What just happened?" Matthew asked.

Father Andrew answered, "It was a self-destruct mechanism. Explosives scattered throughout the tunnels were set off to cause a cave-in, hopefully crushing whatever was after us."

They heard a soft groan nearby and were horrified to see Gloria lying in the grass. Dark blood flowed from a deep gash that stretched across her midsection.

"Glorianna!" Father Andrew cried out as he rushed to her. He dropped to his knees and cradled the fallen angel in his arms, "My God! What happened?"

She coughed and wheezed as she tried to talk, sending blood streaming down her chin, "Blood fiends—", "out of nowhere—", "a Dark Disciple…"

Another coughing fit overtook her, bringing more blood flying from her mouth.

She looked at Matthew once her breathing had calmed, "Give me your hand."

Matthew placed his hand in hers, and immediately felt an intense heat shoot up his arm and wind its way through his body. When it reached his brain, he was bombarded with a flurry of images and symbols, most of which he had never seen before. He looked at her in surprise.

She struggled to speak, "I gave you…a small piece of myself…to help you. Be brave."

Her body convulsed violently, sending an anguished cry from her lips. Then she went still and died. A loud crash of thunder suddenly tore through the sky as all of Heaven mourned her death.

CHAPTER 8

The time to mourn came to an abrupt end when a figure walked out of the building and looked around intensely, surveying the surrounding area. Father Andrew and Grace let out a simultaneous gasp when they saw him. Tall and thin, wearing a black robe with blacker sigils interwoven throughout, the figure had a determined and sinister look in his eyes.

As they crouched lower into the grass Matthew whispered, "Who is that? You act like you know him."

Father Andrew didn't answer

"It's Father Gideon," Grace said. "At one time, we thought he was our friend."

"That doesn't matter right now," Father Andrew said. "But we need to get out of here."

Matthew glanced toward their car, which was buried under a pile of rubble. "It doesn't look like we're leaving the same way we got here."

Father Andrew said, "If we can get to the back of the building there's an emergency vehicle parked there."

As if to emphasize just how quickly their time was running out, they heard a loud banging from beneath the escape hatch that drew the attention of Father Gideon.

A second later, a bolt of lightning scorched the ground a few feet from them. Matthew quickly jumped up, twisted his ring, and shot a fireball at the man. The blast hit Father Gideon squarely in the chest and dissipated, leaving him unscathed.

"Well, that didn't work out like I'd planned," Matthew muttered.

Father Gideon laughed as he ran toward them, his arms raised high with sparks of energy crackling in the air between them. "Like a fool, you rush headlong into battle with no idea of what you're playing with. I'm going to really enjoy annihilating you."

Panic flew into Matthew's brain for a second until a calmness settled into him, and he heard Glorianna utter a single word in his mind: *earthquake.* He understood immediately. He turned the ring again and pointed at the ground near Gideon's feet. The earth began to roll, and a large chasm opened up, swallowing the man.

A second later, the escape hatch flew into the air and out sprang a nightmare. Standing nearly nine feet tall, it had a thick, scaly hide that shimmered a deep black, making it appear more like a shadow that something solid. Its four arms ended in claws that had three long, boney fingers and an equally long thumb. Sharp nails dripped a black, oily poison.

It opened its mouth and emitted a high-pitched shrill. Immediately, Matthew felt his strength fading. He only had one shot at killing the blood fiend, and if he failed, they'd be ripped to shreds in seconds. He turned his ring and pointed at the beast. Instead of a ball of fire this time, a stream of flames shot out. Matthew concentrated with all of his remaining strength. The impact sent the creature crashing to the ground, where it flailed its arms and gnashed its teeth feverishly. Then it exploded, leaving a pile of smoking ash.

"Impressive," Gideon said as he finished pulling himself out of the chasm. "It seems you've learned a couple of tricks after all."

Father Andrew stepped forward, "Enough of this, Gideon. You can't possibly hope to win this war. Good will always triumph over evil."

Gideon laughed, "You always were naïve, Father. Not only will we win, but we will flourish. Lucifer's reign will be magnificent, and you'll have been the one to bring it to pass."

A look of shock crossed Father Andrew's face.

"Think about it," Gideon said. "Remember, I sent you to find him and bring him to me. Now that you've fulfilled your duty, you can die knowing that you have played a significant part in Lucifer's plan. Nothing will stand in Vizibir's way as he brings about the end of days."

The thought that he had been used as a pawn made Father Andrew angry. He whispered to Grace and Matthew, "When I give the word, I want both of you to run for the car while I take on Gideon."

Grace started to plead, "But Dad—"

"No arguing. Just go when I say!"

Although she clearly didn't like the plan, she silenced any further objection. For the first time, Matthew saw the true depths of her love for her father. For a moment, he envied their relationship.

Father Andrew walked forward a few steps to put himself between them and Gideon. As he did so, he pulled a crucifix from his pocket and mumbled a prayer to himself.

"Your prayers won't save you, Father. In the end, they're as pathetic as the God you serve."

Father Andrew replied, "I think you underestimate the

power of faith."

"Keep telling yourself whatever you need to, in order to help you sleep at night. The scriptures are stories and lies, made up to spread propaganda upon an unsuspecting world. In the end, your so-called faith will prove as weak as your futile attempt here."

Matthew heard a soft click come from the Priest's direction and saw a small blade spring from the bottom of the crucifix. A quick glance back from Father Andrew told them that they needed to be ready.

Gideon continued forward until he was a few feet away.

"Let them go," Father Andrew said, "and I'll do whatever you want."

"Now, why would I do that? We both know the boy has to die. It's his destiny. And if I just happen to kill you and your daughter in the process, all the better."

"Your arrogance will prove to be your downfall, Gideon," Father Andrew said. He brought his hands together in prayer, then he lunged forward, catching Gideon unaware. The blade caught him in the throat, slicing a three-inch gash. But, even with blood gushing down his chest, Gideon grabbed Father Andrew by the arm, twisting him to the ground.

As he hit the pavement, Father Andrew yelled, "Run!"

When Grace hesitated to move, Matthew understood all too well. The memory of his mother's own sacrifice instantly sprang into his mind.

Even from his prone position Gideon raised his hands, electricity springing from his fingertips once more, as he readied for another attack. Matthew fumbled with his ring, knowing that it would be too late.

Suddenly Gideon was flailing on the ground with streaks of lightning flying everywhere from his hands. Father

Andrew had staggered to his knees and lurched onto Gideon.

Somehow, Gideon twisted his body around, sending electricity surging through Father Andrew. Matthew and Grace watched in horror as thousands of volts of electricity convulsed violently through the Priest, wracking his body in pain.

Matthew had no choice but to grab Grace and pull her toward the corner of the building. She cried out as he yanked her away, "Pops, no!"

When they rounded the corner to the back of the fallen building, a plain white cargo van was waiting for them. Instead of heading for the passenger's seat, Grace wiped the tears from her eyes and steeled her resolve before jumping in the driver's seat. As she stepped on the gas and peeled away, another explosion rocketed through the structure. Matthew turned to look back through the rear window and saw the final pieces of the building leveled to the ground.

CHAPTER 9

They drove for miles in silence. Matthew could feel the torment winding through Grace as she struggled with the thought that her father had just sacrificed his life to her. He knew the feeling all too well. He needed to say something to her, he just didn't know what. When he opened his mouth to talk, she immediately cut him off.

"Don't," she warned. "Don't say it. I don't want you to say a word. There's still hope he's alive. If we talk about it, that takes away that hope."

He turned his attention back to the road, determined to sit there in silence until they reached their destination, wherever that was. A few minutes later, Grace broke the silence and said matter-of-factly, "You better turn your ring back on."

He had completely forgotten the ring. Quickly, he pressed the button, hoping that he had done it soon enough to prevent anything from following them.

"In case you're wondering," Grace said, "we're heading to a safe house about twenty miles from here. It's where my dad —"

She started to break down, but quickly recovered, "It's where we're supposed to go if there's ever any trouble."

Twenty miles certainly didn't seem far enough away to keep them safe from the horror they'd just seen. "Are you sure it's safe there?" Matthew asked.

She looked at Matthew, and he knew she couldn't hold it together much longer. "I hope so. I don't really have anywhere else to go."

Tears started pouring down her face. She tried using the sleeve of her jacket to wipe them away but it was no use.

"Why don't you let me drive for a bit?" Matthew offered.

She nodded and pulled over to the curb. The horizon was just about to swallow up the last bits of the sun, and cast a purple glow throughout the sky. As the shadows outside grew deeper, Matthew's paranoia went into overdrive, causing him to glance about nervously while he walked around the front of the van. Grace passed him without even glancing up, but when she reached her door, she stopped for a second, then rushed back and grabbed him tight.

"Thank you," she said as she buried her head in his chest.

The screech of an owl jumped them back to reality and they pulled away from each other. Matthew cast a glimpse toward Grace as he jumped into the driver's seat, hoping she was going to be alright, but knowing the answer was probably aa resounding 'no', Thirty minutes later they were parked in front of a small, white house nestled in a cul-de-sac on a quiet suburban street.

"Now what?" he asked as they walked up the steps to the front door.

"Beats me? I was only told where to go. I've never actually been here before. I guess we ring the doorbell?"

She pressed the button and waited. A minute later, they heard a shuffling sound inside the house. A gruff voice from the other side of the door said, "For God so loved the world..."

Grace answered, "That, on the seventh day he rested."

"A secret catch-phrase?" Matthew asked. "Are you kidding me?"

"Hey, it's what I was told to say."

The voice said, "hold on to your hats."

Grace and Matthew looked at each other in confusion. Then the floor beneath them suddenly dropped open, and they were plunged down a dark and twisting tunnel that felt like they should have been at Disneyland instead of a secret hideout. After a stomach-wrenching drop, they hit open air, just before landing on a soft pile of down and feathers. Both of them sat up quickly, spitting feathers from their mouths and shaking them from their hair.

They both looked around in panic to discover they were in some kind of underground bunker. The walls were solid concrete, florescent lights lined the ceiling, and a row of shelves stood against one wall filled with canned goods and supplies. An arrangement of cots filled one corner of the room. The craziest thing in the room, though, was the sight of Solomon wearing a purple and yellow tie-dye t-shirt playing solitaire at a table in the center.

He jumped from his chair, "Matthew, Grace! I'm so glad you're here. Where's Andrew?"

Tears started to well up in Grace's eyes, so Matthew quickly interjected, "There was an attack right after you left. The H.O.M.E. building was destroyed. We barely escaped with our lives."

"That explains why I was summoned here. Who attacked you?"

"It was Gideon," Grace said bitterly. "He betrayed us. He betrayed us all."

Solomon was silent for a minute, then spoke, "I always had my doubts about him, but I still gave him a chance. This is my fault. In my zest to believe in his goodness, I was blind to his deceit."

"It's not your fault, Sam," Grace said. "We were all fooled."

"But I shouldn't have been. I above anyone else should've seen him for what he really was."

Grace went over and hugged him tight. After a minute, he pulled away, "What happened?"

She took a deep breath, "After the alarm sounded, we barely made it through the tunnels and out of the escape hatch before Pops set off the self-destruct. Then we found Glorianna lying in the field injured. She died a few minutes later."

"Glorianna is dead?"

She nodded sadly. Then it was Solomon's turn to cry.

Grace continued, "Gideon came out of the building at the same time that a blood fiend erupted from the hatch beside us. While Matthew was destroying the demon, Gideon attacked us. Pops sacrificed himself so we could escape."

"I'm so sorry," Solomon said.

Everyone was silent, as Grace and Solomon held each other tightly. Then a red warning light started flashing in the ceiling.

"Now what?" Matthew said, his voice tinged in fear.

"It means we have company," Solomon replied guardedly.

Seconds later, a figure emerged from the chute and landed with a thud on the pile of feathers. A soft groan ushered from the person on the floor.

Grace walked over to the figure laying in a heap and dropped to her knees in tear-filled surprise. "Dad, you're alive!"

CHAPTER 10

Father Andrew was alive, but just barely. The whole left side of his face was burned and bleeding, and a large patch of flesh on his jaw dangled down, held on only by a few strands of tissue to expose the bone beneath. His left eye was swollen shut, and his hair was singed down to his scalp. His hands looked worse. Somehow, he had managed to wrap them in rags that were completely soaked with blood and looked like two bloody stumps at the end of his arms.

Blood flew from his mouth as he tried to speak. Instead, he ended up in a coughing fit. Solomon cradled the priest's neck. "Don't try to talk," he said.

Together, the three of them lifted him up and carried him to the other side of the room. Even though Death hadn't claimed him yet, everyone knew that the Reaper waited a breath away, ready to snatch his soul in an instant.

Solomon said, "Grace, can you bring that box to me?" He indicated a plain brown wooden crate sitting on one of the shelves. "Matthew, under the sink there are some towels. And I need some hot water."

As they both rushed frantically to retrieve the objects, Father Andrew opened his one good eye and said to Solomon sadly, "Glorianna."

Solomon replied softly, "I know."

A seizure wracked violently through the priest's body. "Stand back. I need some room!" Solomon said.

Grace and Matthew shrank back, watching as Solomon worked to save him, using a combination of ointments and salves while performing a series of complicated hand gestures and chanting in a barely audible tone. A soft, white light began to cover Father Andrew's head and then extended downward until it enveloped the rest of his body, blanketing him completely. Then Father Andrew smiled thinly and slept.

"How is he?" Grace asked.

"He's resting now. I think the worst is over. His wounds are pretty bad and will take time to heal, and I think he may have lost his vision in his left eye. But he'll live."

Grace was silent for a minute as she tried to hold herself together. Then she said with trembling lips, "Thank you, Sam, for everything."

"Come here," he said. She slid over to him and they hugged tightly. After a minute, he said, "Now we need to figure out our next move, and quickly."

Solomon looked at Matthew, "What did Glorianna give you?"

Matthew was shocked. "How did you know?"

He chuckled, "It's not magic, if that's what you're thinking? I simply saw the mark on your hand."

My hand? Matthew thought.

He glanced down to see what Solomon was talking about. What he had passed off initially as a scratch, upon closer inspection was actually some sort of symbol—a lot like a capital B, with the rounded sections changed to sideways triangles.

"That's the rune Berkano, the symbol for wisdom and secret knowledge. I suspect that Glorianna passed on some sort of special knowledge to you?"

"I'm not really sure what it is? At first, I just saw a bunch of images flying around in my head. Then, when the demon attacked, the answers just came to me. I knew all of its strengths and weaknesses. I knew exactly what I had to do to kill it."

Solomon thought about it for a minute. "She gave you the knowledge of all creatures known to man, as well as those yet unknown."

It made sense. It was weird, but it made sense. "Now what?"

Grace said, "I think we need to go see my mom. She may be able to help."

"Do you think that's wise?" Solomon asked.

"I don't see any other choice."

"She's not going to be thrilled to see you."

"Oh well. She'll get over it. Are you going to stay here with my dad?"

"As long as needed."

"Then I know he'll be okay."

"Right now," Solomon said, "you two need to get some rest. You've both been through a lot."

He was right. As soon as he said that Matthew's eyes suddenly felt heavy, and exhaustion threatened to overtake him.

They settled into a couple of the cots at one corner of the room. A few feet away, Father Andrew slept and healed. Grace was lying on her side watching him. While she prayed for his quick healing, Matthew fell asleep in seconds.

***

* * *

When Matthew woke up, Solomon was gone. Father Andrew lay still in his cot, breathing slowly. He was surprised that Solomon had left him alone, even for only a short time.

He was shocked even further when he saw his mom and dad sitting at the small table, with Grace beside them.

"Matthew, you're awake," Mary said. "How are you feeling?"

Matthew replied, "Okay, I guess."

"Why don't you come and join us?"

He shuffled more than walked over to the table, still groggy and heavy-headed. When he sat down on one of the empty chairs, Michael asked, "Can I get you anything?"

"No, I'm fine."

"Good," Grace said. "We have a lot to talk about. In fact, I have some great news. Michael and Mary just told me that the threat is over. Isn't that fantastic?"

Matthew was shocked. "What do you mean? How can the threat be over? We haven't even found Caleb yet."

"We were wrong. It was Gideon all along. He was the demon we were after, not Caleb. Now that my dad has killed him, the threat is over."

Something didn't make sense. "But we figured out that Vizibir was Caleb, or was with Caleb. It doesn't make sense that it's Gideon. He doesn't have anything to do with the prophecies."

Michael looked at Grace, "See, I told you that angle wouldn't work. I knew he wouldn't believe you."

"He always made things harder than they should be," Mary said. "Nothing was ever easy with him."

Matthew couldn't believe his ears. His lips started quivering as they verbally attacked him.

"It's true," she continued. "Look at all the crap you put me through. You lied to me. You stole from me. You hurt me. And you continuously disappointed me."

The words stung Matthew. But it was true. All of it. However, something didn't seem right. He recalled how his mom and dad had been when they visited him in Solomon's lair. These weren't the same people."

Grace turned to Michael, "Why, I think he's starting to figure it out, Father."

Matthew did a double-take to make sure he heard her right, "Why did you call him 'Father'?"

Grace suddenly morphed into Elizabeth, the girl from his dreams. She smiled at him and winked before changing once more, this time into Jeremy, also from his dreams. Terror stormed through his brain as he stared at the demon, Vizibir. And next to him sat Lucifer and his demon queen, Lilith—the demon's mother and father.

"As you can see," Lucifer said, "there's no hope for you to win. Your pathetic attempts will only end with disastrous results. So, I'll give you something you really don't deserve: a choice. You can end your foolish pursuit of this worthless cause, or you can die a horrible death. The choice is yours."

The room suddenly burst into flames and the three of them disappeared. A deep, rolling laughter echoed throughout as Matthew searched desperately for an escape. The only way out that he knew of was the same way in, only he couldn't see anything. The flames grew angrier, and the smoke grew thicker with each passing second. In a few minutes, he wouldn't be able to breathe. Then he remembered that Father Andrew was still in the room with him!

Suddenly, he heard a voice above the crackle of the flames, urgently calling his name. This only elevated his fear, as he realized that someone else was in the room!

The voice grew louder and his body started shaking

violently. Then his consciousness shifted, and he shot up from his nightmare. Solomon was there shaking him, while Grace kneeled beside him, holding his hand.

"It's okay, Matthew," Solomon said. "You're safe now. It was just a dream."

Matthew sat there on the cot, shaking terribly. Sure, it had all felt so real, the way dreams tend to do. But what bothered him the most was the way Lucifer had used those closest to him to attack him emotionally. He also knew that he was running out of time.

He looked up at Solomon weakly. "No, it wasn't."

CHAPTER 11

Matthew couldn't sleep the rest of the night. His nightmare had left him shaken. With a sigh, he got up and brewed a fresh pot of coffee. Solomon joined him at the table a few minutes later.

"Couldn't sleep?" Solomon asked.

Matthew shook his head, hoping to avoid any lengthy conversation.

Instead of asking him a million questions he really didn't want to answer, Solomon simply studied him for a moment, then reached into the cupboard for a couple of coffee cups. The smell of coffee roused Grace, and a minute later she was standing next to them stretching herself awake.

Solomon spoke first, "Don't beat yourself up so much, Matthew. Whatever you're going through, remember we're here to help."

"I know. Thanks. I'm just feeling a little down right now. No biggie."

"Do you want to talk about it?" Grace asked.

He didn't, really. The more he dwelled on things, the more depressed he felt. But he found out in that moment that he had a weakness. And that weakness was Grace. He just couldn't say 'no' to her.

"I guess what's bothering me the most," he finally said, "is that Lucifer used my mom and dad to attack me. He destroyed the last images I had of them. Grace, you were there too, and I felt completely safe. Then suddenly you changed into Vizibir, my dad was Lucifer, and my mom was Lilith."

Everybody was silent for a moment before Solomon spoke once more, "He's scared."

Matthew was shocked. How could the Prince of Darkness be scared? If anything, it was the exact opposite!

"It makes sense," the ancient hippie continued. "Think about it. Why else would he attack you like this? He's trying to shake you up."

"Well, it's working."

"Look at it this way...if he believed that you had no chance to succeed, he wouldn't waste his time on you. He'd let you go until you finally gave up or were dead. But he remembers what your father did—how he defeated Belial—and is afraid that you have the power to do the same."

"But I'm not my father."

"Nobody said you were. You're the one putting that pressure on yourself. Just be yourself, trust yourself, and everything will work out fine. Faith is the key."

"I'll try," he said with little conviction.

"That's the spirit. Remember that every attempt Lucifer makes to stop you means that he's growing weaker and his plan is falling apart. Let that knowledge strengthen your resolve, and your faith."

It made sense. All of it. It was just a huge pill to swallow. As he thought about it for a minute, he heard his mom's voice in his head, reminding him, *'You always have a choice, Matthew. You can decide how you let things affect you. Will it be happiness or sadness; love or hate; courage or fear.'* As he pictured her in his mind, he vowed that he would make Lucifer wish he'd never started this war.

"Okay. What's next?" Matthew asked. "You said something last night about your mom."

A gurgled cough sounded from across the room and they all turned in unison. "Do you think that's wise?" Father Andrew croaked.

Immediately Grace shot over to him, throwing herself onto him. He winced noticeably as she touched him, but still managed to return the embrace. "Daddy!" she cried. "I was so worried. I thought I'd lost you."

He coughed a couple of times, then said, "Me too. I wasn't sure you guys made it."

"But how did you survive?" Matthew asked.

"To be honest, I don't really remember. After a few minutes, I blacked out. When I woke up, I was lying on the front porch here. I'm sure a little bit of Divine Intervention is involved, though." He looked at Grace, "Now about your mother?"

"Look, Pops, we don't have any other choice. I know she can help. Besides, I'm not sure there's anyone else we can trust."

"She won't be happy to see you."

"Oh, well."

***

An hour later, they were ready to go. Grace said goodbye to her dad, while Matthew sat talking to Solomon, "So, once we locate Vizibir, what's our next step?"

"I wish I knew. There are only two known weapons that can kill the Demon Son. One was the medallion that Lilith destroyed. The other is a dagger that was lost during Vizibir's first attack. Without the dagger, you'll have to hit him with everything you have and hope something works. Remember to trust the knowledge Glorianna passed on to you. It will be a key to your victory."

"You mean 'our' victory? I couldn't do any of this by myself."

Solomon smiled, "I stand corrected—our victory."

Grace came over, "Okay, I'm ready."

Solomon nodded, then reached under the table and pressed a button. One of the shelving units slid aside to reveal an elevator. As they stepped inside the metal chamber, Matthew couldn't help but think that somehow, they were trapped inside a Tom Clancy spy novel—with all the secret passageways and hidden rooms—instead of fighting for the salvation of the world.

"Be safe, and may God be with you," Solomon said as the door closed and they began a slow ascent. The elevator stopped about thirty seconds later. When the door slid open, they were surprised to see that they were inside a dimly lit garage. The only other occupant was a silver metallic beast that smiled at them expectantly.

Matthew rushed over to the driver's side and climbed inside the Mustang convertible before Grace could object. It felt like magic as he turned the key in the ignition and felt the machine come to life. Grace looked at him jealously for a second before climbing in the other side.

He backed out of the garage and was shocked to find that they were coming out of the property directly across from the safe house.

The sun rained down on them from a cloudless morning sky as they drove away. Grace pulled her phone out and tapped in a couple of commands. She studied the screen for a couple of minutes.

"Any idea where we're going?" Matthew asked.

"Yeah," was all she replied. Then she touched the screen for the GPS located in the center console. A few seconds later, he saw their destination: Madison Square Garden.

He gave her a questioning look, but got no more from her. He flipped on the radio and immediately AC/DC started belting out 'Highway to Hell'. *How fitting!* He thought.

CHAPTER 12

If the nasally voice of the GPS lady told them to stay in the left lane one more time, Matthew was going to rip the console right out of the dash.

Finally, they reached their destination, or at least as close as they were going to get. They ended up at a parking garage on the corner of 8th and 30th street—about a five-minute walk from The Garden.

After taking the elevator from their fourth-floor parking spot to the main level, they hunkered down into their jackets as they started walking down the block toward MSG.

As they walked through the crowds, Matthew considered asking Grace about her mother, then decided against it. She'd been through enough recently and he didn't want to push her. He figured she'd tell him when she was ready.

When they reached the corner of the block and he saw the massive sprawl of architecture that is Madison Square Garden, Matthew stood there speechless. It looked more like a fortress than an entertainment venue, and he was sure that it could house a small city if needed.

His confusion mounted when he saw a hundred-foot marquee on the front of the building with the famous slogan,

'The Greatest Show On Earth!' Below it was an image depicting the Ringling Brothers, Barnum and Bailey Circus.

"When you said the circus," Matthew exclaimed, "I thought you meant a small, County Fair, Shriner's type of circus. I never imagined something like this."

"Don't get too excited," Grace answered. "I don't plan on staying long."

"Okay, so what's the deal with your mom?"

"You mean, besides the fact that I stole her car, got her arrested, and basically ruined her life?"

Her statement hit far too close to home and Matthew immediately regretted saying anything. "I'm sorry I brought it up."

She sighed, "Don't worry about it. After all, everyone makes mistakes, right?"

When her eyes misted up, he knew exactly how she was feeling. Before he got the chance to say anything, though, she had gathered her emotions together and was charging across the street with a purpose.

When they reached the opposite corner, Matthew automatically started walking toward the main entrance, unaware that Grace was walking the opposite way. He quickly spun around and ran to catch up to her just as she entered a place called 'Jimmy's Burger Shack'.

He had no idea what they were doing in a place that served drinks in fishbowls with rubber alligators in them, but he learned early on that it was usually best to just let Grace do her thing. It also meant that he had learned to trust her.

She went directly to the bar, which was being run by a young guy with long brown hair and a contagious smile. "Hey, Garrett," she said.

"Grace! It's been a long time. How's it going?"

"It's going okay," she obviously lied.

"What can I get you?"

"How about a walk in the park?"

The surfer bartender eyed Matthew warily.

"It's okay," Grace said. "He's cool."

The whole exchange flew completely over Matthew's head. "Is that a new drink or something? I thought we were in a hurry?"

She just rolled her eyes while Garrett gave her a little grin. Then he nodded toward the back of the room where an older black man was sitting at a booth. Grace grabbed Matthew's hand and pulled him back toward the man.

When they got close, the man stood up and directed them through a door in the back of a small hallway marked 'Employees Only'. This brought them to the kitchen area, where they crossed to a back office amidst the curious stares of the kitchen staff present.

The office was barely more than a walk-in closet, with most of the space taken up by a gray metal desk along the left wall. Another door faced the entrance, and the black man, who hadn't said a word the whole time, walked over and fished a ring of keys from his pocket. After opening a series of three different dead-bolts, he opened the door.

"Thanks, Frankie," grace said. The guy just smiled and walked away.

"What a strange guy," Matthew said, stating the obvious.

"He's actually really sweet. Doesn't talk much, though."

"No kidding."

The opening loomed before Grace like a dark abyss threatening to devour her. She sighed as she shuffled through the door. "Might as well get this over with," she mumbled.

"Hey, it might not turn out too bad," Matthew suggested.

She turned on him with a steely, cold stare and he let it drop. After a second, she turned back and trudged down what seemed to be a service hallway with several doors lining each side. A small elevator at the end took them down a couple of stories, where they emerged into another hallway that sloped slightly downward.

The terrible stench hit them right before they heard the loud trumpet of an elephant resounding through the building.

They exited the hall into the main arena and heard a man exclaim, "My god, Edna, what have you been eating?"

The elephant snorted triumphantly and continued forward, being led by her trainer, a middle-aged woman with dark hair, wearing a red jacket. The man with the task of cleaning up after the animal was a gray-haired skinny man in his sixties. His jaws were lined with stubble, and a pair of small glasses sat atop his nose.

"Grace!" he shouted when he saw them. In his excitement, he nearly stepped into the steaming pile that Edna had just deposited.

"It's good to see you, Charlie," she said as they hugged.

Charlie gave Matthew a quick look, "Who've we got here?"

"This is my friend, Matthew," Grace said. Then, after a pause, "Is my mom around?"

Charlie gestured toward a small tent near the rear of the circus. As they walked through the arena, they passed several performers practicing, from clowns and jugglers, to acrobats and men on stilts. Each of them waved at Grace like she was a member of the family returning after a long hiatus.

Grace returned their greetings, forcing herself to smile even though it was the last place on earth she wanted to be.

A minute later they were standing outside a tent with a sign on it that read, 'Zelda the All-Knowing'. Matthew gave Grace a questioning look.

"Don't look at me like that," she exclaimed. "Her real

name is Priscilla. Zelda's just her stage name."

"And I suppose she's some kind of fortune teller?"

"Actually, she prefers the term 'medium'. And she's totally legit. In fact, that's the reason I kept getting in so much trouble. I could never hide anything from her, no matter how hard I tried. And believe me, I tried."

Matthew didn't know what to expect when they entered the tent, but it certainly wasn't the woman sitting at the table, looking into a small mirror while putting makeup on. Her wavy, black hair hung down the middle of her back. Large golden hoops dangled from her earlobes, and a myriad of bracelets wrapped around her arms. The low-cut ivory blouse completed the gypsy image.

"I knew you'd show up eventually," Priscilla said without even looking up. "What took you so long?"

"We ran into some trouble," Grace said. "Dad got hurt."

Priscilla stopped her grooming and looked up at Grace, concern now covering her face. "What happened?"

"I'll tell you later. He's okay, though. Sam's taking care of him."

"And you want me to help you figure out what to do next?"

Instead of answering, Grace just stared at her mother, unwilling to verbalize her need for help. After a few seconds, her mother turned to Matthew, "So, you're the one?"

Matthew grinned. Like Mother, like Daughter, apparently.

"Mom, this is Matthew," Grace said. "Matthew, this is my mother, Priscilla."

Priscilla gestured to the chair opposite her, "Well, don't just stand there. Have a seat."

Matthew glanced at Grace questioningly, who responded with a nod. He sat down nervously, unsure of what to expect.

Priscilla said, "Give me your hands and close your eyes."

He reached his hands toward the center of the table and closed his eyes as instructed. A second later, he felt Priscilla's hands on his. Immediately, a blinding light shot through his head right before everything went completely black.

262

CHAPTER 13

The pain was nearly unbearable, yet somehow Matthew pushed through until he was able to open his eyes. His head hung low so that his chin rested against his chest.

Slowly, he managed to look up and see through eyes tinged red with blood that he was in the sanctuary of his church looking down at the pulpit where Pastor Brown usually stood. He tried to move and realized that he wasn't actually standing there. He looked to his left, and then to his right, and was horrified to find that his hands and feet were nailed to the cross that hung high on the sanctuary wall. Blood streamed down his head where the thorns had pierced his scalp. Panic quickly set in as he struggled to get free. But with every move, the pain grew more intense.

Then a voice sounded nearby, "Matthew! I'm so glad you could join us."

Matthew looked and saw Lucifer sitting in the front pew with his arms stretched out along the top. Vizibir sat next to him posing as Caleb with a wicked smile on his face, while Lilith sat on the other side.

Lucifer leaned forward, "I imagine you're wondering what's going on here?"

Without giving Matthew a chance to reply, Lucifer shot forward, "I thought I'd give you a firsthand experience of what happens to anyone who defies me. It seemed fitting to remind you of another one who thought he could oppose me."

Desperation set in as Matthew tried to fight through the pain and free himself from his torture. Then he heard voice calling him; urging him to still his mind and quiet the panic inside. Then a thought occurred to him, "You should probably look back at history, you piece of shit! I seem to remember that after you tortured and killed him, Christ came back stronger than before."

Lucifer's eyes filled with rage, "I think it's time you learned your true place in the grand scheme of things."

A large spear appeared in his hands, and in a flash, he plunged the tip deep into Matthew's side. A loud scream issued from Matthew's lips as the blood flowed from the wound like a waterfall onto the floor beneath.

"Since you think you're so special, let's see if you can duplicate the feat of your cursed savior?"

Then, just as everything was about to go black, he heard the voice once more calling him. Then there was nothing.

***

As the voice slowly broke through the silence, Matthew realized it was Grace calling out his name. Her voice was desperate and scared. He tried to open his eyes, and for a second, everything was tinged with red, bringing the nightmare back in full force.

When his vision cleared, he looked across the table and saw Priscilla staring at him in shock. She didn't move for a second and Matthew feared the worst. Then her lips quivered as she slowly spoke, "I saw it. I saw everything." Her eyes grew wide, "He crucified you! He actually put you on a cross and crucified you!"

Matthew knew that she was on the verge of losing it, and grabbed her hands. Fearfully, she pulled back.

"It's okay, Priscilla," Matthew said.

Priscilla closed her eyes for a second and took a deep breath to calm herself. When she opened them, she caught Matthew wincing in obvious pain. She turned to Grace and gestured toward a shelf to the left of the entrance. "Grace, dear, can you bring me that blue bottle on the shelf?"

Grace grabbed the bottle as directed and brought it to the table. Priscilla opened the bottle and poured a couple drops of the liquid into a small cup. Then she added what looked like tea leaves to the concoction and it started to bubble. After a few seconds, the bubbling stopped, and she handed the cup to Matthew.

"Drink this," she said. "It'll help with the pain."

Matthew sipped the drink slowly while memories of him holding his nose as a kid trying to force down nasty cough syrup came rushing in. He was pleasantly surprised by the sweet, fruity taste of the elixir, though, and quickly gulped the rest down. Almost immediately, his brain started to tingle. Then the tingling spread to his whole body, like he was getting a full body massage from the inside. Within a few seconds, he was feeling better.

"Wow!" he exclaimed. "What's in that?"

"You really don't want to know," she replied as she reached down beside her and brought up a long, narrow box made of weathered oak. The only thing of note on the box was the brass lock that bore the same symbol as Matthew's ring. She took a pin from her hair and inserted it into the lock. The lid sprang open to reveal a bundle of white cloth.

"Where did you get that?" Grace asked.

Priscilla replied with a sly smile, "I took it when your father came back from that terrible fire. Something told me I would need it someday."

"But...we thought it was lost."

"It was...in a way. I was afraid that if anyone knew we had it, certain elements would come visiting, so I hid it."

Matthew was totally lost. Then Priscilla took the bundle out of the box and unwrapped it. Inside was a long dagger with a charred handle and a tarnished blade.

Priscilla said, "This is the only known weapon left that can destroy the Demon Son. But I suspect that you'll only get one shot at it. It will need to be a perfect strike right through the heart."

A million questions ran through Matthew's mind. Where had the knife come from? Why was it blackened and burned? Is a demon's heart in the same place as a human's?

They suddenly ran out of time when his ring started glowing. Then they heard Edna trumpeting loudly again, and this time she sounded mad.

Priscilla wrapped the knife back up and handed it to Matthew. "You need to go. Now!"

She looked at Grace softly.

"Mom?" Grace questioned.

Priscilla smiled at her, "Don't worry about me. I'll be fine. Besides, it looks like it's time for us to have a long talk when this is all over."

She jumped up and quickly ushered them toward the back of the tent. As they went through the rear opening, Matthew glanced back and saw her grabbing a few things off of the shelves before rushing out the front opening.

For the second time in twenty-four hours, Grace watched as one of her parents rushed headlong into the face of evil in order to save her.

CHAPTER 14

Cries of terror erupted throughout the arena as Matthew and Grace ran for the exit. The floor started shaking as crazed Edna went into a full-on rage.

When they rounded the side of one of the tents, they found themselves near one of the trapeze towers. The massive beast stopped when she saw them. Her eyes glowed an unnatural red, then she lowered her head and charged.

Twelve thousand pounds of raging elephant flesh quickly closed in on them, forcing them to dodge out of the way at the last moment so that the trapeze tower took the brunt of the attack. Although the tower creaked and groaned, threatening to come crashing down, it luckily held together, preventing any sort of catastrophe. Edna's momentary disorientation from the blow gave Matthew and Grace just enough time to run out of the arena.

They raced out onto 8th Ave., expecting Edna to give chase. Whatever demon had influenced her must have disappeared, because there wasn't any pursuit. They breathed a sigh of relief as they made their way back toward the parking garage.

Paranoia surfaced at every corner, doorway, and shadow

that they crossed. Luckily, they made it back to the car without further incident. This time Grace jumped into the driver's seat, and Matthew didn't have the strength to argue.

"Now what?" he asked.

Grace just shrugged as she leaned against the steering wheel for a minute. "I guess we need to find out where Caleb is, so we can finish this?"

"Right now, I'd feel better just getting as far away from here as we can."

Grace turned the ignition and was just about to put the car into reverse when there was a loud knocking on her window. They were both shocked to see Priscilla standing there, gasping for breath.

Grace opened her door quickly and jumped out, "Mom! What are you doing here?"

"I couldn't exactly let you run headlong into the belly of the beast all by yourself now, could I? Right after Edna nearly knocked herself out, I was able to dart out of the building and follow you. I don't think I've run that hard for years."

"You sure you want to do this, Mom?"

"I figure you can use all the help you can get right now."

"That's for sure."

Matthew got out and climbed into the back seat so she could sit next to Grace. Once he was settled in, Priscilla sat down and closed the door. His breath caught in his throat for a second when his ring glowed bright red, but then it died out, and he let out a sigh, hoping the nearby threat had passed.

"Do you know where you're going?" she asked.

Grace replied, "Right now, I just want to get out of here before something else crazy happens."

They exited the parking garage and entered the early afternoon traffic. Grace zigged and zagged like she had driven those streets forever. While they were driving Priscilla seemed intent on studying Grace carefully.

They drove for a few miles when Priscilla suddenly exclaimed that she was hungry. Grace glanced in the rear-view and gave Matthew a stern look that squelched the objection he was just about to voice.

"There's a McDonald's up on Canal Street. Does that sound okay?" Grace said.

Priscilla replied, "That sounds fine, Dear."

Grace turned right onto 7th Avenue. After continuing onto Varick Street, she turned left onto Canal Street, and two minutes later they pulled into the McDonald's parking lot.

As soon as they stepped into the lobby Matthew's mouth began to water. In all the excitement, he hadn't realized how hungry he was. They approached the counter and a tall, lanky red-headed boy with freckles named Spencer greeted them with a bored 'I really don't want to be here' look. Instead of asking for their order, he just stood there, waiting. Grace rolled her eyes at the boy and looked at Matthew to go first.

"Big Mac, fries, and a chocolate shake," Matthew said.

Grace turned to Priscilla, "You want your usual Filet-O-Fish?"

"That sounds good," Priscilla said.

Matthew caught a hint of disappointment on Grace's face as she turned back to the freckled cashier, "Two Filet-O-Fish, two small fries, and two large drinks."

Grace handed the boy some cash and then went over to the side of the counter while they waited for their food.

"I'm just gonna check on my dad," she said as she pulled her phone from her pocket.

Spencer's demeanor remained unchanged as he slapped the tray onto the counter with their order a few minutes later.

Now it was Matthew's turn to roll his eyes at the boy who was obviously a model employee.

Matthew grabbed the tray and headed for the nearest booth. Grace joined them a second later. Then they both watched in awe as Priscilla ripped open the box containing her sandwich and practically devoured it in one bite.

Priscilla looked up at them with a smear of tartar sauce on the corner of her mouth. "What? I was hungry."

Grace said, "Mom...you kind of have something on your face..."

Priscilla grabbed a napkin and wiped her face, but failed to remove all the sauce. "Better?" she asked.

Grace shook her head.

"I'll be right back, then," Priscilla said. She then got up and headed back toward the restrooms.

As soon as she was gone, Grace grabbed Matthew's hand, "Matthew, that's not my mom!"

He was shocked, "What do you mean?"

"For one thing, when we were back at MSG, I noticed that her fingernails were painted black. Now they're red. But I wasn't totally convinced until she started eating."

"Why is that?"

"She hates fish."

Matthew was just about to ask more questions, but then Priscilla showed up.

"What are you two talking about?" Priscilla asked.

"Grace was just telling me how her dad was doing," Matthew replied.

"And how is dear old dad doing?"

Grace answered, "He's doing okay."

"And where are they treating him? Once this is all done, I'd like to pay him a visit."

"He's at Mercy Hospital right now. But they said he might

be able to leave in a couple of days."

"Well, hopefully this will be all over by then."

Grace snatched their trays up and emptied them into the trash, signaling that they were done even though Matthew had barely touched his food. "Time to go," she said. We need to get moving before traffic gets heavy."

Minutes later, they were loaded back into the car. Grace started the engine, but before they left, she pressed the button to put the convertible top down. Matthew didn't know what she was up to, but Priscilla, or whoever/whatever she was, didn't seem to mind.

Matthew shivered as they drove with the top down, but he trusted that Grace knew what she was doing. They turned right onto Lafayette Street and continued onto Centre Street until they merged onto the Brooklyn Bridge. Traffic slowed for a moment and he could sense that the lack of movement was making Grace nervous. He caught a slight movement from her as she tapped her right ring finger on the steering wheel, signaling him to be ready.

Then the Priscilla-thing said, "So, how long have you known?"

"Long enough," Grace answered.

"Then you know that you have no chance to defeat me, let alone win this war."

Grace gritted her teeth, "We'll see about that, demon. What did you do with my mother?"

The fiend laughed and licked her lips, "I assure you; she was quite delicious."

Grace cried, "You bitch!" Then she stomped on the gas. Unfortunately, traffic hadn't cleared enough for her to go very far before she had to step on the brake. The doppelganger shot her left hand out, which now ended in long, sharp claws, and grabbed Grace by the throat.

"No tricks," the demon hissed, "or I'll snap your neck like a twig, right before I disembowel your boyfriend here. Her head swiveled completely around to look at Matthew, while her hand kept a firm grip on Grace's neck. Her mouth was now filled with a row of sharp teeth that dripped green saliva as she spoke, "And you better not get any ideas of your own, Little Man."

Matthew's left hand grabbed his ring, and he heard a voice in his head, *'Drown it'*. It was a good plan, except the creature still had hold of Grace's neck. Anything he did would put her life at risk. He glanced in the mirror and their eyes locked for the briefest of moments. He knew that look. She was about to do something stupid. Then she brought her right arm up quickly so that it smashed the demon's elbow. Both of them cried out at the same time.

Immediately, Matthew turned the dial on his ring and pointed it at the thing's head. A bolt of energy shot out and enveloped the creature. He raised his arm, and it flew upward out of the car. An overhead sign provided the perfect opportunity to knock the thing out. Then he lowered his hand and plunged the creature into the East River.

When the traffic finally broke, Grace floored the gas pedal and raced across the bridge. Once across, she made a couple of turns until they ended up on Plymouth Street, where the Brooklyn Bridge Park loomed on the left.

Grace pulled over to the curb and put the car in park. When she slumped against the wheel, Matthew saw that she had a series of long gashes running up her neck and onto her cheek. Blood poured from the wound down her whole left side. She tried to smile at him as she said weakly, "Okay, your turn to drive."

CHAPTER 15

Matthew jumped out quickly and rushed over to the driver's side. Grace was a mess. Blood was everywhere. Somehow, he managed to scoop her up and carry her around to the passenger's side, where he set her down as gently as he could. Her eyes were rolling back into her head as she started going into shock.

Matthew slapped her hand repeatedly, "Stay with me, Grace! I'll get you to a hospital, just don't die on me!"

Her eyes snapped open for a second. "My bag..." she mumbled.

He glanced back and saw her backpack in the back seat. "Don't worry. Your bag is still there."

He raced over and jumped into the car, fumbling with the GPS. His hands were trembling too much that he kept hitting the wrong buttons.

"Dammit!" he said. "All I want is the nearest hospital."

"No time for that," Grace coughed. "Poison..."; "blue bottle..."; "backpack..."

He finally understood. The demon's claws had injected her with poison. Glorianna's voice told him that Grace only had minutes to live.

Matthew reached back and quickly rummaged through the bag until he found a small bottle with a blue liquid inside. he unscrewed the cap and poured the liquid into her mouth, praying that he was in time.

Almost immediately, her shaking stopped and her breathing calmed. She closed her eyes and then whispered, "Thank you."

The thought that he nearly lost her devastated him. It took a minute for his hands to stop shaking. "Now, can I get you to a hospital?" he asked.

She shook her head slightly and opened her eyes. "No hospital...just sleep." Then her eyes closed, and she drifted off to sleep.

A few minutes later, he pulled up in front of a nearby motel. He was hesitant to leave Grace by herself in the car, but didn't have any other choice. He relaxed when he returned to the car a few minutes later, thankful that she was exactly the way he had left her.

He had requested a room in the back corner of the building, away from prying eyes so he could carry her inside without incident. He placed her gingerly on the bed and noticed she was running a slight fever. After placing a cold cloth on her forehead, he went to work cleaning her wounds. Once all the blood had been cleaned off, he was shocked to see that most of her cuts were already closed.

He laid down on the bed next to her so that his back was against the headboard and closed his eyes for a minute, reflecting on everything that had happened. *So much blood. So much death. So much loss.* He hadn't been strong enough to stop any of it. *And I'm supposed to be something special?*

Doubts filled his head as he drifted off to sleep.

***

* * *

Matthew was back in the church again, sitting in the last pew at the back of the sanctuary. A man dressed all in white was addressing the congregation with an open casket off to one side.

"Dearly beloved," the man said. "We are gathered here today in memory of a strong and courageous man, and to celebrate his passing as he journeys toward enlightenment."

A chorus of praise and cheer erupted from the crowd.

The preacher continued, "He was a brave man, who fought with a warrior's might. Now, as he prepares for the next phase of this battle, we must bless his spirit so that he may have the strength to endure."

Matthew watched as a thousand angels filed down the aisle one by one. Each one stopped at the casket for a minute to bend down and kiss the deceased. When they had all paid their respects, the preacher looked at him and smiled, "Your turn, Matthew."

He was about to protest when he suddenly found himself at the edge of the casket, looking down at his own body lying there. His skin was shiny and plastic looking, and he was wearing the same kind of white suit as the preacher. "I don't understand. Does this mean I'm dead?"

"Not in the conventional sense. Consider this your first step toward becoming the man you need to be in order to win this battle."

"So, this means that I'm going to die? That's why you're showing me this. It's a premonition, right?"

"What I'm trying to say, Matthew, is that in order to grow, you need to let go of your past. Your former self must die, so that you may live. Cast aside all of your doubts and fears. Release all the hurt inside, and have faith in yourself."

"That's easier said than done."

The Preacher put his arm around Matthew's shoulder, "Just remember, that we are never given more than we can handle."

***

Matthew opened his eyes to find that he was still lying in bed with Grace. He had scooted down, so that he was lying flat, and Grace had rolled over onto her side so that her head rested on his chest. He ran his hand gently through her hair, the silky strands sending a pleasant charge through his body. In response, Grace nestled closer to him. *I could get used to this!* He thought.

Every inch of him wanted to give in to his feelings, then he heard his mom's voice in his head, *'Now is not the time, Matthew.'*

Embarrassed, he gently lifted Grace's head from his chest and slid out from underneath her. She stirred for a second before slipping back to sleep. Then Matthew scooted off the bed and brewed a pot of coffee.

He remembered Grace's backpack on the table in the corner of the room. After plugging her laptop in, he was met with a password screen. For a couple of minutes, he tried every possibility he could think of, to no avail.

He was just about to close the lid, when Grace said, "Try angry birds."

Matthew turned around and saw Grace lying across the bed. "What? I like the game," she said.

"How are you feeling?" he asked.

"Other than the gong pounding in my head, I think I'm okay."

"I made coffee. Want some?"

"Sure."

"How do you like it?"

"Just black."

He smiled, "A woman after my own heart."

After pouring a couple cups and handing one to Grace, he sat down in front of the computer and typed in her password. The splash screen promptly came up. "So, how did you know that thing wasn't your mom?"

"It was just a guess. I suspected something was up when I noticed the fingernail thing. When I made the call at McDonald's, I was actually talking to Solomon. He warned me what might be going on."

"You knew what was going to happen, didn't you?"

Instead of answering, she just sat there on the edge of the bed staring down into her cup of coffee. Her silence was her answer.

"And the poison? You knew that the slightest movement would put you at risk, yet you pulled that crazy stunt, anyway."

"I did what I had to," she said.

"You almost died."

"But I didn't."

Grace then changed the subject, "What are you looking for?"

"I figured we needed to find this Caleb guy and finish this once and for all."

She slid off the bed and staggered a little before finding the chair next to Matthew. As she sat down, he noticed that the cuts on her neck and face had completely healed. The only traces were a series of three light scars on her cheek.

He lost himself in her eyes for a minute, "I was scared to death that I'd lost you."

She smiled at him before grabbing the computer, "Here, let me try."

After typing a few commands, a search came back with several entries pertaining to Caleb Albright. She clicked on a couple of them and scanned the articles. Finally, she said, "I think we found him."

Matthew peered over her shoulder and saw a page for the United States Institute of Peace. "I didn't even know there was such an organization.

"Well, there is, and apparently our boy has an office there."

"So now that we know where he, we can get this over with."

"Unfortunately, it won't be quite that easy."

"Why is that?"

"Look at the address."

She pointed to the left side of the screen and his heart sank. It was in the heart of Washington, DC. The most fortified city in the U.S.

"What's the plan?" Matthew asked.

Grace looked at him indignantly, "Why am I the designated tactician here?"

"Because you've been doing this a lot longer than me, and you're obviously better at it than I am."

She tilted her head and smiled, "I guess you're right. I bet it hurt to admit that? Does that mean I'm the brains of this outfit, and you're the brawn?"

It was obvious that she was feeling better. "I see you're back to your ornery self."

"Getting there. Of course, you leave yourself open pretty readily, so it's hard to resist."

"Hey!"

Her smile grew so that it lit up her whole face. Matthew found himself unable to resist anymore. He bent over and kissed her. She responded with equal passion as they explored each other's mouths. But then she broke away, "I can't do this right now. Not with everything that's going on."

She grabbed her phone and quickly headed to the bathroom. Matthew's heart clanged to the floor like a frying pan lid. He understood where she was coming from, but couldn't help it. He had never felt like this before; like he had found someone special.

A few minutes later, she returned from the bathroom looking dejected.

"Any news yet?" Matthew asked.

She shook her head, "Nothing."

"Let's not give up hope, okay? I'm sure she's fine."

"But you heard the demon in the car."

"That could just be a ploy to upset us."

She wasn't buying it, but he didn't know what else to do. When she didn't respond he thought that maybe she was also troubled about the kiss. "Look, about earlier—"

She cut him off, "I don't want to talk about it right now. Let's get through this shit. Then we'll talk."

Matthew's heart plummeted even further, but he knew he had to put his feelings aside and concentrate on the task at hand.

She resumed her seat next to Matthew and said pointedly, "The way I see it, the first thing we need to do is determine whether Caleb Albright is actually Vizibir. If he's not, then that changes things drastically."

"How do you know so much about all of this stuff, anyway?"

"Some of it I learned from Solomon. But most of it was from Gideon."

When he heard that name, Matthew understood her hatred. Betrayal is, in some ways, worse than death. Death is something that is easy to believe in. It's all around us. But to pour your love and hope into someone, only to have them turn and shove a dagger into your heart, brings your spirit even lower. In the end, it's easier to forgive an enemy than it is to forgive a friend.

She continued, "When I was six, something pretty bad happened that my dad won't talk about. Whatever it was, eventually led to my parent's divorce. That's when my dad joined the Church. Gideon took him under his wing and immediately recognized that he had a natural affinity for the supernatural. Before long, I found myself immersed in a world most people don't even know exists." She sighed deeply, "Then he stabbed us in the back."

"Try not to think about that right now."

"That's easy for you to say. He didn't almost kill your father."

Matthew almost said something he shouldn't. But he held his tongue. The last thing they needed was more tension between them.

He changed the subject quickly, "So, what's your plan?"

Grace pressed a few buttons on the laptop and a map of DC popped up. She studied it for a minute then said, "This is not going to be easy. It looks like our man is giving a lecture on Global Islamic Studies in two days."

"That sounds exciting."

"I know, right? Not exactly my idea of a good time, either. But it should be a good way to check out Caleb and see what's going on. The problem is that it's located right across from George Washington University in a very busy part of town. According to the Institute website, there isn't any onsite visitor parking."

"So that means we're not going to have transportation handy in case anything crazy happens."

"Exactly."

With the way things had been going, crazy was pretty

much expected.

The plan was simple: park the car at Central Parking, walk to the Institute, sit in on a boring lecture to determine if Caleb was the Antichrist or not, then walk back to retrieve their car and return to their room at the River Inn. It seemed like a good plan until they saw Gideon in the hotel lobby.

They had just turned the corner when Grace stopped and then backed quickly into the hallway. As they peered around the corner, they watched as Gideon, dressed in a dark shirt and khaki pants, talked to one of the desk clerks. The clerk, a young college-age girl, with long dark hair and an eyebrow piercing, didn't take any particular interest in what Gideon was saying. This really seemed to piss him off. He got agitated and started pointing at the girl, who basically ignored him. As he pointed, they saw that his left arm was all bandaged up.

Matthew whispered to Grace, "How did he find us?"

"It must've been the doppelganger," she whispered back. "I bet it put some kind of tracker on the car."

"Well, that sucks. That means we can't use the Mustang anymore."

Grace scowled at him, "Are you serious? With everything

going on, you're worrying about the car? Now, be quiet or he'll hear us."

They both held their breaths and shrank back into the shadows. Gideon stopped talking to the girl and turned in their direction, looking around like he was Darth Vader and had just felt a disturbance in the force. A minute later, he stormed out of the hotel in frustration. The desk clerk grinned as he left.

A sigh of relief escaped both of their lips when he walked out of the door, but was short-lived when they realized their plan was completely ruined.

"Any ideas?" Grace asked.

Matthew replied, "Follow him?"

He walked cautiously toward the front entrance and peered through the door. Gideon was standing on the curb next to a black sedan talking on a cell phone. A minute later, he hung up, got into the car, and drove away.

They rushed outside and found a taxi waiting there. "Follow that car," they said in unison as they slid into the back seat.

The leather-faced Hispanic driver was stunned and started to protest. He changed his tune when Grace waved a hundred-dollar bill in his face. He put the car in gear and pulled away in hot pursuit.

The driver, Geraldo, according to the nameplate on the dash, regarded them in the rear-view mirror, "You kids okay?"

Matthew replied, "We're fine. We just need to follow that man."

"You don't look fine to me. You look like two kids in trouble."

Grace interjected, "Look, let's just say that the man we're following is dangerous and we need to stop him before a lot of people get hurt."

"So, you're cops, then?"

"Not exactly."

The driver let the subject drop and continued following Gideon. He was actually quite adept at keeping a safe distance without being detected. Only once did Grace warn the guy not to follow too close. When the driver scowled at her through the mirror, she kept her comments to herself.

They soon found themselves in a residential area of Georgetown. Geraldo parked about a block down from the driveway they had seen Gideon drive into. The money had barely changed hands before the guy drove away.

"I guess there's no turning back now," Matthew said.

She grunted her agreement. "Come on, let's get a closer look."

They only made it a few yards when a voice stopped them, "Where do you think you're going?"

They were startled to turn around and see Father Andrew standing there. "What? You didn't think I'd let you take all the credit for saving the world, did you?"

He had a patch over his left eye and a large burn mark that extended from his jaw down to his neck. His wound was an exact mirror of the injury Grace had received from the demon.

Grace exclaimed, "Dad! What are you doing here? And how did you find us?"

When you called Solomon from McDonald's, we cued in on the GPS tracking on your phone. Something told me you'd need my help."

"But shouldn't you be resting?"

"Solomon's a pretty amazing healer. Besides, it's time Gideon gets what he deserves. So, fill me in. What's going on?"

Grace said, "We were planning on checking out Caleb during a lecture at the Peace Institute to determine if it was really him or the demon."

Matthew butted in, "Then we saw Gideon in our hotel lobby and followed him."

"He pulled into this driveway," Grace said. "We were just about to check it out when you showed up."

Father Andrew said, "We need to be careful. We don't know who or what might be in there with him."

They walked cautiously down the sidewalk, holding close to the six-foot concrete wall surrounding the property. When they got to the driveway, they were frustrated to find a heavy metal gate blocking their entrance.

Grace looked around. "I think I see a way." She pointed to a large oak tree jutting out over a section of the wall.

She turned to Matthew, "Can you climb?"

Matthew smiled, took a second to gage the height and distance and then charged the wall. He leaped forward, and when his foot touched the concrete, he pushed upward while spinning back toward the street. He grabbed a branch hanging low and swung himself up into the tree.

Grace smiled, "Impressive. Now move so I can show you how it's really done."

Matthew stepped backward onto another branch and watched as Grace duplicated his move perfectly.

Father Andrew looked up at them, "Don't expect me to try that. I'd probably fall and break my neck. I'll circle around and try to find another way in."

They watched him disappear around the side of the property, then inched their way down into the lower boughs of the tree. After scanning the area and seeing no immediate threat, they dropped down softly to the ground.

They were on the east side of the long driveway, about fifty yards from a large, white colonial house. Gideon's car was parked in front of an attached two-car garage.

A couple of smaller oak trees provided cover as they scurried to get closer to the house. They made it to the side of Gideon's car and crouched down beside it. Matthew was just about to edge around the front of the car when a large, black hairy spider, the size of a Bulldog scuttled out from around the car.

Instinctively, he stomped down on the creature, smashing it into a gooey mess. The moment he felt the crunch of its bones under his foot, a banshee cry came from the house. A second later, the stick figure of Lilith erupted from the building on her long, spindly legs.

Her mouth was open in a viscous scream as she raced toward them. Half-way there, her lower abdomen morphed into a giant spider.

As he scrambled to get away, Matthew stumbled backward and fell to the ground. Lilith leaped on top of the car and snarled, "Foolish boy! Did you actually think your pathetic plan could succeed?"

Grace was just about to circle around the back of the car when she was confronted by Gideon. She crouched down and pulled a long dagger from her boot.

Gideon chuckled, "Ah, the little kitten is finally showing her claws. How cute."

Grace replied, "You won't think it's so cute when I gut you like a fish."

Gideon's smile turned into a sneer, "I think it's time you learn what happens to those who oppose the Prince of Darkness."

Matthew was powerless to help as Gideon lunged at her, because at the same moment Lilith leapt off the car toward him. He tried to scramble backwards, but she was on him in an instant. A set of gruesome fangs gnashed at him from the mouth in her stomach.

He brought his hand up, but before he could use the ring, Lilith swung one of her spider legs forward and caught him in his side, sending him flying through the air. He landed with a hard crash against a tree and felt several snaps inside his chest. A cry of pain shot from his mouth as he lay there huddled tight, trying to fight through the agony of his broken ribs.

Lilith scurried quickly over to him and reared up, preparing to deliver the killing blow. Matthew heard Grace cry out beside him, and that gave him a shot of adrenaline. He brought his ring up and shot a blast of holy fire into the chomping mouth. Lilith flew backward and crashed into the side of the car. Her spider body twitched and smoldered as it crumpled to the ground.

Matthew looked over at Grace and saw her take a hard kick to the stomach that sent her flying to the ground. He climbed to his feet and staggered toward her. Then he heard a loud buzzing sound right before he found his path blocked by Vizibir, who was still posing as Caleb.

Vizibir pointed at Matthew, "You'll pay for hurting my mother, you fucking twit!"

A bolt of energy shot from his hand and hit Matthew in the chest, sending him crashing backward into the same tree they had used for cover a minute before. He felt his right shoulder dislocate on impact, causing him to cry out in pain again.

As Matthew slumped to the ground, Vizibir walked forward. "Others have tried to kill me before, and all have failed. Now you'll join them," he said.

Matthew struggled to his feet, trying desperately to keep from falling unconscious. This was his only chance, and he knew it. If he failed, then the whole world would die. With his left hand, he slowly pulled the dagger from inside his jacket.

Vizibir was now close enough that Matthew could smell death on his breath when he talked, "So tell me, Matthew, are you ready to die?"

With his last bit of strength, Matthew plunged the knife deep into the demon's chest. "I think I'll stick around a little longer."

A look of shock came over Vizibir as a white light started glowing in his chest. He turned and stumbled over to where Lilith's limp body lay. Falling to his knees in front of her, he cried out, "Mother!"

Lilith opened her eyes and looked in horror as the light engulfed her son completely. Vizibir reached out and grabbed his mother's hand. At the moment of contact, the light spread to her. They both glowed white-hot for an instant before exploding in a blinding flash.

Matthew closed his eyes to avoid being blinded. When he opened them a moment later all that was left of Lilith and Vizibir was a fire-blackened outline on the driveway. Grace was lying on the ground a few feet away, struggling to get up. He went over and helped her to her feet.

Gideon was nowhere to be found.

"Is it over?" she asked.

"Yeah, I think so."

Just then, Father Andrew emerged from behind the garage, completely out of breath. "What did I miss?" he gasped.

Grace and Matthew just looked at each other and smiled.

CHAPTER 17

Just as they finished telling Father Andrew what had happened, the sound of sirens filled the air.

"Time to go," Grace said.

"Follow me around back," The priest said. "We'll be less noticeable there."

As they started toward the side of the garage, Matthew's foot clanged against something. He bent down and saw the knife laying on the ground that had destroyed Vizibir. As he picked it up, he couldn't help feeling a sense of sorrow. The truth that evil was so rampant in the world had opened his eyes and sobered his heart. It had brought death to so many innocent people. And he realized sadly that evil almost always hides in the shadows, working undercover like a cancer spreading throughout your body, unseen by the naked eye.

Matthew tucked the blade back inside his jacket and followed the others through the back of the property. There was a break in the wall behind a thick row of shrubs. The whole top had collapsed in a five-foot section, giving them a chance to escape. As he climbed over, he saw another giant spider, only this time it was on its back with all eight of its legs curled in and shriveled. That it was dead didn't make it any less creepy.

Behind the property was an empty lot with the first stages of a new construction showing. The foundation of a large home had been poured and framing had started. Unfortunately, a group of about a dozen construction workers milled about.

Grace said, "Well, this could be a problem. How did you get by?"

Father Andrew said, "They were all on a break when I came through. No one saw me."

"I have an idea," Matthew said. "Give me your hands."

He didn't know if it would work, or if using the ring with Vizibir and Lilith dead would still bring demons to them? With their hands locked together, he reached over and twisted the ring, making them all invisible, so that they walked right past the crew. When they were far enough away, he deactivated the ring and pressed the center just in case.

They rounded the block and found Father Andrew's car parked along a side street. They sped away just as a couple of police cars flew by heading toward Caleb's house.

With Gideon out of the way, they headed back to the room at the River Inn. They parked in the front and walked silently through the lobby. Everyone was numb as they rode the elevator up to their second-floor room in silence. Sleep seemed to be calling to each one, and they were hopelessly caught in its tractor beam.

Plans changed the second they opened the door and saw Priscilla sitting on the edge of one of the beds, waiting for them.

Grace rushed over to her, "Mom! I thought you were dead."

Both women were crying as they hugged. "I thought so, too," Priscilla said. "After Edna went on her rampage, I found myself face to face with my twin. I tried to fight the demon, but it was too strong. At one point, it threw me up against the wall. I guess I passed out, because I woke up hours later at the hospital."

"But how did you find us?"

"I called Solomon from the hospital and he told me what was going on. Once I found out where you were, I used a little bit of my own special magic to get the desk clerk to let me in here. I've been waiting for hours, hoping you'd make it back okay."

Grace was still a little apprehensive. "Well, I'm certainly glad you're okay," she said. "Are you hungry?"

Priscilla answered, "I could go for a bite."

"How about a Filet-O-Fish?"

Priscilla snorted, "You go right ahead. I'm not eating that shit."

Grace smiled and hugged her again, "I love you, Mom."

Priscilla gave Matthew an 'am I missing something?' look, to which he only smiled.

Instead of heading out, they ordered room service. While they were waiting for their food, they filled Priscilla in on everything that had happened. She almost started crying again when Grace recounted her near-death experience, easing any reservations still lingering about her true identity.

****

At some point, they all fell asleep. The weight of the battle had taken its toll on all of them, mentally, physically, and emotionally. When Matthew woke up in the chair, his body was sore from the position he'd fallen asleep in, but he felt surprisingly refreshed. For the first time in a long while, the nightmares had stayed away.

When he looked around the room, he was disappointed to find himself alone. But he wasn't surprised. On the table next to him was a letter from Grace. Beside it was her cell phone and the keys to the Mustang.

He opened the note:

Matthew,

Considering everything that's happened recently, the three of us have decided that we need to spend some quality time together. It's been a long time since any of us have talked, and I'm hoping that this will help us reunite as a family.

I know it hurts, leaving you on your own like this. Please, don't be mad. Maybe in a little while we can get back together and see how things go? In the meantime, Pops put another key on the key ring that goes to a safe deposit box at the Bank of America on Lexington Avenue, in New York. He says that the Church has set something up for you in honor of your mother and father. It should help you get by

See you soon,

Grace

P.S. I removed the tracker in your car. You can thank me later.

Matthew sat the note down and just stared at the wall. For the first time since all of this craziness had started, he felt completely alone. What would he do? Where would he go? Sure, he had been plodding through life pretty aimlessly for the last few years. But someone had always been there to nudge him back on track, whether it was his, mom, a teacher, or even a police officer. None of these people were there anymore. Now he was completely on his own.

He sighed and headed to the bathroom. After a long, hot

shower, he got dressed and said goodbye to the River Inn. A few minutes later, he was sitting in the Mustang and saw that Grace had left another note on the passenger's seat. It simply read: *look in the glove compartment*. He did so and found an envelope with some cash inside.

Traffic was fairly light as Matthew made the trek to New York. He was tempted to put the top down, but then decided that he needed to feel the security of a small enclosed space for a while. The world had grown so large in such a short period of time that he suddenly felt like a tiny guppy swimming in an endless sea.

Matthew got to the bank a little after two. Since it was Friday afternoon, the bank was a little busier than he had hoped. After waiting in the small lobby area for fifteen minutes, a small, pudgy man in his forties escorted him to the outer vault, where the safe-deposit boxes were located. Matthew presented his key, and the man withdrew a key of his own. Then he placed both keys in and turned them simultaneously. He withdrew the box from its slot and placed it on the table, sending a soft clang echoing through the small room.

"Just press the button on the wall when you're done and I'll escort you out," the bank manager said before he left the room.

Matthew slowly opened the lid, not sure what to expect. Inside he found another envelope with five thousand dollars cash inside, a prepaid Visa with another five thousand, and two manila envelopes with legal documents inside.

He pulled the first one out a little before quickly shoving it back inside. It was a life insurance policy for his mother and he wasn't quite ready to deal with that. The second envelope contained a key and a lease agreement for an apartment at 1510 Lex.

An hour after he had entered the bank, Matthew left with everything he needed to start a new life. But he knew before he could look to the future, he had to take care of the past.

295

CHAPTER 18

Going home was hard, but necessary. His mother deserved a proper burial and a proper goodbye. The yellow tape crossing the front door of the crime-scene made it almost too much to take. Instead of getting out of the car, Matthew continued driving until he ended up at the police station.

After a long talk and some heavy scrutiny by the detective in charge of the case, he found out that his mother's body was lying in the morgue, waiting to be claimed. The official report was a burglary gone wrong. If only it were that simple.

His head was pounding by the time he left the station and drove the mile and a half to the hospital. In the past he would've found himself desperate for a hit of something that would ease his apprehension. But after all the shit had gone down, he'd sworn off drugs and was committed to turning over a new leaf. It's what his mom would've wanted.

The only parking space available was way in the back forty, so the long walk to the front entrance made him feel like he was a death-row inmate on his way to the gas chamber.

Once inside, Matthew trudged along the main corridor until he came to the elevator that would take him to the basement. When the elevator opened, he was staring down a long hallway with several doors on each side. Most of them appeared to be various labs. A couple of them were unmarked. The one at the end of the hall had a placard on the wall next to it with a simple M on it.

With a heavy heart, Matthew knocked on the door. A minute later, a tall, thin lady opened the door. Her nametag read Dr. Mora, and she was a lady in her mid-forties with streaks of gray running through her black hair.

"Can I help you?" she asked.

Matthew swallowed, "I'm here to see my mother."

Her expression softened, "I see. Come in."

She opened the door, and he was immediately hit with an overwhelming chemical smell. Instinctively, he wrinkled his nose.

"You get used to it," the Doctor smiled. "What's your mom's name?"

"Mary Carpenter."

She nodded and led him to a long wall filled with rows of cabinets. She opened one and pulled out the table where his mother's body rested. A few seconds was all he could stand before he had to turn away.

Every emotion Matthew had been holding in for the last week poured out like a waterfall. He fell to his knees and cried uncontrollably.

The doctor came over and put her hand on his shoulder. "I'm sorry," she said. She gave him a minute to mourn, and then asked, "Have you made funeral arrangements yet?"

Matthew shook his head.

She walked over to a small desk and came back with a business card. "This is the number for Cahn Funeral Home. They do a very nice job, and are highly recommended. I can call to have the body transported there if you'd like?"

As he left the morgue, the door clanged behind him, echoing through the hallway. Seeing his mom lying there on a cold metal slab had been hard, but pouring his heart out had finally lifted a big weight off of his chest.

***

After running around like a lunatic for a couple of days, Matthew was completely exhausted. He had finalized the funeral details, dealt with the insurance company numerous times, and packed a whole house worth of stuff all by himself.

It was no wonder then, that when the alarm clock buzzed loudly at eight o'clock, he dreaded the thought of getting out of bed. The funeral was scheduled for eleven, and he wasn't looking forward to it at all. Finally, he forced himself out of bed. It was the least he could do.

Matthew arrived at the funeral home early to go over the details of the proceedings with the funeral director. The elder gentleman took him in so he could spend some time alone before guests started showing up. As he looked at her, he was amazed at how great a job they'd done making her look like the angel she truly was.

The service started right on time, and from the first word Matthew was totally oblivious to everything. The only thing he could do was stare at his mom sitting beside him, watching her own funeral. She placed her hand on his, and even though he couldn't feel her solid flesh, he felt the warmth of her love flowing through him.

Before he knew it, the service was over and they were leading the long procession through town toward the cemetery. The sky overhead was dark and dreary, with rain threatening to break through any minute, as if Heaven were mourning as well.

Finally, they reached the cemetery. Matthew followed the pall-bearers to the burial site and then looked around for a minute to see who was there. When he saw Grace and her parents there, he nodded to thank them for their support. Just seeing Grace there made him feel better.

He didn't really know anyone else there, but he assumed that most of them were members of her church. After the Preacher had said his last words, everyone filed forward to give their condolences, and he found himself hugging strangers as if they were old friends. At one point, his ring glowed bright red for a moment before fading. The woman in front of him was a short, old lady, with curly gray hair and small round glasses. She smiled a sly smile at him before shuffling off.

A sobering thought entered his head: it wasn't over. They had won this battle, but surely Hell would try again. He would have to be ready.

***

Two months after Matthew buried his mother—even though he knew she was in a far better place—it was still hard to accept the fact that she was gone. Couple his loss with the battle he had just fought, and it was easy to understand just how emotionally drained he was. Most days, he had a hard time just getting out of bed.

He started writing a journal, documenting everything he had gone through hoping it would provide the catharsis he needed. Writing the events down brought his emotions out into the open so he could deal with them. That had helped him heal. But it would take time to restore his soul completely. All he could do was to push forward one step at a time.

He switched on the TV, hoping to take his mind off things. Instead, he was instantly plunged right back into his nightmare. Looking back at him was Gideon, dressed in his priestly robes and acting very sanctimonious.

Matthew turned the volume up and was horrified when he heard Gideon talk about Father Andrew. He went on to talk about Father Andrew's part in the death of a prominent Senator. As a result, the Church had stripped Andrew of his priesthood.

Gideon said into the microphone, "I am confident in the justice of the Almighty. Our former priest will get what he has coming to him. In the end, everyone must atone for their sins." a smile crossed his lips before the news report switched to another subject.

Matthew remembered something his mother had said some time before: 'A demon can smile at you, but it's still a demon.' He hadn't understood it then, but he certainly did now.

"You'll get yours, Gideon," he said.

The End

Hellish Book Five:
Saving Grace

CHAPTER 1

Hecate hated her life and what it had become. She sighed as she looked around the small broken-down house on the West side of town that she and a couple other squatters were calling home at the moment. It wasn't always this way. At one time, she lived in a wonderful house, with wonderful parents, had a wonderful sister, and a wonderful dog. It was all just wonderful.

That was before the nightmare happened that tore everything apart.

She went to take another swig from the whiskey bottle sitting on the floor next to her, and was disappointed to find it empty, just like her life. She tossed the bottle back on the floor, where it landed with a clunk that woke up Josh and Kerry, the brother and sister runaways that were her temporary roommates.

Josh sat up groggily, the effects of the alcohol still lingering in his fifteen-year-old brain as he struggled to grasp where he was or what was happening. Kerry, on the other hand, stirred a little, looked up at Hecate for a second, and immediately passed out again. Even though she was two years older than her brother, it was apparent she couldn't hold her liquor as well.

"What's going on?" he asked with slurred speech.

Hecate replied, "Nothing. We're out of booze. I'm gonna go get some more."

Josh just kind of nodded and slunk back to his alcohol induced slumber.

Hecate got up, walked into the bathroom, where she lit a little candle on the vanity top and looked at herself in the mirror. She was a wreck, and she knew it. Her hair was matted to the side of her face, her eyes were bordered by dark circles, and she could feel the bad breath coming out of her mouth as if it was something she could hold. She just wasn't in the best frame of mind to do anything about it.

Although it had been over a year since the brutal attack that had taken her father and sister from her, she still couldn't come to grips with the reality of the situation. It hadn't helped that her mother had blamed her for everything. How would she have been able to stop a monster from entering their house and destroying their world? If anything, the blame should be on her for not locking the fucking door!

Hecate took a deep breath. Just thinking about everything was making her angry again, and when she got angry, she tended to do stupid things. And in her present situation, stupid could have disastrous results.

She lifted the toilet lid and immediately started to gag. The downfall of living in an abandoned house was that there wasn't any running water. She held her breath long enough to piss, and when she was done, she closed the lid quickly, blew out the candle, which helped mask the smell just a little, and left.

Hecate crossed the backyard to the small opening in the privacy fence at the rear of the property. She scampered through hole and down the alley until she reached the street. Her destination was a small liquor store at the end of the block.

She knew the guy was a dick as soon as she saw him pull up, but she didn't have any choice. Dressed in jeans and a black leather jacket, the guy climbed out of his beat-up Camaro and strode toward the door with his chest puffed out like he was God's gift.

Hecate sauntered up to him, putting on her best pouty face. "Hey, mister," she said sadly as she batted her best puppy-dog eyes at him. "Do you think you could help me out?"

The man eyed Hecate up and down for a minute, grinning, "Okay, I'll bite. What you looking for?"

"Just a couple bottles of some hard stuff. My friends and I ran out a little while ago." She pulled some bills from her pocket and flashed them at the guy, "I got money."

The man replied, "I tell you what. You can keep your money. How about you climb into my car and give me a blowjob and I'll get you whatever you want?"

Hecate glared at the man, "How about if you go fuck yourself instead?"

The man just shrugged his shoulders and sneered, "Suit yourself."

As he walked inside the store, Hecate muttered under her breath, "Asshole!"

She stood outside the building waiting for another opportunity, when she suddenly caught a flash of movement out of the corner of her eye. She turned and thought she saw a dark figure disappearing down the alley the same way she had come, but she couldn't be sure. She shrugged it off and resumed her stakeout.

When she saw an older lady pull up, she followed her into

the store and immediately slunk into the corner, out of sight of the clerk and the security camera on the wall. She quickly grabbed the closest bottle of booze she could reach and stuffed it under her shirt.

The alarm sounded as Hecate exited the building right on the heels of the woman. Then, in the confusion, she slipped away unseen.

When she was far enough away, she pulled the bottle out from under her shirt and looked at what she had grabbed. She was a little disappointed when she saw that it was a bottle of peach schnapps, not her first choice to get drunk, but it would do. The trick was going to be getting the security cap off. She figured if she got desperate enough, she'd just break the damn thing off.

That all became a moot point when she walked toward the back of the house and saw the door torn off its hinges. Her brain screamed for her to turn and run away. Then she remembered Josh and Kerry.

Slowly, Hecate approached the broken door, holding the bottle of booze upside down like a makeshift mallet. She entered the house quietly and listened for a moment. Nothing but silence. She didn't know if that was a good thing or a bad thing.

Every hair on the back of her neck was standing upright as she ventured from the kitchen into the living room. The darkness seemed blacker than normal, as if all the energy had been sucked from the room, leaving a massive void that encompassed the world. A heaviness covered her chest as she inched her way forward.

For a brief second, the moonlight broke through the window, casting a sliver of light into the room. That's when she saw it and her whole world changed.

It was crouched down, bent over Josh's body. Hecate cried

out, and the beast turned toward her. As it stood up, it spread a pair of dark wings that stretched out from one end of the room to the other. A fierce roar bellowed from its blood-soaked mouth before it charged at her.

Hecate stood paralyzed with fear for a second, before something inside her gave her the strength to move. She quickly hurled the bottle at the beast, which bounced off its chest harmlessly. But the action gave her a brief second to turn and run for the back door.

She made it just outside the house when the thing grabbed her. Sharp claws dug into her flesh as it held both arms tight. Then she felt its hot, acrid breath on the back of her neck as it brought it mouth close.

Suddenly, she heard a thump, and the creature released its hold on her. Hecate turned around as its body fell to the ground next to its severed head. Confused, she looked up to find an older gentleman with a long, white beard, wearing a tie-die shirt and holding a bloody hatchet.

"Hello, my name is Solomon," the man said with a smile.

CHAPTER 2

The sun's roaming fingers slipped through the splinters of the boarded-up windows to cast just enough light into the room for Hecate to see how grisly the scene was. Josh's body had been savagely ripped apart. One of his arms lay five feet away, torn from its socket, and he had a gaping hole in his chest where his heart used to be. Kerry's death hadn't been nearly as brutal, but she was dead nonetheless.

Hecate rushed to the bathroom to vomit. When she returned, she immediately ran out of the house, this time through the front door.

"Wait," Solomon called out as he chased after her. "I want to help."

She thought about running away from this madness, just like she had run away from everything else before, but something told her to stop. She turned around and looked at Solomon. Her eyes were wide and her lips were trembling, "What the hell happened here?"

Solomon replied, "You were attacked by a demon."

"A demon! Those things really exist?"

Solomon nodded, "They do. Actually, most of the monsters in human lore are really demons, and you, my dear, had set up shop in this one's lair."

"How did you know it was here?"

"I'd been hunting this one for a while, but lost track of it for a moment. I just wish I'd arrived in time to save your friends."

Hecate thought about the kids she'd only known for a couple of days. The kids who had been abused by their parents and had run away to escape the horror, only to find themselves in the middle of a worse nightmare. The kids who were now dead. "Are there more of them?" she asked.

Solomon thought about it for a second, "In this area? No, I don't think so. Out there in the rest of the world? Yes."

Hecate sat down on the porch steps and picked at a loose patch of cracked cement. "So, what do I do now?" she asked quietly.

"Do you have any place you can go?"

She shook her head, "Not really."

Solomon closed his eyes and took a deep, slow breath. He concentrated for a moment, before opening them. He looked at Hecate curiously. "You can come with me if you want? I can give you a place to stay and maybe teach you more about this stuff. But only if you want to?"

Hecate was shocked. "You can teach me how to protect myself from those things?"

"Yes, but only if you tell me your name first."

Hecate was silent for a moment, gauging whether she could trust the hippie monster hunter. But anything would be better than being at home with her mom. "It's Hecate," she finally said.

"It's a pleasure to meet you, Hecate. I must warn you, though, that if you really want to learn, you must totally commit yourself. It's not going to be easy. You've already had a little taste of what's out there."

A realization hit her. What was really at the heart of her troubles was that she felt helpless and weak. She hadn't been there to save her dad and sister, and wasn't strong enough to stand up to her mom. Instead, she ran away and almost got killed. That was the moment she decided not to be weak again.

"I'm ready to do whatever I need to do."

"Good. Then follow me."

Solomon led her down the block to a black sedan parked at the side of the curb. She hesitated for a second, just to make sure she wasn't being led to her doom, but something told her Solomon could be trusted.

"Where are we going?" she asked as she slid in.

"Have you ever seen Touchdown Jesus?"

The question was a little weird for her, "Only on TV."

"Well, you're about to get a firsthand look, sort of."

Hecate learned quickly that Solomon was a quirky man who said quirky things, and that the best way to handle him was to go with the flow. So, she rode in silence as they drove through town toward the Notre Dame campus, wondering what in the world she'd gotten herself into.

After a few minutes, Solomon turned off of North Michigan Street onto Angela Boulevard. The sun was just beginning to overtaking the darkness as they passed the golf course and saw a few dedicated golfers already hitting the links. *They have no idea what's really out there,* Hecate thought bitterly.

When they turned left onto Eddy Street, she found herself entering the campus for the first time. Growing up in the area she had always been indifferent to the school. She didn't love it, and she didn't hate it. It was just there. Who would have thought her first visit would be under such strange circumstances?

Solomon continued slowly down the street until he pulled into a parking garage near the Hesburgh Library. As they approached the massive structure, Hecate was captivated by the mural that had been dubbed 'Touchdown Jesus', a name that it had been given because of the way it faced the North end of the football stadium.

"It's actually called 'The Word of Life' mural," Solomon said. "Ara Parseghian is the one that gave it the nickname 'Touchdown Jesus' way back in nineteen sixty-four and it stuck. He was always a little bit of a smartass."

"And how do you know that?"

"Because I was here."

Hecate looked at him questioningly, but when he just kept walking, she let it drop.

Instead of entering the library through the front doors, Solomon led her around the east side to a small set of stairs. A door at the top of the stairs opened to a small hallway leading south with a couple of doors on the west side.

As Solomon stopped at one of the doors and fished a set of keys from his pocket, a middle-aged man in a sport coat came around the corner. "Morning, Sam," the man said. "How's it going?"

Solomon replied, "It's good, Aaron. How are you?"

"Busy already. Is this a new one?"

"Maybe. We'll see how it goes."

Aaron turned to Hecate and extended his hand, which Hecate took hesitantly. "I'm Aaron."

"Hecate."

"Well, Hecate, if there's anything you need while you're here, just ask."

"Ok?"

Aaron smiled at her and walked away, exiting the same door they had entered from.

"I thought you said your name was Solomon?"

Solomon replied, "It is. I just prefer Sam. It's much more current."

Hecate found the statement odd. *What the hell does current mean?*

Solomon opened the door and stepped into the room. Hecate followed and was surprised to see the room completely empty.

"I suggest you brace yourself," Solomon said.

Solomon extended his hand, and Hecate saw the massive gold ring on his right hand. He pressed the center of the ring and immediately the floor of the room started to descend. Hecate couldn't believe what was happening. The whole room was a giant elevator like in some spy movie.

They seemed to descend forever, or at least that's how Hecate felt as she wondered into which beast's belly she was being delivered. Final they stopped and the wall on the west side flew up.

When she followed Solomon out of the room, she couldn't believe her eyes. They were in a large, cavernous room built out of the earth itself. Shelves lined with books spanned one of the walls, while a long altar ran along another. A couple of tunnels ran in opposite directions on the far wall. But what was so amazing about the place was the number of people milling about. A few were sitting at desks, pouring over ancient texts, while others were off in the corner practicing various forms of martial arts.

"Welcome to our training facility," Solomon said.

AUTHOR BIO

Growing up in the shadow of Notre Dame's Golden Dome, Scott Dokey developed a strong affinity for the arts, learning at a young age the joy of transforming an empty page into something magical. Eventually, as an adult, his creative endeavors expanded to include writing and filmmaking. Focusing primarily on subjects with horror and supernatural aspects, he became an award-winning screenwriter, and has produced and directed several short films and a no-budget feature film.

Scott currently lives in Southern California with his wife, Jennifer, and their daughter, Kaylee, enjoying the sweltering 120° summer heat. Of course, 85° in January more than makes up for it.

To find out more about his work visit his website at www.scottdokey.com

* * *

Be sure to check out the rest of the Hellish series:
Hellish Book One: Tortured Souls
Hellish Book Two: The Chosen
Hellish Book Three: Unholy Religion